BACK ROOM GIRL

Francis Henry Durbridge was born in Hull, Yorkshire, in 1912 and was educated at Bradford Grammar School. He was encouraged at an early age to write by his English teacher and went on to read English at Birmingham University. At the age of twenty-one he sold a radio play to the BBC and continued to write following his graduation whilst working as a stockbroker's clerk.

In 1938, he created the character Paul Temple, a crime novelist and detective. For thirty years the radio serials were hugely successful until the last of the series was completed in 1968. In 1969, Paul Temple was adapted for television and four of the adventures prior to this had been adapted for cinema, albeit with less success than radio and TV. Francis Durbridge also wrote for the stage and continued doing so up until 1991, when *Sweet Revenge* was completed. Additionally, he wrote over twenty other well-received novels, most of which were on the general subject of crime. The last, *Fatal Encounter*, was published after his death in 1998.

Also in this series

Send for Paul Temple
Paul Temple and the Front Page Men
News of Paul Temple
Paul Temple Intervenes
Send for Paul Temple Again!
Paul Temple and the Tyler Mystery
Design for Murder
Paul Temple: East of Algiers
Another Woman's Shoes
Dead to the World
Paul Temple and the Kelby Affair
Paul Temple and the Harkdale Robbery
Paul Temple and the Geneva Mystery
Paul Temple and the Curzon Case
Paul Temple and the Margo Mystery
Paul Temple and the Madison Case

FRANCIS DURBRIDGE

Back Room Girl

PLUS

Light-Fingers

AND

A Present from Paul Temple

WITH AN INTRODUCTION BY
MELVYN BARNES

COLLINS
CRIME
CLUB

COLLINS CRIME CLUB

An imprint of HarperCollins*Publishers*
1 London Bridge Street
London SE1 9GF
www.harpercollins.co.uk

This paperback edition 2018

First published in Great Britain by
John Long 1950

'Light-Fingers' and 'A Present from Paul Temple'
first published in the *Daily Mail Annual for Boys and Girls*
by Associated Newspapers 1950, 1951

A catalogue record for this book is available from the British Library

ISBN 978-0-00-824203-9

Typeset in Sabon LT Std by Palimpsest Book Production Ltd, Falkirk, Stirlingshire

Printed and bound in Great Britain by CPI Group (UK) Ltd, Croydon CR0 4YY

Introduction

When *Back Room Girl* was published in July 1950, Francis Durbridge (1912–1998) had long been the most popular writer of mystery thrillers for BBC radio and was soon to become a 'brand name' on television and in the theatre. In 1938 the BBC had broadcast his serial *Send for Paul Temple*, and the novelist-detective and his wife Steve cemented their cult status in the sequels *Paul Temple and the Front Page Men* (1938), *News of Paul Temple* (1939), *Paul Temple Intervenes* (1942), *Send for Paul Temple Again* (1945) and many more. These first five radio serials were all novelised, published by John Long between 1938 and 1948, and most recently reissued in 2015 by Collins Crime Club.

Back Room Girl, however, was markedly different. It was Durbridge's first book not to feature the Temples, and neither was it based on a radio serial. Instead it was an original one-off novel, which by the end of Durbridge's writing career still compared only with *The Pig-Tail Murder* (1969) in this respect, although he had penned several standalone Sunday newspaper serials in the 1950s.

The Temple mysteries had invariably seen the sophisti-
cated couple pursuing and unmasking murderers, so they
all had a 'whodunit?' element. *Back Room Girl*, on the
other hand, was not a detective mystery but an adventure/
espionage thriller concerning skulduggery in a rural English
setting. From the somewhat whimsical opening sentence, 'It
was early on the highly appropriate day of Friday that Roy
Benton first saw the footprints in the sand,' it must have
been immediately obvious to any Paul Temple fan that this
was not going to be typical Durbridge fare.

The year is 1947, and Fleet Street crime reporter and SAS
hero Major Roy Benton begins a new life by retiring to No
Man's Cove in Cornwall to write his memoirs. He anticipates
peace and quiet, but this seems increasingly unlikely when
he discovers that a disused tin mine has become a research
laboratory for a top secret project. He finds that the brilliant
scientist Karen Silvers is heading the operation, and that his
friend Chief Inspector Wilfred Leyland has been seconded
from Scotland Yard because a sinister organisation is intent
on stealing the plans.

The ringleader is Fabian Delouris, and he and his henchmen
are Nazis ('the worst Gestapo types') who use extreme forms
of torture to extract the information they require. 'I have
been,' says Delouris, 'a dealer in mass murder and the means
to it for more years than I care to remember.' This could
account for the fact that *Back Room Girl* has not been trans-
lated and in particular has never been published in Germany,
where Durbridge is otherwise a great favourite and where
almost all of his novels have appeared.

The book has some themes that remain relevant today.
For example, it speculates about the morality of Karen's
work on developing a weapon of mass destruction. 'A curious

way of preventing war,' comments Roy, 'to have a bigger stick than the other fellow, but . . . it's the best we can do until we learn more sense'; whereas Karen believes that 'This thing is so deadly, so devastating, that its very existence ought to prevent anyone ever going to war again.' Underlying the story is also an element of surprise that a woman has been put in such a powerful position, although feisty Karen has always believed that 'men had been merely people with whom she had to work because there weren't enough women scientists.'

Back Room Girl therefore showed Durbridge in a new and unusual light, and he followed it up with two more novels that appeared to continue his move away from Paul Temple. But this was illusory, as *Beware of Johnny Washington* (April 1951) was a re-write of his first novel *Send for Paul Temple*, with some plot changes and a new set of characters without Paul and Steve, while *Design for Murder* (November 1951) was a novelisation of his 1946 radio serial *Paul Temple and the Gregory Affair*, but again with new characters instead of the Temples. (Both books, originally published by John Long and out of print for over sixty-five years, have now finally also been reissued.)

A key factor in Durbridge's success as an entertainer, however, was his astuteness in recognising what his audience wanted. For the rest of his career as a novelist, apart from his standalone *The Pig-Tail Murder*, he concentrated on two reliable publishing categories. The first was the Paul Temple mysteries, which resumed in 1957 until 1988, of which five were based on his radio serials and three were original novels: *The Tyler Mystery* (1957), *Paul Temple and the Harkdale Robbery* and *Paul Temple and the Kelby Affair* (both 1970). The second category was adaptations of his phenomenally popular television serials, sixteen of which he novelised between 1958 and 1982. There were also two further instances of nifty recycling when Durbridge turned the radio serials *Paul Temple and the Gilbert Case* and *Paul Temple and the Jonathan Mystery* into the non-Temple novels *Another Woman's Shoes* (1965) and *Dead to the World* (1967).

It transpired that Durbridge never again wrote a novel that resembled *Back Room Girl* in any way. Truly a one-off, it is a book that few among his legion of fans will have had the opportunity to read until now. The bonus short stories 'Light-Fingers' and 'A Present from Paul Temple' at the back of this book will be similarly unfamiliar to the modern audience. They appeared in consecutive editions of the *Daily Mail Annual for Boys and Girls* in 1950 and 1951, shortly after the publication of *Back Room Girl*, and show the lighter side of Francis Durbridge writing for younger followers of his radio series.

MELVYN BARNES
May 2017

Contents

I.	Strange Visitors	1
II.	Discovery of No Man's Cove	7
III.	A Man's Life	15
IV.	Rude Awakening	20
V.	Chief Inspector Leyland Explains	31
VI.	Bait for a Trap	39
VII.	Atomic Secrets	44
VIII.	A Shot in the Dark	53
IX.	Smugglers and Monks	58
X.	The Man with the Handcart	66
XI.	Attempted Murder	74
XII.	Strange Behaviour at the Inn	80
XIII.	Midnight Rendezvous	92
XIV.	Coffee for Three	99
XV.	The Man in the Combe	109
XVI.	Charlie gets a Shock	120
XVII.	Two Casualties	125
XVIII.	The Old Priory	139
XIX.	Ordeal by Torture	149

XX. This Way Out   157
XXI. Council of War   165
XXII. The Bolt Hole   170
XXIII. Through the Tunnel   180
XXIV. Trapped Again   187
XXV. No Exit?   202
XXVI. Curtain for Delouris   219

Light-Fingers   235
A Present from Paul Temple   243
Solution to Light-Fingers   257

CHAPTER I

Strange Visitors

It was early on the highly appropriate day of Friday that Roy Benton first saw the footprints in the sand. The surprise of it brought him up dead. Again, appropriately enough, the first thought that came into his mind as he stood staring down at them was that he was probably feeling now as Alexander Selkirk felt when he first looked on human footprints in the sands of Juan Fernandez.

But, Roy reminded himself, as he continued to stare and Angus, his Cairn terrier, sniffed excitedly up and down, this wasn't an inaccessible desert island hundreds of years ago – it was a Cornish cove in the year 1947 and anyone had a right to come there. True, it was called No Man's Cove, and since he had first made his home there four months ago in the disused tea chalet he had not seen anyone, or even traces of anyone, nearer the beach than the road, which roughly followed the line of the coast at the head of the wooded valley a quarter of a mile inland.

That was why the footprints were such a surprise, and why Roy's second reaction was one of annoyance and

1

resentment that anyone had dared to invade the privacy he had enjoyed there. His third reaction was to glance round apprehensively to see if there was anyone in sight, for he was not wearing any clothes, so sure had he become that no one would disturb him. He was relieved when he did not see anyone. It wasn't *his* cove, he reminded himself, as his eyes traced out once more the line of the footprints and Angus looked up curiously, as if asking what he was going to do about it, but he was realizing now that during the past months the absence of any other human beings had led him to think of this cove as a little domain of his own upon which, as time passed, and no one, not even an occasional tripper, came near, he had come subconsciously to feel no one would ever intrude. It was absurd, of course, and now these footprints had pricked the bubble of his little world as a sharp finger-nail punctures a balloon at a Christmas party. At the moment Roy was feeling an acute sense of deflation.

The footprints appeared to come out of the sea and curved away to his left, where, as he followed them, they gradually petered out as the sand gave way to coarse grass and then to turf. Roy wondered why he had not seen them when he went for the early bathe he had enjoyed every morning since he had come to the cove. Then he remembered that, instead of running down the beach into the sea as he usually did, he had gone a little way along the point to the natural rock diving platform which jutted out into deep water. It was only when he had waded out of the sea on his way back to the chalet and had seen Angus – who wouldn't do more than wet his paws – running frenziedly up and down like a bloodhound on the trail, that he had discovered what all the fuss was about.

When had they been made, then? They could not have

been there when he had walked down to the beach, smoking a last cigarette, at eleven o'clock the night before, or he would almost certainly have seen them, for there was a bright moon, and if he had missed them Angus would undoubtedly have drawn his attention to them. He had been out for his bathe by 6.30 a.m., so the prints must have been made during the night, or very early that morning.

He bent and examined them more closely. They had been made, he judged, by several pairs of boots, probably sea boots, and it was impossible, except perhaps for an expert tracker, to say how many pairs of feet there had been, though Roy would have hazarded several. They were deep prints, he noticed, especially the heels, and as the sand here was never very soft even when the tide had just uncovered it, that probably meant – he harked back to his scouting and, more recently, his Special Air Service days – that the wearers were carrying heavy loads.

Roy walked down to the sea's edge, Angus hanging cautiously behind a little, looking for signs of a boat, or boats. There were two indentations a few yards apart which might have been made by a keel dragged up out of the water, possibly during an unloading operation, but the tide had washed over them and he could not be sure. But why on earth, he asked himself, should anyone want to unload anything at this isolated spot? There could not be any point in fishermen landing their catches here when there was a perfectly good harbour at Torcombe, the nearest village five miles up the coast.

Smugglers? Well, there had been plenty of them here in the old days, and it was, of course, possible that their modern counterparts were active now, for lots of Black Market stuff from the Continent was being got past the Customs somehow. No Man's Cove would certainly be a good place for that sort of thing, but if some of the Torcombe men were involved – and from what he had seen of them Roy thought it unlikely – they would be running the risk of his seeing them, and he had not noticed anything suspicious. It was generally known in the village, to which he went for his supplies once a week, that he was living in the old chalet, and his presence there had at first caused a good deal of talk, though they seemed to have accepted him now. No, Roy felt that neither fishermen nor smugglers supplied a completely satisfactory solution to the mystery, though he saw that if he ruled out both these possible explanations the problem became even more puzzling.

He followed the footprints back up the beach, Angus trotting jauntily after him. Their course, he noted again, was not straight up the beach, which would have taken the people who made them direct to the chalet, but to the right and slightly inland, though he could not think of any place in that direction to which men carrying heavy loads (assuming that he was right and they were so burdened) could be going. The nearest village in that direction was Torcombe and the going was pretty rough. He and Angus had explored the immediate coast pretty thoroughly during their wanderings together, and at the moment he could not think of any place between the cove and the village which would supply the answer he was seeking.

Roy whistled Angus, who, tired of watching his master mooning around, had wandered off on a private and more enthralling expedition of his own, and turned to go back to the chalet for a delayed breakfast, but he stopped again as his eyes fell on marks in the sand he had not noticed before. They – by Jove, yes! – they looked very much like

4

the imprints of the heel of a woman's shoe, a broad one; a walking shoe, perhaps. Now how the devil . . . Roy walked back again alongside the prints to see if there were any more of them, but although there were one or two similar indentations they were blurred by the tracks of the sea boots and were not as clear as the first he had seen near the grass.

'This is getting really interesting,' Roy said aloud to himself, a habit he had acquired since he had been living alone, hearing the sound of human voices only when he went to the village, or the Cliff Top Inn on the coast road. 'A woman and sea-fishing sounds a bit unlikely; but smuggling . . . that would attract plenty of women.' His mind began to play about with all kinds of interesting possibilities. 'Now don't go jumping to conclusions,' he told himself. 'You're not a Fleet Street crime reporter now, and there aren't any glamorous women Secret Service agents at large any more outside books. If you're going to finish those confounded war memoirs of yours, you've got to work like blazes, without starting up any crazy hares about smugglers. Stick to real life, my boy . . .'

But he couldn't get those neat feminine footprints out of his head. What on earth would bring a woman to No Man's Cove? One woman and two or three men? Landing from the sea . . . They must have had some definite purpose . . . it wasn't just a pleasure trip.

Ideas churned through his mind in quick succession, and he realized that he would do little work that day until he had found out more about the mysterious footprints.

'What about a nice walk after breakfast, just to clear the brain, old son?' he asked Angus, skipping along beside him. The terrier barked eagerly as he recognized the familiar word.

'Right you are, then,' nodded Roy. 'But breakfast first. The most languorous female spy in christendom isn't going to spoil my appetite.'

Angus barked his approval.

CHAPTER II

Discovery of No Man's Cove

As he followed the dog, Roy found himself tingling with an anticipatory excitement he had not known since his Fleet Street days. He had been getting a little tired of crime reporting even before the war came along, so that when he joined up it was not the wrench he had thought it might be. Still, it was a fascinating job; it had something which 'got' you, and the old spell was on him again.

He had been lucky in the Army – if you could call it lucky to be one of the last off the Dunkirk beaches, parachute into enemy-occupied territory and fight with the underground forces. Any way, he'd come through some pretty tight corners without a scratch and collected a DSO and Bar and an MC on the way, though none of his newspaper colleagues, when he saw them during his rare leaves, could ever get him to talk about his experiences. Damn it all, was Roy's attitude, there were some things a man should keep between himself and his God – if he had one. Roy wasn't sure whether he had or not, but all the same he had kept his war-time experiences to himself hitherto. It was only during the past few months that he had felt an overwhelming urge to put them on paper.

He paused to help Angus extricate himself from a rabbit hole and they went on towards the chalet. They had all been glad to see him back in the *Daily Tribune* office, and having had his fill of physical excitement for the time being, he had returned quite happily to his old job, though it had taken him some time to pick up the threads again. There were several new faces in the office and in the police force with whom he had to deal, and the number of new rackets that had sprung up in the wake of rationing and other controls was unbelievable. Investigating them had kept him pretty busy, but after a time their meanness and pettiness had begun to pall on him and he had become restless and discontented.

'What you need,' Bill Darkis, one of the Home Office pathologists Roy had met while working on a poisoning case, had told him, 'is six months' vegetating in the country. Why don't you rent a cottage in Devon or Cornwall and write your war experiences? Do you good to get 'em out of your system. But don't spend all your time indoors writing and smoking cigarettes. Get out and walk or dig. Do something with your hands instead of that thing of yours you call a brain.'

Roy had laughed and said he would think about it. He had done more. The summer before this he'd used his holiday trying to locate a suitable cottage. Again acting on Bill's advice, he had bought a bicycle and gone riding along the south-west coast, or over the moors, just as the fancy had taken him.

He had been nearing the end of the fortnight's trip when he had found himself in Shingleton, where he stayed the night. He had set out next morning for Torcombe along the cliff road. It had been a lovely day and he had dismounted to rest and enjoy a cigarette at the head of the combe, or valley, which led down to what he saw from his map was No Man's Cove. Through the trees from where he had leaned against the wall that ran along the seaward side of the road he could see an inviting stretch of sand, and as there was no one in sight, he had decided to slip down for a quick bathe, leaving his cycle behind some bushes on the roadside.

Going down the combe, he had been surprised to come across the chalet, which had not been visible from the road because of the trees that flanked each side of a pretty little stream which ran down the bed of the valley to the sea. After his bathe he had gone to look at it more closely. A quick glance round showed that, apart from needing a coat of paint, a few new window-panes and some other minor repairs, the place seemed sound in wind and limb, so to speak. Indeed, it looked to be the very place he was seeking; remote, prettily situated, just the spot apparently if one didn't want to be bothered by people. (It looks as if you've been bothered now all right, Roy reflected a little grimly.) In one of the windows there had been a faded, dirty notice:

TO LET – CHEAP

Appy Barwell & Co.
Caterers
Harbour Road, Shingleton

So back to Shingleton he had immediately gone to call on Barwell and Co. He vaguely remembered the name, and they had turned out to be the firm whose tea-shops and cafés he had seen dotted about the coast roads and villages like a rash, with their 'Beautiful Barwell Teas' signs. Ugh! Still, he'd been grateful for a cup more than once.

He recalled the breezy smart-Alec of a manager, who had told him that the chalet had been a great disappointment to them. If it hadn't been for the war, of course . . . The manager had shrugged. They'd opened it in the summer of 1939, and at first hadn't done too badly, considering all the war scares, but after that season it had been hopeless. Then the evacuation from the south-east had begun and for a time Shingleton Rural District Council had installed a couple of families from London there, but successive visitors had found that the loneliness and quiet of the place had got on their nerves more than the fear of the *Luftwaffe's* bombs and they had drifted back to London. Since then the chalet had been empty. The evacuees had made rather a mess of the place, but if Mr Benton was interested they could soon have it cleaned up for him and made habitable.

Roy had told him he was interested, but he had not said why except that he had been ordered by his doctor to take a long rest following a serious illness. He had said he would like to look over the place and the manager had given him the key. As he had peered into the dirty interior of the chalet, Roy had reflected that the manager had been right in one respect at least – the evacuees had made rather a mess. But it wasn't beyond reparation if the manager would be as good as his word.

Roy had found himself liking the place from the first. It was a one-storey building, square except for two bulging outhouses, the kitchen and the usual 'offices', which were a trifle primitive but would pass if one hadn't too finicky a sense of smell. The doorway faced the sea, and a covered verandah ran round three sides of the square. That, presumably, had been so that teas could be served outside, but it had also struck Roy that it would be an admirable place for writing and for sleeping out on fine nights. The interior, apart from the kitchen and the 'offices', consisted of one big room, with a counter and shelves running the length of the left-hand wall as you entered. The counter, of course, would have to come out, but the shelves would be sure to come in handy. In the centre of the back wall was a large, rough, but serviceable brick fireplace, which, despite the filth that had accumulated in it, looked as if it could be made very inviting.

Not bad, Roy had mused, as he had stood in the centre of the big room looking around him. A few structural alterations, a good clean-up, some paint and distemper and lots of elbow grease, a few pieces of furniture – he was determined to live as simply as possible, though he would permit himself two luxuries in the shape of the divan, which would make an ideal bed, and the easy chair from his flat – and the place would be reasonably habitable.

It was, in fact, such a retreat as every Fleet Street journalist, with ambitions towards authorship, dreamed about – 'far from the madding crowd'.

So he had cycled back to Shingleton once more, haggled with the manager a little over the rent, and as he didn't want to move in until the following April, paid in advance so that in the meantime no one else would snap up the place. A year, he had thought, would be long enough to enable him to get the book written, but the English climate, even in the south-west, was not such as to make him want to start living the open-air life in the winter, at least to begin with. After he had got acclimatized it might not be so bad, and if he liked it he could stay on after he had finished the book.

The rent and what it would cost him to live wouldn't make too big a hole in his war gratuity, still untouched, and even if he didn't succeed in selling the book he'd be able to hang on for a while at any rate. He had no intention of returning to Fleet Street without making a fight to avoid that fate.

Besides, as he intended to grow as much of his own food as possible – there was a plot of promising land by the side of the chalet – he might be able to make a little pin-money by selling his surplus to the shops in Shingleton and Torcombe. If he did not move in until the following spring, Barwell and Co. would have ample time to get the place renovated and cleaned up. He had arranged to let the manager know well in advance the exact date, and the manager had promised to get one of the village women to go in and light fires, air the place and lay in some food for him.

Roy had gone back to Fleet Street feeling very pleased with himself. He had not told anyone except Bill of his plans. The latter thoroughly approved of his arrangements, got quite enthusiastic about the chalet, and threatened to come and stay with him when he could get away from the 'blasted corpses' he had to dissect from time to time. 'OK,' Roy had said, 'but don't you come popping down every weekend; I'm going down there to work, not keep a hostel for pals who are too mean to pay for their holidays.'

Roy had found his crime routine during the winter wearisome and stale. He had been surprised to find how eagerly he was looking forward to going to No Man's Cove and seeing what transformation – at least he hoped it would be a transformation – had been wrought in the chalet and to get to work on finishing it. It had been with a peculiar glow of satisfaction that he had gone to see Jim Tailby, his news editor, and told him he was resigning.

Jim had been thunderstruck. Roy had thought that he regarded him a little oddly as he said: 'Look here, old man, are you sure you're all right? If you're not feeling up to the mark – and I shouldn't be surprised if you weren't after all you went through during the war – take a couple of months sick leave, but don't chuck up your job altogether. We should find it damned difficult to replace you; no-one else has got your contacts. If it's money—'

'No, Jim, it isn't money and I'm perfectly well,' Roy had told him. 'It's just that I feel I've got to get away. It's that book I told you about. If I don't get it out of my system now, I never shall.'

'Well, I suppose you know your own business best,' Jim had replied ruefully, 'but I take a damned poor view of it. I'll bet you're back here inside a month asking if your job's been filled.' He shook his head somewhat ruefully, then smiled. 'Well, if it has I'll fire the bloke who's got it. You know that as far as I'm concerned you can come back any time.'

'Thanks, Jim,' Roy had said. 'That's very handsome of you and I won't forget it, but I doubt if I'll be back. I'm going to finish with crime reporting once and for all. After that – well, you know as much as I do. Maybe I'll wander round the world a bit – if I've anything left to wander with.'

'Any*one* you mean,' Jim had countered with a laugh.

'No, not *any*one,' Roy had replied, 'and you ought to know me better than to think there's a woman behind all this, so don't get any romantic ideas into your head. I love the ladies, when I've time for 'em and nothing better to do, but not enough to get myself entangled with one of 'em. Confirmed bachelor and man's man, that's me.'

'Your sort always fall the hardest,' Jim had said. 'I've seen

13

it happen to more than one. And mark my words: one of these days you'll fall good and proper. You'll pick up some nice girl somewhere and you'll find you can't put her down.'

'To hear you talk, anyone would think I was going on the halls with an acrobatic act,' grinned Roy.

'There are worse ways of making a living,' grunted Jim, dismissing him with a significant nod, as both his telephones rang simultaneously.

CHAPTER III

A Man's Life

Was he as woman-proof as he had boasted? Roy asked himself as he went into the chalet and set about getting breakfast. Fine man's man you are now, he reflected, getting all excited about seeing a woman's footprint in the sand. Ah well. He flipped Angus a couple of biscuits from the table's edge – he seemed to prefer them served that way – and as he ate he looked around the chalet. A trifle bare, he thought, but pretty comfortable on the whole and a darned sight better than some of the dumps you were in during the war. *And* you're on your own, with no one to please except yourself. Then he suddenly realized that he was not alone, that visitors had passed within a stone's-throw of his door not so long ago. He found the thought somewhat disturbing.

He'd had to pig it a bit the first week or so while he was moving in and getting the place to rights, and had felt that the whitewashing, the distempering and the painting, which he had done himself, would never be finished, especially the cleaning up afterwards. At first he had been too tired at night to do much writing, but gradually existence here, as in Fleet

Street, had settled into a more or less regular routine, with this difference – it was a routine of his own choosing. No one told him what to do or where to go. He got up when he liked, ate when he liked, worked at the book when he felt like it, or in the garden he had made; slept, walked, swam, sunbathed, or just loafed around as the fancy took him. He observed only one general rule – when it was fine he stayed outdoors as much as possible, saving the indoor jobs for when it was cool or wet.

After the hurly-burly of Fleet Street it seemed an ideal existence, so much so that he was thinking of staying here indefinitely. If he could make enough money out of his writing to live, not luxuriously, but simply as he was doing now . . . That was the snag, but he had high hopes of the book, which was going well, and maybe the *Tribune* would serialize it before it was published – if it ever was. He had also had one or two promising ideas for other books.

'I could think of a hell of a sight worse existence than this, couldn't you, Angus?' he asked the dog. Angus amiably chuntered agreement in the way Cairns do, for all the world as if they were talking. Angus, in fact, was having the time of his life. All through the war he had stayed with Roy's sister in Cheshire, seeing his master only when he came on leave and then not for long. He did not know what had led to his being brought to this seventh heaven, but he was all for staying here as long as possible.

Roy had found him an ideal companion, for the dog had kept him from feeling too lonely. The thing he had missed most had been the sound of other human voices – he had thought that would be the cacophony he would be most glad to get away from – and he had slipped into the habit of talking aloud both to himself and to the dog. When he thought he was doing too much of it – he'd heard it was one of the first signs of madness! – he got on his cycle and, with Angus running alongside him and barking madly, sped off along the cliff road towards Torcombe to spend the evening in the smoke-room of the Cliff Top Inn playing darts, draughts or dominoes and drinking ale with the fishermen, with whom he sometimes went out in their boats.

He knew that they thought him a bit of an odd bird, but gradually they had come to accept him, and he found himself looking forward to their company. Ruddy-faced Tod Murdock, the landlord, a retired deep-sea fisherman, his wife and daughter Modwen, always made him feel at home there. For the rest, when it was fine (and he had been very lucky in the weather that summer, the villagers told him) he worked in the garden he had made alongside the chalet. The soil, previously uncultivated, was rich. He had grown some fine peas and beans – Tod told him he ought to have entered some in the Torcombe Allotment Association's show, and had bought most of his surplus – and the other vegetables were looking fine. He had also planted various flowers in nooks and crannies along the banks of his little stream, from which he got his water, which flowed clear and cold past the chalet. It looked a picture now.

When it was too hot for gardening, he sunbathed or swam in the deep blue water of the little cove. At first he had worn bathing trunks, but as the days went by and he did not see anyone near the cove, he discarded them, and most of the time he went about naked, feeling a freedom of body movement that he had never known before. He had been fit enough when he was in the Service, but two years of Fleet Street life, irregular hours and too many cigarettes had taken the edge off that. Now, however, there was again no trace of flabbiness on any part of his six foot, well-knit frame and his skin was a rich golden brown.

He had found that outdoor work had caused the rhythm of his life to slow down – he had soon discovered that gardening can't be rushed – except when the fury of creative writing caught him in its grip, sometimes for hours at a stretch, so that he neither ate, drank nor slept, but worked on in the soft light of his oil lamp until either inspiration failed him, or his back and fingers ached so much that he could no longer sit at the typewriter at the desk he had rigged up on the verandah. After a long spell such as this he was more physically tired than any amount of digging or sawing up logs in readiness for the winter could make him. After such a phase, he would fling himself down on the divan on the verandah and sleep the sleep of exhaustion until the early morning sun on his face woke him.

As he cleared away after breakfast, Roy's mind switched from considering his mode of existence to the effect the discovery of the footprints had had on him. He was vaguely disturbed to find that it had aroused once more all the sense of curiosity which had made him one of Fleet Street's crack crime reporters. He had imagined he had lost that during the months of his Crusoe-like existence in the Cove, but perhaps it was true as they said, 'Once a newspaperman, always a newspaperman'. Already he was beginning to sense a story in those footprints.

'Blast, blast, blast!' he exclaimed aloud. 'Why the hell did this have to happen just when things were going so well?'

Angus looked up inquiringly, and then followed him out to the pool Roy had made in the stream and watched him wash the breakfast things. When they were clean Roy stood up and looked around him. In the pale morning sunlight the cove looked its loveliest. It was going to be another hot day, just right for sunbathing followed by a good long swim.

'Well, go ahead and swim,' Roy told himself again aloud. 'Forget you ever saw the footprints. You don't *have* to try to find out where they go. There's no news editor badgering you now. Try minding your own business for once. Don't get tangled up in anything that may spoil all this and take your mind off the book. That's what you've come here to write – not hectic news stories about glamorous women smugglers. You're not a crime reporter any more. You're really enjoying yourself and living your own life at last. Why spoil it?'

He turned to walk back to the chalet, and as he went the crime reporter answered him. 'It won't do any harm to find out where the footprints go,' this voice insisted insidiously. 'Besides, you may not be able to find out. You're no Boy Scout and you can't go and ask the Yard about it. Those prints have rather spoiled your beautiful dream, haven't they? You know you'll never rest now until you get to the bottom of it all, so you might as well get on with the job.' He could almost hear Jim Tailby's voice echo – 'And mind it's a good story!'

The crockery in his hands had dried in the sunshine by the time he got back to the chalet. Mechanically, his mind still on other things, Roy replaced it on the shelves. Then he put on a sports shirt and a pair of old flannels just in case he met anyone. He went outside again, closing the door behind him and locking it. Angus ran ahead, knowing he was going for a walk. Roy had gone a few yards towards the beach when he realized that this was the first time he had locked the door of the chalet since he had got out of the habit after the first week he had been there.

'Idiot,' he muttered to himself. But he didn't go back.

CHAPTER IV

Rude Awakening

The man on the camp bed groaned, stirred, opened his eyes and found himself looking at a pair of trim, silk-stocking-clad ankles. He blinked and tried to raise his head. Pain leaped like a striking beast, clawing at the back of his head and neck. A little moan escaped him and he lowered his head and closed his eyes once more. The pain seemed to take an age to subside.

When it did he opened his eyes again. The ankles were still there. The man realized at last that he was lying on his right side. He could feel a bandage round his head. He tried, more cautiously this time, to raise himself on his elbow, but at once the pain returned and forced another groan from him. As from a long way off, he heard a woman's voice.

'Ah,' it said softly, 'I think the inquisitive Major Benton is coming to himself again.'

The man on the bed heard someone move towards him, and a hand rested softly for a moment on the bandage on his forehead. So, he thought, the ankles, the voice and the hand are real. He opened his eyes, moved his head slightly and this time found himself looking up into a face framed in dark hair. The face seemed vaguely familiar, but for the moment he could not place it. The voice, pleasantly melodious he noticed, spoke again.

'Feeling better?' it asked.

'I could hardly be feeling much worse and still be alive,' Roy heard himself saying, though the voice didn't in the least sound like his. 'Where the deuce am I? What happened? Was I run over by a tank or something?'

'Not quite so bad as that,' said the woman, who sounded a little amused, 'though I must say Joe doesn't go in for half-measures. He was a Commando, I believe. Anyhow, I thought you were supposed to be pretty tough.'

'Oh, I am, am I? And who, may I ask, is Joe?' inquired Roy, thinking he would like to get his hands on him – though not just yet. 'And how do you know who I am?'

'Joe,' said the girl, ignoring the last part of the question, 'is just one of the boys we keep here to make sure that too curious people don't get poking their noses into something that doesn't concern them.'

That's one for me all right, thought Roy. Well, he supposed it served him right for not staying at home and minding his own business. But, damn it, she might be a bit more sympathetic about it, instead of so cocky and self-assured, almost as if she were delighting in his discomfiture. Perhaps she was at that. He looked her over coolly. Pretty good-looking, he decided. Not exactly a film-star profile, but still, not bad . . .

She looked as coolly at him and then spoke again. 'I gather you didn't see him.'

'See whom?' asked Roy absently. He had just decided he rather liked the tilt of her head, even if it did give her rather a haughty air; she could carry it.

21

'Joe, of course.'

'I did not. If I had, do you suppose I should be here like this? But I would very much like to see him sometime – when I'm feeling a little less like a mashed potato. Joe wasn't the only one who had Commando training, you know. If I'd had a little warning, there's just a chance I could have dealt with him.'

The girl laughed.

'It may be very funny to you,' said Roy, as sarcastically as he could, 'but at the moment I don't feel exactly like rolling in the aisle.'

'Well, it was your own fault,' the girl retorted. 'You shouldn't have been so curious. I suppose it's the news-paperman in you.'

'I can't say I care a lot for the contemptuous way in which you said the word "newspaperman", even though I have retired from the profession, but we'll let that pass for the moment. What I'm really curious about at the moment is how the devil you know so much about me.'

'We make it our business to know all about the people who come near here. We knew all about you long before you moved into the chalet.'

'Oh, you did, did you?' said Roy rather lamely. 'And you talk about *me* being curious. You've got a nerve, I must say. What business was it of yours or anyone else's, might I ask?'

'I'm afraid you'll have to wait a little longer for the answer to that question.'

'All right,' said Roy with patient resignation, 'I'll play mysteries for a while, anyhow, but how about telling me where I am and how I got here and who you are? I think we ought at least to be introduced, don't you? Seeing how intimately you know me, that is.'

'You don't remember what happened?'

'All I remember is that I set out with my dog for a perfectly innocent walk and that, just as I was getting near the entrance to the old mine – the existence of which I'd almost completely forgotten, by the way – someone or something, I don't know who or what, came up behind me and hit me good and hard for six.'

He started up suddenly, forgetting his head. He winced and gingerly felt the bandage.

'What is it now?' asked the girl.

'My dog,' said Roy. 'I've only just remembered. What happened to him? Where is he? If your damned Joe laid a finger on *him*, I'll—'

'Now don't get impatient. The dog's perfectly all right. He's in the kitchen at the moment making crooning noises at the steward. As for Joe laying a finger on him, it was the other way round. Joe wasn't at all pleased when he bit him in the juicy part of the calf.'

'Good for Angus,' nodded Roy with great satisfaction.

'Angus.' The girl repeated the name. 'Rather sweet.'

'A pity his master isn't equally popular around here, then he might get a little well-deserved sympathy.'

The girl ignored the remark. Roy gave her another long look. Despite her manner, which still annoyed him, he had to admit she was damned attractive. She was tall and slim and the business-like white coat she was wearing did not altogether conceal the by no means inconsiderable curves of her body beneath it. She returned his gaze coolly and then looked away again.

'Well,' said Roy after a pause, 'at least I was right in one thing. They *were* a woman's footprints. Yours, I presume?'

'You presume correctly, but you should never have been

23

given the chance even of seeing them. It was gross carelessness. The culprit has been suitably dealt with.'

Roy laughed. 'You sounded just like a headmistress then. I suppose you had him hung, drawn and quartered?'

The girl smiled. That's better, he thought. Why didn't she do it more often?

'Not exactly,' she said, 'but he won't have the chance to make the same mistake again. We can't afford to take the slightest risk.'

'Who are "we" and why can't "we" afford to take any chances? You really do make the most curiosity-rousing remarks and then you don't satisfy it. What *is* this place, anyway – the smugglers' lair or something?'

'No,' said the girl, 'and I don't propose to satisfy your curiosity either. I've nothing to do with the security aspect, only the scientific. You'll have to wait until the Chief gets back and you'll probably have another surprise when you see him. I hope it will be a pleasant one – for both of you.'

'Security? Scientific? The Chief? I don't get it. The war's over – or is it?'

'Not our part at any rate.'

'And what is your part?'

'It's no good your going on asking me questions. You won't get any more information out of me. I'm afraid I've said too much already, I don't know why, and to a complete stranger.'

'For one who's a complete stranger to you, you seem to know a heck of a lot about me,' retorted Roy, slowly and painfully raising himself to a sitting position. The effect made his head swim. 'Are you a first-aid expert, too?' he asked the girl, who, he thought, seemed to be eyeing him a little more sympathetically. From this position she was even better-looking than he had surmised earlier. He was sure he had seen her somewhere before, but he could not recall where.

He looked around him. He appeared to be in some sort of a cave, but it was lit by electric light and the air, he noted, was warm, not cool and dank. The cave was sparsely furnished, if you could call it that. There was the camp bed on which he was now sitting, a table covered with papers and documents and a portable typewriter. There was a shelf fixed against one wall. It contained some massive books, probably scientific works, he guessed. Underneath it was a steel filing cabinet. Behind the door was a small mirror, the only touch of femininity. Apart from this and the square of coconut matting covering the floor, the cave was devoid of decoration.

Roy's eyes came back to the girl. She had been watching him curiously as if not quite sure how to treat him.

'You still haven't told me who you are and where I am,' he remarked.

She hesitated a little before replying. 'I'm Karen Silvers, if that conveys anything to you,' she said finally, 'and we're in the old tin mine, but I can't say anything more about that. You have to—'

'I know, I know,' interposed Roy, 'I'll have to wait till the Chief gets back. I'll wait, but that's no reason, is it, why I shouldn't go on trying to solve the Karen part of the mystery?'

'I don't know that there's any mystery to solve about me,' said Miss Silvers.

'There is for me. I've heard your name before and I'm sure I've seen you, too, though I don't think we've met.' Roy repeated her name thoughtfully. 'Sounds nice, anyway.'

She laughed, and he looked at her, liking it, trying to remember. She returned his gaze steadily. Suddenly he slapped

25

his knee and exclaimed: 'Of course, that's it – or, rather, you. You're the girl scientific wonder who got the George Cross for that magnetic mine job. I remember seeing your photograph in the paper at the time. He frowned and added, 'It didn't flatter you.'

Roy thought he saw the suspicion of a blush. He went on: 'Brilliant career at Oxford, took all the degrees there were and a few others besides, didn't you, or something like that? I remember Dick Thomas, one of our reporters who tried to interview you when the award was announced, coming back to the office disgusted because you wouldn't talk. But he wrote a nice little piece about Britain's prettiest blue-stocking.'

'I remember it,' nodded Miss Silvers grimly. 'Typical of the popular Press. It annoyed me very much indeed.'

'Why should it? He was right – as far as the "prettiest" part goes, anyway. Not having any degrees myself and darned little knowledge of science, I wouldn't know about the blue-stocking part of it. But what on earth are you doing here now in an old tin mine, of all places?'

'Still working for the Government.'

'I see; one of the back room girls, eh?'

'I suppose *you* would call it that. It's what I should expect from the newspapers, I suppose.' She said it as if she didn't think much of newspapers – or newspapermen.

'Or perhaps you'd prefer to be called one of the old tin mine girls,' suggested Roy banteringly.

'That would hardly be accurate, though, of course, I shouldn't expect a journalist to bother much about accuracy. I'm the only woman here.'

'Overlooking the outrageous slight on my profession, or ex-profession, you are telling me, bit by bit, what I want to know, but you're still far from being really co-operative. I understand now why our Mr Thomas was so disappointed in you, in one respect at least.'

'And are you disappointed in me, Major Benton?'

'It couldn't be, could it, that you're fishing for compliments? No,' Roy went on hastily, seeing her indignant reaction to his question. 'No, of course not. By the way, please don't call me Major. The name is Roy – but you probably know that as well – and I'm not disappointed – yet. Unlike Mr Thomas, you see, I haven't to get a story out of you, at least not for publication in the papers.'

'You'd better not try,' said Karen Silvers, 'or you'd get into very serious trouble.'

'As hush-hush as that, is it? Hence all the security – and my poor head. What are you researching for now – a super atomic bomb to blow the world to bits?'

Roy thought he saw her give a slight start, but she recovered quickly. 'I've already told you,' she said firmly, 'that I can't answer questions about my work.'

'Nor why you do it in an abandoned Cornish tin mine?'

'No.'

'But surely I'm entitled to some sort of explanation and apology after the brutal way I've been treated when I was out for a perfectly innocent walk?'

'Was it so innocent? You couldn't by any chance have been plain nosey-parkering?'

'Really, Miss Silvers,' exclaimed Roy in mock indignation, 'how could you suspect me of such a thing?'

'You were a crime reporter, weren't you?'

'Does that mean you're engaged in something criminal? I *was* a crime reporter, but I'm a reformed character now. I don't seem to have been able to conceal any of my past from you, do I?'

'I told you we made it our business to know. We couldn't have anyone living so close as you were who might possibly, for all your war record, be an enemy agent—' She broke off, realizing that she had said more than she intended.

Roy was quick to seize the point. 'So that's it,' he said. 'I wondered why it was necessary for the disembarkation to take place in the dead of night. What *were* your boy friends bringing ashore, anyway?'

'That's enough,' retorted Miss Silvers determinedly. 'You've pumped me too much already. I often wondered why people let themselves make such stupid statements in the papers. Now I know. You'd worm anything out of anyone, but you'll get nothing more out of me. The sooner I hand you over to the Chief the better.'

'Hand me over? I like that. You don't really suppose you can keep me here, do you? Ever heard of *habeas corpus*? Why shouldn't I get up and just walk out, I'd like to know?'

Roy got up and took two or three determined steps towards the door. At least, he had meant them to be determined, but he swayed and clutched at the table. Miss Silvers took his arm and led him firmly back to the camp bed, on which he gratefully sank down again.

'That's one reason why you won't just get up and walk out. Secondly, you'd never get out without a guide. Thirdly, if by some miracle you did find your way to the exit, the guards wouldn't let you out without a pass signed by the Chief. We all have to have them. Now, would a cup of tea and a bun preserve us from more of your questions?'

'It's an idea,' agreed Roy thankfully. 'Now you're being human. I was wondering what I had to do to be offered some real hospitality.'

Miss Silvers ignored this and pressed a button on the table.

28

In a moment or two a white-jacketed steward entered the cavern through the curtained door.

'You rang, Miss Silvers?' he said quietly.

'Yes, Tom. Tea for two, please, and make it fairly strong. Our guest here is feeling a trifle faint.'

Tom glanced at Roy and a shadow of a smile passed over his weather-beaten features. 'Very good, miss,' he said, and went out as quietly as he had come in.

'That's what I call service,' commented Roy. 'Where did you get him? The Savoy?'

'Not exactly. Tom was a steward in the *Queen Mary* before the war. Then he joined up. His first ship was the *Rawalpindi*. He was torpedoed three times after that, I think. The last time he suffered so much from exposure that he was invalided out. Now he's here. All the servants and guards here are ex-Servicemen. And *very* reliable,' she added significantly.

Tom entered silently once more and placed a tea-tray on the table. 'I've brought some hot water,' he said. 'Do you think you'll want anything more, Miss Silvers?'

'Thank you, no. I'll ring if we do. Oh, you might let me know as soon as the Chief gets back, will you?'

'Certainly, miss,' said Tom, and vanished.

'Nice man, Tom,' said Miss Silvers, as she poured out tea and passed a cup to Roy; 'I don't know what we'd do without him, expecially since Pat disappeared.'

'Pat? Disappeared?'

'Another steward. Went about a week ago without saying anything to anyone. We're rather worried about him. That's why the Chief's been away today. We haven't replaced him yet. It's not easy to get people for a job like this. The conditions are so abnormal and they have to be very carefully vetted.'

'Like me, I suppose,' said Roy with a rueful grin. 'But do you mean the other steward left without any explanation?'

'Yes, one or two rather odd things have happened round here lately. That's why we arrange special receptions for curious strangers.' There was a smile about Miss Silvers' lips as she said this.

'So I've noticed.' Roy sipped his tea thoughtfully. 'This is an odd business altogether,' he said reflectively. 'A little while ago I was living what I fondly imagined was an idyllic life in a little cove far from the madding crowd. You ought to come and see my chalet, by the way, it knocks spots off this place. I set out for a perfectly innocent walk, get knocked out and dragged into a disused tin mine – at least I thought it was disused – and wake up to find myself being entertained to tea by a very charming hostess in the most unconventional setting you could imagine. You must agree it's all very unusual. What puzzles me is where I go from here.'

'That's for the Chief to say, and here he is now.'

CHAPTER V

Chief Inspector Leyland Explains

Miss Silvers rose as a short, rather shabbily dressed, sandy-haired man came into the cavern. Roy uttered a startled exclamation as the man's face came into the range of the electric light and he saw him clearly. He tried to get up from the bed, but lost his balance and sank back. 'Well, I'm damned,' he said. 'If it isn't old Wilfred!'

'I gather there isn't any need to introduce you,' remarked Miss Silvers to the grinning little man.

'There is not,' said Roy as 'old Wilfred' came over to him and they shook hands.

'And if it isn't our Roy, in trouble as usual,' said the newcomer in an unmistakable Yorkshire accent. 'And how the heck did you find your way in here?'

'I didn't,' retorted Roy indignantly. 'I was knocked out and dragged in. Ask Miss Silvers. She knows all about it.'

Miss Silvers recapitulated briefly what had happened. 'Joe hit him a little too hard,' she concluded, 'and it was quite a time before he came round.'

'I should have thought you Special Air Service lads were

31

tougher than that,' said the little man. 'Nosey-parkering as usual, were you? I thought you'd retired from newspaper work to become a famous author.'

'I had, damn it! I suppose Bill Darkis told you. But can I help it if I go for a stroll and am set on by thugs and vagabonds and heaven knows who? You're a fine one to talk, anyway, if it comes to that. What are you doing here? You're supposed to be in London tracking down criminals.'

'Wilfred' – Chief Inspector Leyland, to give him his full name, – smiled. 'I was, I was,' he said, 'but the Government found me another little job, and Scotland Yard's having to carry on without my invaluable services for the time being.'

Though he was joking when he said 'invaluable services', Chief Inspector Leyland was right, as Roy was well aware. They had met on a score of cases which he had been covering for the *Tribune* and Roy knew him as one of the most astute officers at Scotland Yard. Few equalled, and none surpassed, his knowledge of London's underworld. His shabby, shambling appearance belied him, for beneath that sandy head was a first-class brain, which Roy also knew had been employed during the war on the side of the counter-espionage branch of the Secret Service. What Roy did not know was how many spies had faced the firing-squad as a result of the little man's efforts. Was he still doing that kind of work? he wondered. Would that account for this strange reunion?

'Well, come on,' he said impatiently, 'how much longer do I have to wait for an explanation? What's it all about?'

Leyland looked at Miss Silvers. 'How much have you told him?' he asked.

'Not as little as I intended,' she replied, a trifle sheepishly, 'but you know what newspapermen are.'

Leyland smiled. 'I do, I do,' he said. He had a habit, which some people found irritating, of repeating the first phrase of a sentence. 'Especially this one,' he added.

'Yes, but I never broke a confidence,' Roy reminded him, 'so you might as well come clean. You know that if you don't tell me, I'll never rest until I find out what it's all about.'

'I know, I know,' snapped the Chief Inspector. 'That's what's worrying me, and if it were any routine job you might be able to help us. But this is rather different. It isn't a matter of cat burglars, safe-cracking, or even murder – yet. It's something far more important. I'd be for the high jump good and proper if they thought I'd whispered a word of this to anyone, however well I knew him, or however trustworthy and reliable he might be. But I don't quite see how we can keep you here indefinitely. He hesitated a moment, then added, 'There's just a remote chance that you might – I say might – be able to help us.'

'I should damned well think you can't keep me here indefinitely,' retorted Roy indignantly. 'Of all the nerve!'

'All right, all right,' said the Chief Inspector soothingly, 'there's no need to get excited. Well, here goes, though if you so much as breath a word that I've told you anything I'll have your hide. This tin mine has been converted into a secret Government laboratory – at least we thought it was secret – with Miss Silvers in charge of quite a large scientific staff. It was begun before the war ended. After Miss Silvers had finished her work on the magnetic mine, about which I expect you know, she was put in charge of a small group of scientists to work on an atomic radio-controlled rocket, with a speed and explosive power which are quite unprecedented.'

Roy whistled quietly. 'So that's it,' he said. 'No wonder you didn't want any visitors. I don't blame you.'

'I didn't think you would,' went on the Chief Inspector, 'when you knew. Just one of these things could completely wipe out a city as big as London or New York, and a hell of a sight more besides. I don't know all the scientific details – those are Miss Silvers' department; I'm concerned only with the security side of it – but I know enough to realize that no one inside or outside this country must get the secret, especially now that the work is nearly finished and the first completed rocket is being assembled.

'Every man Jack here,' he continued, 'scientific staff, servants, guards, all hand-picked and vetted, is sworn to absolute secrecy. Only a very few people, not even their own relatives, know where they are, or what they are doing. Indeed, only a few of the staff know why they are here. The guards and servants certainly don't.

'And only Miss Silvers among the scientists here knows the whole thing from A to Z. The others know only their own particular part of the work. No one leaves here, or returns, except at night. All supplies and parts are brought in at night, quietly by sea, not by noisy lorries which might attract attention. No one has any contact with the village life. At intervals they are allowed to go home, leaving at night and returning at night on foot.'

'What about plans?' asked Roy. 'Isn't there anything on paper?'

'There is,' said the Chief Inspector, 'but there's no complete plan, not even in London. The plans are divided into a dozen sections, each in a different part of the country, but they're not even under lock and key.'

'Good God!' The exclamation came from the shocked Roy. 'Why ever not?'

'We thought it would be better that way. For instance, there's one part in an ordinary envelope in the tobacco jar on my mantelpiece at home. There's another in a deed box in a solicitor's office in Taunton. There's a third among the manuscripts in the British Museum, and so on. Any ordinary person, if he happened to see them, would not understand the first thing about them, though a scientist who had worked on atomic projects might get a glimmering. But we couldn't take the risk of anyone getting hold of the complete plan, so it was divided, as I've told you. And it's a good thing it was.'

'Oh, why?'

'Because we have reason to suspect that there's a criminal organization in this country that's doing its damnedest to get the plans of the atomic rocket.'

Roy whistled thoughtfully.

'This must be since my time in Fleet Street.' He smiled a trifle ruefully at the thought that things had already moved on so far since his crime-reporting days.

'I'm not saying it's generally known,' put in Leyland quickly. 'We're not giving them any publicity – in fact we daren't.'

'Any idea who's behind it all?'

'Leyland frowned.

'Not a word about this, mind,' he repeated.

'Of course not,' said Roy, somewhat impatiently.

'Do you think we ought to tell him all this, Inspector?' queried Karen Silvers anxiously, a gleam of apprehension in her grey-blue eyes. 'After all, what's to stop him ringing up his old newpaper as soon as he gets out of here—'

'I'll take a chance on that, Miss Silvers,' replied Leyland drily. 'He's always played straight with me, and he's a useful man to have around at times.'

'Thank you, Inspector,' said Roy ironically. 'But I won't be of much use unless I know the person I'm up against. You know my weakness for facts.'

The Inspector slowly filled his pipe and lit it.

'This may come as a bit of a surprise to you, Roy,' he said slowly, as he held a match to Karen's cigarette. 'And you must realize it's quite off the record. There's a lot to be checked yet before we can grab this customer.'

'I take it there's no time to be wasted,' said Roy meaningly as he took three fierce puffs at his cigarette. 'Come on, Inspector – who is this mystery man?'

Leyland passed his hand over his thin sandy hair, and said in a casual voice, 'You've heard of Fabian Delouris, I suppose.'

Roy looked up quickly.

'Delouris – the armaments king?' he exclaimed with a low whistle. 'But I thought he was worth millions.'

'He is worth millions,' nodded Leyland.

'Then why should he go in for crime at his time of life?'

'There are other things besides money – such as power, for instance,' murmured Leyland. 'As to crime – well,when a man's been in the armaments racket for twenty years I don't suppose he has many morals left. He did quite a bit of gun-running and stirring up revolutions in his young days, you know . . . before he dealt in a really big way.'

'A case of "once a crook", eh?' mused Roy, looking across at Karen Silvers, who was smoking her cigarette and apparently lost in her own thoughts.

'Why do you think Delouris should suddenly break out at this stage?' he continued. Leyland shrugged.

'Don't ask me to define his motives. Maybe he thinks the man who controls the atom will be the king-pin of existence . . . maybe it's just a fit of panic that rifles and machine-guns won't count for much in the armaments market from now on, and he simply wants to corner atomic weapons to keep 'em off the market.'

'What makes you suspect him, anyhow?'

The Inspector smiled. 'I'm not going into all that now, Roy. As you know, we've our own methods of finding out things, and several men we've been checking on have led us straight to Delouris in one way or another. As far as we can judge, he's got a pretty hefty organization behind him, and it's going to be none too pleasant when we get to grips with them. They're a tough lot of boys – several ex-German prisoners who escaped, a sprinkling of deserters from the American Forces when they were over here, one or two old lags we know well enough, and a couple of pilots from the Australian Air Force, who fly his special private 'planes, Oh yes, it's quite a set-up, I can tell you. Quite a set-up!'

Roy shook his head a trifle dubiously.

'I'm still surprised that a man like Delouris, who can make his millions without much effort, would think such a gamble is worth the risk.'

The Inspector carefully stubbed out his cigarette.

'How many of us would resist the opportunity to become a world dictator?' he slowly demanded.

Roy glanced across at Karen. 'There are other things in life,' he murmured.

'Not for him. He's had all the women he wants . . . all the money . . . the worldly goods . . . He saw how far Hitler went – and I reckon he means to profit by his mistakes.'

Roy eased his bandage a little. The throbbing had almost stopped now, and the hot tea had cleared the fuzziness from his brain.

'Well, I can see I'll have to bolt my doors and windows in future, Inspector,' he said lightly.

'I should strongly advise it,' declared Leyland, with surprising seriousness.

'Eh – what d'you mean?'

'I mean,' replied Leyland deliberately, 'that we have reason to suspect that the headquarters of this organization is somewhere within five miles of where you're sitting.'

CHAPTER VI

Bait for a Trap

Roy was too staggered to say anything for a moment. Then
he burst forth: 'Well, for crying out loud! If you know that,
why on earth don't you round 'em up?'

'Well,' said the Chief Inspector with a smile, 'it's not
quite so simple as that. For one thing, I'm not sure exactly
where they are, and for another, and the most important,
Delouris, to the best of our information, isn't with them
– yet.'

'What do you mean by "yet"?' asked Roy.

'Just that he isn't wherever the others are. Our latest report
says that he was seen two days ago in the north of England,
but we're rather expecting him to pay us a visit soon when
they're ready to move. You see, to some extent, indeed to
a very large extent, we're using this mine and what's going
on here as bait for a trap. We must be sure that when it's
sprung they're all in it, but especially Delouris. He's the man
we want most of all. He's dangerous.'

'Sounds a bit risky to me with all this at stake,' said Roy,
'but I suppose you know best. But what makes you think

they're in the neighbourhood, anyway? And how did they get to know about this place? Has somebody talked?'

'I think they're in the neighbourhood because within the last few months a Ministry of Food depot, located here during the war, has twice been robbed of substantial supplies. A number of farms have also missed food and clothing, and some weeks ago a coal pit not far from here was robbed of tools, props, and even a few tubs.'

'I see the point about the food and clothes,' said Roy, 'but why the mining tools?'

'Well, this is a mine, isn't it?' asked Karen Silvers, rather impatiently – 'and one way of getting into a mine, especially if you don't want to be seen going in at the front door, would be to mine your way into it – if you'll forgive the pun.'

'But surely that would attract attention, wouldn't it?' objected Roy. 'You can't start mining even in a spot as quiet as this without somebody spotting you. Or can you?'

'Forgive me for pointing out that mining is an underground occupation,' said Karen drily.

'It's certainly a possibility we've got to watch,' said Leyland, 'but so far we haven't found any trace of it, or, indeed, of any of them. No one has even reported seeing any strangers, and you know what Cornish villagers are about strangers. That's where you may be able to help. The Cornish police know, of course, that I'm down here, but they think it's just to investigate the robberies. I've kept out of the public eye as much as possible because I don't want any gossip about my being here. You're pretty well known in the village by this time and you could make enquiries for me without attracting attention. I'd also like you to keep your eyes and ears open for anything suspicious, and let me know.'

'But how can I do that without coming to the mine?' asked Roy.

'Leave a message addressed to me at Torcombe police station. I make a call there some time or other every day or night, usually night.'

'Right,' said Roy. 'I could do with a little excitement again. Perhaps I've been stagnating too much here.'

Chief Inspector Leyland smiled. 'I wondered how long you'd stick it when Bill Darkis told me you were here.'

'Now don't get me wrong,' protested Roy. 'I'm going to stay until I finish that book, if I bust in the attempt, and perhaps longer if Scotland Yard will leave me in peace, but a change of routine may do me good. Besides,' he added, with a smiling glance at Miss Silvers, 'there *are* other attractions about the job.'

The Chief Inspector shot a look at them. Roy grinned.

'One point that still puzzles me,' he went on, 'is how Delouris and his gang got wind of this in the first place and how they all knew where to make for when they got out.'

'We're not sure about that, but about six months after this place began to operate we rounded up a spy not ten miles from here. He was shot, of course, but he might have got a radio message away before we picked him up. That could have been sent back to Delouris, who had escaped a couple of months earlier. We think that – with help, of course – he engineered the escapes of the other men he wanted for his scheme and told them to meet him in this locality. Since then, they may have got some information from Pat, one of our stewards, who disappeared a couple of weeks ago. He knew a little of what was going on here – not much, thank God, but knowing Delouris and some of the gang he's got

41

with him, including a couple of the worst Gestapo types, I shouldn't imagine they'll stop at anything to get what they can out of him.'

'Poor Pat,' said Miss Silvers. 'I liked him almost as much as Tom. And I'm sure he wouldn't talk.'

Roy glanced questioningly at Leyland.

'I'm afraid,' he said to the girl 'that you don't know the habits of our late enemies very well. You should have been in France with me once or twice. It's surprising what a man will do if he's merely hit across the throat with a rubber truncheon. Of course, Delouris probably hasn't got the sort of facilities here that they had in France, but I've no doubt he's capable of devising some.'

The girl was looking a bit pale.

'I hope I haven't said anything to shock you,' said Roy, 'but you ought to know the kind of people you're up against.'

He stretched and looked at his watch. 'About time I was getting back to the chalet,' he said – 'that is, if I'm permitted to go.'

Both Leyland and Miss Silvers smiled. Roy gingerly felt the back of his head.

'You must introduce me to Joe sometime,' he said. 'I'd rather like to meet him.'

Leyland also looked at his watch. 'I'd rather you didn't go until it gets really dark, if you don't mind,' he said. 'If I hadn't a hell of a lot of reports to do I'd show you around. Perhaps Miss Silvers . . .' He looked at her with an unspoken question. 'She knows much more about the technicalities of this place than I do.'

She did not look very enthusiastic. 'Well, I've got a good deal of work of my own to do—'

'But you could put it off for one evening, couldn't you?'

pleaded Roy. 'After all, you don't get many visitors here, and you do owe me a little compensation, I think.'

'Very well,' she said, with a well-I-suppose-I-can't-get-out-of-it air, 'but this mustn't be taken as a precedent. Anyway, I don't suppose you'll be coming here again. Will he, Chief?'

'I don't think it would be very advisable,' said Leyland. 'For more than security reasons.'

'And what exactly do you mean by that remark?' demanded Roy, though there was a glint in his eye which told the Chief Inspector that he knew exactly what he meant.

'Nothing at all, nothing at all,' said Leyland airily. 'Well, get off if you're going. I've work to do.'

They went.

CHAPTER VII

Atomic Secrets

'I'm afraid you'll have to put it to me in words of one syllable,' Roy remarked to Miss Silvers as they went along a corridor outside the room they had just left. 'I'm a child where scientific matters are concerned.'

'Only in scientific matters?'

'Miss Silvers,' said Roy with mock severity, 'I'm beginning to think you don't like me.'

She ignored this and stopped at a door on her right. 'I suppose I ought really to have begun showing you the thing from the beginning,' she said, 'but that would have entailed a bit of a detour. It will be quicker this way, but I don't suppose you'll mind.'

'Want to get it over, eh?'

Instead of replying Miss Silvers opened the door. 'This is one of the workshops,' she said.

They were looking into a long low room, or cavern, fitted with lathes and other kinds of machinery. Half a dozen men in overalls were working there.

'They're working on various parts of the rocket,' explained

Miss Silvers. 'It's all highly technical, I'm afraid, but these men are the pick of their kind from the whole country and they love the work.'

'Even though they don't know what it's for?'

'Well, they know the general idea, but this work is so highly skilled and must be absolutely accurate. That appeals to their sense of craftsmanship, as well as their technical skill.'

'Must be a bit dull working in this place, with no opportunities for recreation.'

'Oh, we have a games and recreation room. There's billiards and snooker, table tennis, darts, cards, chess, draughts—'

'Whoa!' said Roy, laughing. 'That's enough. No swimming pool?'

'No swimming pool, though a few of the hardier spirits occasionally slip out for a moonlight bathe, when it's warm enough.'

They went along seemingly innumerable galleries, seeing more workshops and laboratories, all fitted with the latest apparatus, over which men were busily poring. Finally, after they had walked what seemed miles to Roy, they came to a big, central chamber in which a monstrous-looking machine, rather like a cross between a flying bomb and a super-streamlined 'plane, was taking shape under the hands of overalled workmen.

'Well, this is it,' said Miss Silvers, and Roy noted the ring of pride in her voice and saw the light of enthusiasm in her eyes.

'Odd,' he said, and it was almost as if he were talking to himself, 'that a woman as attractive as you are can get so het up about a thing as inhuman as this. I suppose it must be the joy of creating something which no one has ever created before. But don't you ever wake up in the middle of the night in a cold sweat when you think what this thing might do if it got into the wrong hands? What could it do, by the way?'

She was silent for a moment. 'I don't really know,' she said. 'No one knows. But one atom bomb of the Hiroshima type equalled, according to U.S. calculations, the full load of 210 Super Fortresses. The Hiroshima bomb, of course, is now quite out of date.' She paused, as if to let this sink in. When she spoke again it was to ask a question.

'Ever read a book called *Man's Last Choice*, by E. M. Friedwald?'

'Can't say I have.'

'You should. Everybody should. Then maybe they'll realize what they may be letting themselves in for if they don't insist on the nations controlling atomic power. Well, Mr Friedwald estimates that an atomic war – the real thing – would be from 500 to 1000 times as big as the last war. The last war cost over 10,000,000 lives. So work out the cost of the next one. You get a figure of probably 10,000,000,000 fatal casualties – that's only from two and a half to five times as many people as there are on this earth. That should answer another of your questions.

'Yes, I do sometimes wake up in a cold sweat in the middle of the night, especially since I knew about the danger from Delouris and his crowd. Sometimes I almost feel as if I'd like to smash this thing, this dream of mine, to smithereens. I would smash it rather than Delouris should ever get his hands on it. But then I think of what it might do for the peace of the world in our hands. Possession of this weapon, when it becomes known, as it is intended that it shall become known at the right time, ought to deter anyone else from starting another war.'

'A curious way of preventing war,' observed Roy, 'to have

a bigger stick than the other fellow, but human nature being what it is at present, and nations being what they are, I suppose it's the best we can do until we learn more sense. I wonder if we ever shall.'

'But of course,' said Miss Silvers, and her tone admitted of no doubt. 'We must. I couldn't go on working if I didn't believe that. There'd be no point in it. It may not come in our time, of course, but surely we have an obligation to humanity to think beyond our own little lives.'

'Idealist as well as scientist, are you?' said Roy, and he looked at her with a new interest. She coloured a little. Roy reflected that it was a curious interlude in such a setting.

Miss Silvers broke the spell. 'Well, that's that. And now I must get back to my work, if you don't mind.'

'Don't you ever relax?'

'Sometimes.' There was a note of regret in her voice. 'But I haven't had much time for it during the last few years.

'Nor have I. But it's a good thing to do now and again, no matter how busy one is. I've found that all right during the last few months while I've been going back to nature, so to speak. The rhythm of my life's altered completely – at least it had until this morning! It's been slower, deeper, richer, more natural altogether.' He paused and sighed. 'You ought to come and see my chalet and spend a lazy day or two sunbathing. It would do you good, make you forget all this load of responsibility. It's too much for one person to carry alone.'

'Oh, I'm not carrying it alone,' said Miss Silvers. 'There are lots of scientists all over the world who feel as I do. We all share the burden in some degree or other. That makes it easier.'

'Still, you ought to relax more. What about my sunbathing offer?'

47

Miss Silvers laughed. 'Persistent, aren't you? I suppose that's the newspaperman in you. Well, maybe one day, when this is all over, I'll accept your invitation. And now we must be getting back.'

Going back along the galleries Roy stumbled once and nearly fell. He leaned against the wall for a moment. 'Sorry,' he said, 'but I feel a bit faint.'

Karen Silvers was suddenly all contrition. 'What an idiot I am!' she exclaimed. 'I'd forgotten all about your head. And I've been dragging you along for what must have seemed miles.'

'They did,' Roy said, with a rueful grin, 'but a good night's rest should put me right.'

She looked at her watch. 'Good heavens! We've been on the go for nearly two hours. And it won't be dark yet. You must have some supper before you go.'

Chief Inspector Leyland was tidying up his papers when they rejoined him. Roy was glad to drop down on the camp bed.

'Miss Silvers exhausted you?' asked Leyland. 'She's a bit of an enthusiast, you know.'

'Yes, I'm afwully sorry,' said Miss Silvers. 'I'd forgotten all about the poor man's injury. It won't be dark yet, so what about some supper?'

'Well, I'm ready for it,' said Leyland, 'and I'm sure Roy is. I'll clear these things away while you get Tom on the job.'

He stuffed his papers into a briefcase and Miss Silvers went out to order supper. She brought Angus back with her. He jumped on the camp bed and crawled all over Roy.

'You faithless hound,' said Roy, pushing him off. 'Forget all about me when you're near a kitchen, don't you? I hope Tom hasn't given you all the supper.'

'No, sir, I've managed to save something for you,' said Tom, who had come in and was beginning to lay the table. 'Persuasive little fellow, isn't he?' he added, nodding at Angus. 'Reminds me of a dog we had on the *Rawalpindi*. Went down with the ship, poor chap.'

In a few minutes they were sitting down to a supper of steak and chips, followed by cheese, biscuits and celery, and pints of beer to wash it down.

'I must say you do yourselves well here,' remarked Roy as he drained his glass. 'I'll bet that steak wasn't on the ration. I haven't tasted one like it since the war – and not many of them then.'

'Well,' said Leyland drily, 'the people here *are* doing rather important work, you know. Must keep them equal to the job.'

He filled and lit his pipe, while Roy and Miss Silvers lit cigarettes. They talked for a little about the plan of campaign, Roy promising to begin his inquiries in the morning, and then Leyland, glancing at his watch, said it should be dark enough for them to leave.

'Shall I guide you to the entrance?' he asked, or would you prefer Miss Silvers?'

'Much as I like you,' said Roy, 'there are occasions when I prefer the company of others. Besides, I've adopted Miss Silvers as my special guide in this mine, so if she doesn't mind—'

'All right, all right,' chuckled the Chief Inspector. 'I get your point.'

If Miss Silvers did, she did not show it. Instead, she again began to protest that she must get on with her work.

'That'll keep for a few minutes longer,' said Leyland. 'You haven't been out of this place for a week. You look as if you need a breath of fresh air.'

She did not seem very pleased by this remark and sighed resignedly.

'Very well,' she said, 'but don't blame me if we fall behind schedule.'

'I won't,' said Leyland. 'Good night, Roy. I hope you'll be all right in the morning.'

'Good night, and I hope I'll have some information for you soon.'

'Well, look out for yourself. It's more than possible that you were watched this morning.'

'I will, but two can play at that game. I've done a little watching at times myself, but I'll be careful.'

'See that you are. Don't underestimate the Delouris crowd. They mean business.'

Miss Silvers led Roy down another labyrinth of galleries, Angus following. She did not speak, and he sensed that she was feeling a little resentful. As they neared an opening, through which he could feel the night air, a figure flitted in front of them. Roy caught Miss Silvers by the arm and drew her to one side.

'It's all right,' she said rather impatiently. 'That's only one of the guards.'

'My dear friend Joe?'

'No, Joe will be off duty by this time. It's Spud. He was one of the sea-going engineers who had charge of the spud piers of the Mulberry harbour at Arromanches. That's how he got his name.'

''Evening, Spud,' she said as they came up to the man. He was holding a Sten gun under his arm and stood to one side to let them pass. 'All quiet?'

''Evening, Miss Silvers. Yes, it's quiet as a grave. Not going out, are you?'

'No, just seeing our guest off. I shan't be a minute.'

Spud grinned. "Evening, sir,' he said to Roy. 'I hope Joe didn't hit you too hard. He had a shock when he found out *who* he'd hit. We heard quite a bit about you during the war, you see. But it was nothing to the shock he had when your dog bit him. Plucky little fellow, I must say.' He bent down and patted Angus's head, chuckling. 'Joe was never much of a one for dogs, I'm afraid.'

'And I,' said Roy, 'was never much of a one for being hit on the head. Anyway, you can tell him from me there's no hard feelings – except in my head.'

Spud laughed. 'I'll tell him. Good night, sir.'

'Good night.'

They walked on a few yards until they were out of sight of Spud and at the entrance of the tunnel, which was well screened by bushes and shrubs. Roy stopped, looked up at the clear, star-filled sky and sighed.

'What a lovely night! It's perfect for a walk. I suppose you wouldn't care to see me safely back to the chalet? I think I shall sleep out tonight.'

'It is a lovely night,' said Miss Silvers, a little less grudgingly, he thought, 'but I've got work to do and I've wasted too much time already.'

'Wasted? That's not very flattering.'

'It wasn't meant to be. I regard anything that takes me away from my work as a waste of time.'

'What a slave-driver you are and what fun you're missing! Fancy talking about work on a night like this – the air soft as silk, a sky like black velvet, studded with jewels, the sea murmuring gently in the background. It's perfect – and you talk about work!'

She did not speak. His hand touched hers. It was cold,

and he took it between his own as if to warm it. She did not withdraw it, but it remained limp in his without answering the pressure of his own. He looked at her and in the starlight he could see that she was steadily returning his gaze. He bent his head and the thought that came absurdly into his mind was what Jim Tailby would say if he could see him now.

She did not move away and he kissed her on the mouth, gently at first and then more warmly. But there was no response from the body he held in his arms. The feeling of tenderness died in him like a flower withered in a drought. Damn it all, he thought savagely, as, feeling a complete fool, he let her go and stood silently beside her, what can the woman be made of? It had been like kissing a block of wood, even though she was softer.

It was Miss Silvers who broke the uncomfortable silence.

'I suppose I should feel flattered,' she said, and her voice was cool and calm, 'but I don't. Now, if you've quite finished, I'll go. Good night.'

CHAPTER VIII

A Shot in the Dark

She turned and left him standing there. He had never felt more deflated in his life. The thought uppermost in his baffled mind was that it was as if she had been experimenting with his emotions and her own – if she had any – as coolly and detachedly as if she'd been in her damned laboratory. Was she all scientist, he asked himself, this woman who was unlike anyone he had met before, or was there flesh and blood and a heart in her as well as a brain? He had thought so once or twice in the mine, but to have tried him out like a guinea pig – that was insufferable.

Roy swore, and kicked furiously at a broken branch. Angus, who had stood patiently by during all this, went haring off into the bushes after it. Roy set off towards the chalet. Well, he reflected, he'd take damned good care he didn't make a fool of himself again, or give her the opportunity of making him one. It was incredible that a woman so physically attractive as she was could be so cold and indifferent. Or perhaps he just wasn't her type, if she had a type. Maybe she'd thought he'd just been trying to get fresh with her and resented it in the only way she could without making a scene. Somehow he felt she would dread scenes. Oh, hell, Roy my boy, forget it, he told himself.

He tried to do so all the way back to the chalet, but could not forget the feel of her body in his arms and the touch of her lips on his, cool and impersonal though they had been. Jim Tailby would certainly have had a laugh if he'd been there to see what happened and if he knew how he was still thinking about her. He would have twitted him unmercifully. What was it he had said – 'Mark my words, one of these days you'll fall good and proper. You'll pick up some nice girl somewhere and you'll find you can't put her down.'

Well, Roy reflected bitterly, it certainly hadn't been a case of his putting Miss Silvers down. The boot had been on the other foot. She'd done it to him in very decided fashion and he hadn't liked it one little bit. He had a sneaking feeling, too, that Jim would hardly approve of the way in which he was thinking of Miss Silvers now. He would probably regard it as a danger sign. Perhaps it was. He was surprised to find that, despite the rebuff, he didn't care. After all, he'd been in some pretty dangerous spots before – but, he had to admit, none quite like this.

Angus broke into his train of thought by yelping excitedly as they neared the chalet.

'Shut up, you idiot!' Roy told him angrily as he put the key in the door and turned the lock. Angus took no notice and Roy bent to slap him, pushing the door open as he did so. Then the whole world seemed to explode in his face.

It took Roy a little time afterwards to recall the exact sequence of events, but it worked out something like this – first a flash of orange light with fiery red in its centre, which completely blinded him for a moment or two; then a cracking explosion, a whistle in the air over his bent head, and finally a faint clattering noise.

Instinctively, from his stooping position, he dropped flat on his face on the verandah. He remembered thinking as he fell, and feeling rather pleased about it, that he hadn't forgotten his Service training. When, in the next few moments, as he lay there nothing else happened, he began slowly to worm his way on his stomach into the chalet, where he could hear Angus scuffling excitedly to and fro.

In the darkness he felt for the table in the middle of the room and cautiously raised himself. He reached up and his groping hand found the matches near the lamp where he always kept them. He waited a few moments, listening, then struck a match. A quick glance told him that the room was empty. He sighed with relief, got to his feet, lit the lamp and quickly closed the door.

Then he looked around, and on the mantelpiece, facing the door, he saw what he had expected to find. Lying on its side was a still-smoking pistol. It had been the central part of a neatly made booby trap, the sort of thing he had often come across during the war, arranged so that the pistol would fire immediately anyone opened the door.

He thought: If I hadn't stooped to smack Angus I'd be a dead man now. Suddenly he felt clammily cold. He poured himself a stiff whisky and drank it. That made him feel better. You must have gone soft, he told himself. You never felt like this during the war. But that had been different. You expected this sort of thing then. Your life hung by a thread which might snap at any moment. But you didn't expect to find booby traps in a little chalet tucked away in a quiet spot like No Man's Cove.

He examined the pistol again. It was a German Luger

and the trap had been very neatly arranged. The Germans were experts at booby traps, and Leyland had 'guessed' that Delouris and his other escaped friends were within five miles of the old mine. This looked like something more than a guess, but if Delouris and his crowd were responsible for this, how had they got on to him so soon, and why?

Angus was still sniffing all round the chalet, especially near the side window. Roy went over to it. One of the panes of glass near the catch had been neatly removed. So that was how they'd got in, if it was 'they'. Quite simple, of course.

He stood holding the pistol in his hand, pondering his best line of action. His first impulse was to go back to the mine and tell Leyland what had happened, but, he reflected, he might still be under observation by the person or persons who had set the trap to see if it had claimed its victim. He decided that news of the incident could wait until morning when he went into Torcombe. He could leave a message for Leyland at the police station.

Roy turned down the lamp, walked to the door and looked cautiously out. It was a beautiful night. The air was soft and still warm. He could hear the sea murmuring quietly along the beach. On any other night he would have gone for a bathe before he went to bed, but the idea did not tempt him tonight. Orion was flashing jewelled messages in the sky and the perfume of the night-scented stocks he had planted near the stream was pleasant in his nostrils. This was a night for romance, if ever there was one, not for shootings and what-have-you, but all he'd got was something akin to a slap in the face. He sighed a little, turned and went inside.

He didn't sleep on the verandah that night. Instead he locked the door of the chalet, saw that all the windows were securely fastened, took out his old Service revolver from his pack and saw that it was loaded. Then he lay down, but without taking off his clothes.

It was a long time before he got to sleep, though the night was calm and peaceful, except for Angus's sighings and snorings. When he did get off, he dreamed an absurd boy's adventure sort of dream in which he chased film gangsters all over England, and rescued Miss Silvers from their clutches in all kinds of extraordinary situations. But every time he tried to claim his due reward, she held him off with a pistol – a Luger pistol.

CHAPTER IX

Smugglers and Monks

Torcombe was almost unique in being a Cornish village which did not figure in the handsomely illustrated *Holiday Haunts* annuals with which the railway companies seek to beguile the jaded city-dweller with vistas of golden beaches and laughing bathing beauties perched nonchalantly on razor-edged rocks, which must have been extremely uncomfortably even to the photographers' models who specialized in the type of work.

True, there was a year before the war when it did achieve a bare mention as a 'quaint village with good fishing', but not even the word 'quaint' was enough to cause a notable increase in Torcombe's population that summer, and as only one of the residents, old Mrs Tregarthy, who everyone thought was a little touched anyway, took advantage of the opportunity to advertise board and lodgings, h. and c., one minute from sea, Torcombe was thereafter left to linger in obscurity, so far as the railway companies were concerned.

The railway guide was correct, however, in saying that Torcombe had good fishing. It had, and it smelt like it, which was probably why the occasional wandering visitors who did find their way there in summer took a look, a sniff and then departed for other points of the compass. That was all right by Torcombe; the inhabitants just went on with their business of fishing.

There were a few regular enthusiasts who came every year to enjoy the excellent offshore fishing, which provided good sport. They generally stayed at the pub on the quayside, the 'Harbour Bar', and 'stayed' was often the correct word so far as the bar part of it was concerned, for Tim Austell's home-brewed ale was something quite unique to those who, for the fifty or so other weeks of the year, knew only the suburban roadhouse concoctions.

Torcombe, although it had been a fishing village for hundreds of years, still wasn't much to look at. Like Topsy, it had 'just growed'. There was the harbour, tiny but adequate, the quayside with its clutter of nondescript buildings that looked as if they were never used; the pub; a few houses straggling up the road that wound from the sea towards the top of the cliff; a few shops, some of which served teas to the few casual visitors who did drop in; and, at the top of the cliff, the village church and graveyard wherein rested the last remains of the sons and daughters of Torcombe who had lived and died there, always excepting those who had gone down to the sea in ships and had not returned; whether from fishing trips or from the Royal and Merchant Navies to which Torcombe had loyally sent its quota in two world wars.

Roy had been in the habit of going to the village at least once a week, to get the supplies he needed from Mrs Lee's general store next to the lifeboat-house, and had grown to like the place and the people, both of which were unspoilt, unlike most seaside places which depend on visitors in summer to keep them going during the winter. He had one or two regular ports of call besides Mrs Lee's – the post-office, the vicar's, Charlie's garage and finally the 'Harbour Bar', where he generally called in for a drink or two and a gossip before setting off back to the chalet.

This morning he followed his usual routine after parking his cycle on the bare patch next to the Fishermen's Institute. He had left Angus behind, much to his disgust.

'Oh no,' Roy had said to him when he was fussing around, sensing as he always did that his master was going out, 'if nasty people are going to pay calls on us while we're away, somebody had better stick around and keep an eye on the place.' Angus's ears had dropped at the negative tone in his master's voice. 'Sorry, old boy. Besides, I'm going on the bike and you always bark your head off at it. You stay here and tell me when I get back if anybody's been.'

Though Roy had slept that night with one eye open, so to speak, there had not been any further incidents. He had typed a brief note about the booby trap affair to the Chief Inspector and had it in his pocket now, intending to deliver it at the police station.

Exchanging a greeting with a few fishermen who were leaning on the quay wall, no doubt waiting for the 'Harbour Bar' to open its doors, Roy started past them up the road and went into Mrs Lees 'General Stores', which always looked as if a hurricane had just visited it. How the old woman ever found anything was a mystery to him, but she did, and the range of goods she stocked was phenomenal for such a place.

As this wasn't his regular day of call, Mrs Lee was surprised to see him, but he told her he had run out of cigarettes and bought three 20-packets. Mrs Lee was always ready for a gossip, and as there was no one else in the shop, she was soon retailing a stream of village trivialities, ranging from the fact that little Willie Carbis (for whom the fishermen and their boats exercised an irresistible attraction) had once more fallen off the quay wall into the harbour and had been fished out howling his head off, to a résumé of the vicar's sermon last Sunday.

'Any visitors in town?' Roy asked casually.

No, said Mrs Lee, there weren't, and was off again on a trail of reminiscences to which Roy listened as patiently as he could until the arrival of a woman, with two grubby children, one of whom he recognized as Willie Carbis, distracted Mrs Lee's attention. In the loud-voiced resumption of the discussion of Willie's fall, Roy was able to make his escape unnoticed.

He drew a blank also at the post-office, where he posted a letter to Bill Darkis. The wizened Mrs Treorchy, who always reminded Roy of a dried apple, prided herself, like Mrs Lee, on the fact that nothing could happen in Torcombe without her knowing about it. Indeed, there was almost as much rivalry between them as there was between two newspapermen to get a scoop, and it was a source of considerable annoyance to Mrs Lee that Mrs Treorchy's official position as postmistress gave her the chance, which she never missed, to acquaint herself with as much of Torcombe's correspondence as she could without actually steaming open envelopes, and Mrs Lee had darkly hinted more than once that she did even that.

But even Mrs Treorchy failed Roy this morning, so after buying a few stamps he walked up the hill to the vicarage, where, as he expected, he found the Rev. Thomas Palmer pottering as usual in his garden.

'Ah, it's you,' said the vicar rather obviously, straightening up from a bed of roses over which he had been bending, as Roy came in at the gate. 'You're just in time for coffee. Come in.'

Roy followed the vicar up the path and through the french windows into his study, which commanded wonderful views of the coast. Motioning Roy to a seat, the vicar rang a bell which brought old Hannah, his housekeeper, shambling in.

'We've got a visitor, Hannah,' said the vicar. 'Can we have coffee now, please?'

'It's almost ready,' said Hannah in a thin, reedy voice. 'I was just going to call you in. Good morning, Major,' she added, turning to Roy. Hannah came of a soldiering family, and always believed in giving officers their proper rank, although the vicar had told her more than once that Roy didn't like it.

'Good morning, Hannah,' Roy greeted her. 'How's the lumbago today?'

'No better, sir, no better,' quavered Hannah, putting her hand to her back, as if Roy's question had reminded her of something she had forgotten, or lost.

'Oh, I'm sorry,' said Roy. 'Did you try that ointment I got for you?'

'I did,' said Hannah, 'but it only made it move somewhere else.' She shuffled out, and Roy smiled.

'Well, what brings you to Torcombe?' the vicar asked. 'This isn't your usual day, is it?'

'No,' said Roy, 'but I had one or two calls I wanted to make and I thought I'd just drop in. Any news?'

'No, nothing,' said the vicar, 'except the usual lack of interest my parishioners show in their immortal souls.'

Roy laughed. 'I've never understood,' he said, 'why a man like you, with your qualifications, and in the prime of life, should have buried yourself in a place like this. If you'd stayed in London you'd probably have been a bishop by this time, or at least a dean.'

'You flatter me, but if I had become one I should have far more worries than I have now. No, I'm quite happy here, with my garden and my books and the sound of the sea in my ears.'

Roy looked round at the book-laden shelves of the study. 'And your archaeology,' he added. 'Been doing any more excavating at the old Priory?'

Roy asked the question as casually as he could. He knew the vicar had done a great deal of research into the history of Torcombe and especially of the old Priory, the ruins of which stood two miles inland from the sea, and where he was aware the vicar had done some digging the summer before.

'No, I've been too busy in the garden,' replied the vicar, 'but I'll get around to it one of these days.'

'You know,' said Roy, as Hannah brought in the coffee and set the tray down on a little table beside them, 'I'd like to have a look round there myself some time. I should imagine it's very interesting.'

The vicar sipped his coffee before replying. 'It is,' he said. 'Perhaps you don't know it, but there are stories that, way back in the good old smuggling days, the monks weren't above receiving a good deal of the stuff brought ashore at your cove. I've one or two old books which hint at quite an elaborate series of underground passages linking the old tin mine with the Priory, and both of them with the Cliff Top Inn.'

'Oh, why the "Cliff Top"?' Roy asked. What the vicar had told him was exciting confirmation of a theory he had been playing with for some time.

'As an escape. The stuff was landed at No Man's Cove, taken into the mine and then to the Priory. The link with the

"Cliff Top" was in case the revenue men got to them and they needed another way of escape. Eventually, of course, they did. The passages are said to have been filled in, but I've an old chart which purports to show where the one from the Priory to the mine begins. I was trying to find the entrance when I was excavating there last year, but it rained so much that I got very little done.'

'Have you been up to the Priory lately?'

'No, not since last year, though I've been intending to do so, but there's so much to do in the garden.'

'Does anyone beside you ever go there?'

'Not that I know of. An occasional tramp, possibly, but that's all, I should say. You seem very interested in the Priory all of a sudden. Why?'

'Oh, no particular reason,' said Roy offhandedly. 'The place just happens to attract me. I always did like delving into the past, and trying to recapture atmosphere.'

The vicar laughed. 'It sounds to me as if you're well on the way to becoming an antiquarian yourself. We'll have a walk up to the Priory one day if you like and I'll show you where I was working.'

'That's very kind of you. I'd love it. And while I'm here, could I have a look at the chart?'

'With pleasure.'

The vicar got up and went across to one of the book-shelves, returning with a dusty old tome which he laid on the table. He opened it and took from the back a faded sheet of paper which was almost dropping to pieces. Carefully he opened it and spread it on the table. Roy bent over it and saw that it was a rough map of Torcombe and the surrounding area. It showed the village, the Cliff Top Inn, the Priory, No Man's Cove and the tin mine, and linking them were dotted lines.

'Those indicate where the passages used to run,' said the vicar, tracing them with his finger, 'but whether they ever were really filled in as they say, I don't know. That's what I was hoping to find out.'

'Whereabouts in the Priory does the passage come out?'

'I don't know for certain, but I think it's somewhere here on the tin mine side of the ruins.'

'Very interesting,' commented Roy, as the vicar carefully folded up the crude map and replaced it in the book. 'It makes me all the keener to have a look round there.'

'Any time. Just let me know.'

'Well, it may not be for a few days,' said Roy. 'I'm in a difficult passage in the book and I want to get that sorted out, but I'll let you know when I can manage it.'

He didn't want the vicar going to the Priory now before he and Leyland had had a chance to investigate. If his theory was right that might spoil everything.

Roy got up to go. 'I must be off,' he said. 'I've a couple more calls to make before I get back.'

'Have one for me, too, will you?' said the vicar, with a twinkle in his eye. 'Goodbye.'

'Goodbye,' said Roy, laughing. 'You ought to come with me. Do you good to get out more among your parishioners in their haunts of vice!'

CHAPTER X

The Man with the Handcart

Roy hurried off down the hill towards the village to deliver his note for Leyland at the police station, but first he decided he must add something of what the vicar had told him. He had the note in an envelope in his pocket, but he had not sealed it up just in case he learned anything that morning which might be of interest.

He paused on the edge of the pavement to see if there was any traffic coming – there hardly ever was in Torcombe, but he still hadn't got out of the habit of looking – and as he stood there he had a feeling that he was being followed. It was one that had often come to him during the war, although he had never had it before, and more than once it had saved his life.

He stood still and casually looked around him. Apart from the fishermen still lounging on the quayside, a woman with a shopping basket over her arm coming out of the post-office, a milk float drawn up outside a cottage and a man in a fisherman's jersey and sea boots, who was wheeling a handcart down the hill behind him, there was no one to be seen. Yet the feeling persisted. Roy waited, pretending to be absorbed in a shop window, until the man with the handcart had gone by and then, after another quick glance round, crossed the road and went in the police station. As he expected, Sergeant Trelawney was sitting there behind his desk.

"Morning, Sergeant,' he greeted him. 'Mind if I write a note here for a friend of yours?'

"Morning, Mr Benton,' said the sergeant. 'Note? Friend of mine? I don't understand, but go ahead. Don't mind me.'

'Thanks,' said Roy. He glanced out of the station window, but could see nothing except the man with the handcart, who had stopped and was bending down, apparently examining one of the wheels. He took the envelope out of his pocket, extracted the note, scribbled a few lines about the Priory, ending with *MUST SEE YOU URGENTLY* scrawled in block letters, put the note back in the envelope, sealed it up and tossed it across the desk to the sergeant.

Sergeant Trelawney put his pen carefully behind his ear, picked up the envelope and read the name on it. The look of surprise on his face was comical.

'And how, sir, might I ask,' he said after a moment, 'do you come to know anything about Chief Inspector Leyland?'

'We're old friends,' said Roy airily. 'I was with him last night.'

'Oh, you were, were you?' said the sergeant.

'Yes,' said Roy, 'but we won't go into all that now, if you don't mind. The important thing is to see that the Chief Inspector gets that note as soon as possible. It's very urgent.'

'It is, is it,' said the sergeant stolidly. 'Well, I don't know that I ought to do this, you know. No one except me and the Chief Constable are supposed to know that Chief Inspector

Leyland's down here, but if you're sure it's all right . . .' He paused and looked up doubtfully.

'It is all right, I assure you,' said Roy. 'And it is very urgent. I can't tell you anything about it now. You'll have to take my word for it, I'm afraid.'

'Very good, sir,' said the sergeant, 'I'll see that he gets it.'

'That's the stuff. Thanks very much, Sergeant. I suppose you can't pop down to the "Harbour Bar" for a quick one, can you?'

Sergeant Trelawney thoughtfully wiped his moustache and smiled. 'Well, sir, I oughtn't to by rights, but seeing it's you and that it's rather a special occasion, you knowing Chief Inspector Leyland, I think we might manage it.' He turned towards the inner door. 'Jenkins!' he bawled.

P.C. Jenkins popped his head round the door. 'You called, Sergeant?'

'Of course I called, you idiot,' said the sergeant irritably. 'What did you think it was, a fog-horn? Just keep an eye on things here while I go out on an inquiry' – he winked at Roy – 'with Mr Benton.'

'Very good, sir,' said Jenkins, abashed.

The sergeant put on his helmet and went out with Roy, who noticed that the man with the handcart was still bending over his wheel. He looked up as the pair walked down the street and then turned his head away.

'Ever seen that chap before, Sergeant?' asked Roy, indicating the man with the cart.

The sergeant glanced across the road. 'No,' he said. 'Can't say that I have. Why do you ask, sir?'

'No particular reason. I just wondered. I thought I knew most of the fishermen here, but he's new to me.'

'And me, sir. He may be off that French boat that came in last night. Shall I have a word with him?'

'No, no,' Roy interjected hastily. 'It doesn't matter.'

The 'Harbour Bar' had just opened when they went in, and the saloon contained half a dozen fishermen.

'Let's go in the smoke-room,' said Roy. 'It'll be a bit less crowded in there.'

They sat down at a table near the window overlooking the harbour. Tim Austell himself came in to take their orders. 'Good morning, Mr Benton. Good morning, Sergeant. What'll it be, gentlemen?'

'Well,' said Roy, 'I can't think of anything better than a couple of pints of your best mild, can you, Sergeant? And one for you, of course, Tim.'

'That'll suit me,' said Sergeant Trelawney. 'By the way, Tim, if you're wondering what I'm doing here in uniform at this time of day, I'm on duty.'

Tim Austell smiled. 'Of course,' he said. 'Thanks, Mr Benton.'

'I'm not kidding,' said the sergeant, 'so none of your jokes. Let's be having that beer. I'm thirsty.'

Two foaming tankards were quickly put before them and they drank.

'Marvellous beer, this,' said Roy, lighting a cigarette and offering the sergeant one, which he accepted. 'Can't think how he does it. If I could transfer this pub to Fleet Street, I'd make a fortune.'

'Well, sir,' remarked Sergeant Trelawney, after demolishing most of what was left of his pint, 'I don't know what's behind all this business about your note to Chief Inspector Leyland and perhaps I ought not to ask. I'd no idea you knew him.'

'Yes,' said Roy, 'I've known him for years. When I was in Fleet Street I was on lots of cases he was dealing with and we met once or twice during the war, too, but I don't mind admitting it was a big surprise to find him down here.' Roy thought the sergeant would have been even more surprised if he had known the circumstances under which he had found Leyland.

'Have you heard what he's after?' asked the sergeant, lowering his voice. 'I know there've been one or two robberies from farms, the food depot and the mine, but I've an idea that's not all he's here for.'

'I really couldn't say,' Roy's voice was non-committal. 'He told me about the robberies, but I've no idea if he's after anything, or anyone, else. Why would a Scotland Yard man come to a place like this?'

'That's what's been puzzling me,' said the sergeant. 'These robberies aren't the sort of thing he'd deal with.' He paused and eyed Roy quizzically. 'Now that note of your'n, sir. I suppose that couldn't have anything to do with the real reason?'

Roy laughed. 'Trying to pump me, eh? Oh no you don't. Besides, that note was purely a social affair.'

'But very urgent,' said the sergeant pointedly.

'That's enough,' warned Roy goodhumouredly. 'I asked you here to have a drink, not to question me. Have another?'

The sergeant nodded. 'Thanks very much, sir, I will. I didn't mean to poke my nose into something that's none of my business, but you must admit, sir, it's a bit queer like.'

'Perhaps it is and perhaps it isn't.'

Roy steered him off on to other topics. It was obvious as they talked and sipped their beer that the sergeant was completely in the dark about the Chief Inspector's real business, nor, Roy was disappointed to discover, had he noticed anything untoward in the village, or seen any strangers, except the man with the handcart, who had gone past the window as they sat drinking and taken the cliff road.

'Well, I must be getting back,' said Roy, when they had

drunk up. 'Nice to have seen you, Sergeant, and don't forget about the note, will you?'

'I won't forget, sir,' the sergeant assured him. 'And thanks for the drinks.'

They parted outside the inn, the sergeant to walk back to the station and Roy to collect his bike. He set off up the cliff road, overtaking the man with the handcart, and parked his cycle outside the Cliff Top Inn while he went inside to have a word with Tod Murdock, his wife and Modwen.

There were one or two fishermen in the bar, but no sign of the Murdocks, who were usually presiding over the beer handles at this time of the day. He stood at the bar for a moment, but no one came.

'Where is everybody?' he asked a gnarled old fisherman seated in the corner.

'Mrs Murdock's bin taken to 'ospital and Miss Modwen's gone with her,' the old man said, 'but Tod's about somewhere and mighty upset he's lookin', too.'

'Taken to hospital,' repeated Roy. 'What's wrong?'

'Got to 'ave an operashun, ah thinks,' said the old man.

Just then Tod Murdock himself came into the bar. Roy had not seen him for a couple of weeks and he was shocked at the change in his appearance. He had lost weight, his face was pale and haggard, and he looked as if he had all the troubles in the world on his shoulders.

''Morning, Tod,' said Roy. 'Sorry to hear the wife isn't well. Nothing serious, I hope.'

Tod stared past him as if he had not seen him and did not speak. There was an embarrassing silence for a few moments. Roy tried again.

'I said I'm sorry to hear your wife's ill,' he repeated. 'I hope it's nothing serious.'

71

Tod started out of his mood, glanced, rather furtively, Roy thought, towards the door through which he had just come as if he felt he were being watched, and then said: 'Sorry, Mr Benton. My mind's been on other things lately.'

'That's all right,' said Roy. 'No need to apologize. I can imagine how you must feel. What exactly is the trouble with Mrs Murdock?'

Tod shot another glance at the inner door before he replied, and Roy, following his look, could almost have sworn that he saw a head bob back out of sight.

'They don't seem to know exactly,' said Tod. 'She's not been too grand for a long time, always complaining of a gnawing pain in her stomach. Finally Doc Tremlow, down in the village, suggested that she ought to see a specialist, so she and Modwen have gone up to London.'

'Well,' said Roy, trying to console him, 'it may not be as bad as they think. When will they be back?'

'I don't rightly know. Doc Tremlow said they might want to send her to hospital to keep her under observation like for a bit. They went prepared to stay. The wife has a sister in London, so Modwen will stop with her if she has to.'

'Must be very worrying for you. What about a drink? You look as if you could do with something to buck you up.'

'Thanks, Mr Benton. I'll have a nip of whisky, if you don't mind. What's yours? Pint as usual?'

'If you please,' said Roy.

Tod got the drinks, and they sipped them quietly for a few moments.

'Are you managing all right while they're away?' asked Roy, to break the silence. 'Pity you can't come and join me at the chalet till they come back.'

'I wish to heaven I could!'

Roy was surprised at the vehemence in Tod's voice. He looked up from his drink. There was a tense expression on Tod's face. 'Well, why not?' began Roy. 'I don't suppose—'

He broke off as he saw that the landlord once more had his eyes on the inner door. 'Excuse me, sir,' he said hastily, and there was something akin to fear in his voice, 'but I must go in the back a moment.' He hurried out of the bar, closing the inner door after him.

Well, said Roy to himself, that's a bit odd even for a man who is worried about his wife's health.

CHAPTER XI

Attempted Murder

Roy finished his beer and went out, pondering on Tod's strange behaviour. There was no one in sight. He wheeled his cycle on to the road, mounted it and set off down the hill towards the chalet. He was still musing on the problem of Tod when there was a popping sound followed by a hiss of escaping air which was so unexpected that he nearly lost control of the machine. He saw that his front tyre had gone flat.

'Blast!' exclaimed Roy, and put on the brakes. Nothing happened, except that the speed of the cycle, now well on its way down the steep hill, increased. Roy tried the brakes again, but the cycle only travelled faster, with the front wheel bumping furiously on its rim.

'Hell!' he exclaimed. He was coming to a sharp bend. On his right was the cliff wall, rising steeply above him. On his left was a sheer drop of a hundred feet to the rocks.

'God!' muttered Roy under his breath. 'You'll never get round that bend at this speed.' The machine was developing a wobble now, and it was all he could do to keep it on the road. This is it, thought Roy, as he neared the bend. How absurd it would be if, after all he'd been through during the war, he was going to be killed in a cycling accident!

Then, out of the corner of his eye, he saw on the right-hand side of the road, where the cliff wall curved in a little, a pile of gravel left by the council workmen. It's that or the sea, thought Roy and turned the cycle towards it. His front wheel hit the pile with a jar that shot him over the handlebars as if he had been discharged from a catapult. The cycle reared up and turned a complete somersault and Roy landed in a slithering dive on the gravel.

He lay half stunned for a few moments, then cautiously picked himself up, gingerly felt himself all over and was relieved to find that, so far as he could tell, he was still in one piece. Blood was trickling from a cut on his cheek where his face had landed on the gravel, and his left side felt as if it had been scraped several times with a sharp-toothed rake. Otherwise he seemed all right.

He moved painfully across to the cycle. The front wheel was badly buckled, the handlebars forced out of alignment, and the machine generally badly scratched. But it was the brakes in which Roy was most interested. They had never given him any trouble, and he was curious to find out, if he could, why they had suddenly failed him on the hill.

Carefully he examined them. There was nothing wrong with the blocks or the grips, so far as he could see, but he whistled under his breath as he saw that the cables were severed. He looked at the ends; he was a Dutchman if those weren't clean cuts, he told himself. They might have been made with a knife, or a pair of pliers. That could only mean that somebody had intended him to crash on the hill, and probably into the sea, and it was only by the greatest good fortune that he had avoided doing so.

He glanced back up the hill towards the inn, but there was no one in sight. 'Someone,' he mused aloud, 'has taken a decided dislike to you, my lad. I wonder if it could possibly be anyone connected with Monsignor Delouris and his boy friends? What about the bloke with the handcart? If he's one of the gang, he'd know I'd have to come down that hill to get to the chalet.'

He bent down, stifled a groan as his left side suddenly felt as if it was on fire as a result of the movement, moved the cycle off the gravel pile and propped it against the cliff wall.

'I shan't ride you again for a bit,' he said aloud, 'and goodness knows how long it'll take Charlie at the garage to put you in running order.'

Roy set off painfully towards the chalet, half expecting that there would be another attempt to dispose of him before he arrived, but nothing more happened, and there were no signs that anyone had been prowling around the chalet when he unlocked the door and released the pent-up Angus, who barked and jumped around showing his pleasure.

'Any more visitors, old man?' asked Roy, as he bent and fondled him. 'No?' A quick look round showed him that the chalet was as he had left it that morning. There were no more booby traps, apparently.

Roy was impatient to see Leyland and tell him of this latest attempt on his life – he was sure it was that – and he was tempted to stroll up to the mine after lunch, but decided he had better not. It was time he did some work on the book, anyway, so he spent the afternoon on the verandah, typing.

Finishing a chapter round about tea-time, he put the cover on his typewriter and went for a swim, much to the disappointment of Angus, who had been anticipating a walk, and showed his annoyance by standing at the water's edge and barking furiously.

Roy knew that he could not expect a call from Leyland until nightfall, so he spent the evening working in the vegetable garden, went for another swim to get rid of the sweat, grime and stiffness, had a meal, took Angus for a walk along the cliffs, and had just settled down to a cigarette on the verandah when he saw a figure approaching from the direction of the mine. It was Leyland, and Roy got up and went to meet him.

'You got my note?' Roy asked him. The Inspector pushed back his worn felt hat.

'Yes, the case is getting more and more interesting,' he mused.

'You're telling me,' said Roy feelingly.

They strolled to the chalet and went inside. Leyland looked round appraisingly.

'Quite a comfortable little place you've got here,' he remarked. 'I wouldn't mind retiring to a spot like this myself one day.'

'You wouldn't have thought it was comfortable if you'd been here last night,' said Roy. 'It was much too unpleasant for my liking.'

He showed Leyland the Luger and pointed out where it had been fixed on the mantelpiece.

'Very neat, very neat,' commented the Chief Inspector. 'Quite in the best booby-trap tradition, in fact. Must have taken quite a bit of arranging.'

'You've no doubt it was our friends, then?'

'Oh, I should say it was pretty certain.'

'But why should they be so concerned about me? They tried again today, you know.'

'They did, did they?' said Leyland in surprised tones. 'How? What happened?'

Roy described his trip to the village, the visit to the Cliff

Top Inn and the crash on the cliff road. He told Leyland of his suspicions.

'It sounds as if you had a pretty lucky escape,' commented Leyland. 'You're positive the brake cables were cut, and hadn't just frayed with wear?'

'Pretty sure. But why are they picking on me? If it had been you I could have understood it.'

'Oh, they probably think they can take care of me in their own good time,' said Leyland. 'Besides, it's apt to attract attention when you bump off Scotland Yard men, and attention, or, at any rate additional attention, is just what Delouris doesn't want just now. You've provided that. You're a complication they hadn't bargained for. They probably know all about you and they're trying to scare you off before you get too interested.'

'Well,' said Roy, 'they're going the wrong way about it. If I wasn't particularly interested before, two attempts on my life have certainly made me interested now.'

He lit a cigarette while Leyland filled his pipe.

'What do you think of the information I got from the vicar?' asked Roy. 'Could there be anything in my theory?'

'Maybe, maybe. I think we'll have to do a little investigating at the Priory, anyway. You say the vicar said there was also supposed to be a link with the Cliff Top Inn?'

'Yes, and I've half an idea there's something funny going on there, too.'

'Oh, why?'

Roy told him about Tod Murdock's odd behaviour and his suspicion that the cycle had been tampered with while he was having a drink there.

'I saw a fisherman, or what looked like a fisherman, who's new to me,' went on Roy. 'I overtook him on the way to the pub. He'd gone when I came out, but he could have done it. Anyway, the brakes had been all right up to then.'

'It certainly sounds a bit odd. Are you going to drop in again?'

'I was thinking of calling tomorrow. Old Tod may have some news of his wife. That will give me an excuse, and I'll try to have a scout round.'

Leyland got up and knocked out his pipe.

'Well, I'll be off. I've got to go up to Town tomorrow to see about one or two things and I want to get away early before anyone's about. Just see you keep out of trouble while I'm gone. I can't be any help to you while I'm at Scotland Yard, so don't get impulsive and try to clear up the whole business yourself.'

'Don't worry, I won't,' said Roy with a smile. 'I've had enough excitement these last few days even for me. When will you be back?'

'Tomorrow evening sometime, all being well. I'll drop in again about this time to see if you've any news for me – or got yourself into any more trouble. So long.'

'So long. I'll try not to do anything you wouldn't want me to do.'

CHAPTER XII

Strange Behaviour at the Inn

After breakfast next morning – it had been an uneventful night – Roy spent some time putting the chalet to rights. He had rather neglected his household chores during the past few days. Angus, too, was infected by the cleaning bug, turning his bed upside down and generally behaving as if there were a rat in it, until Roy cuffed him with a cushion and told him to lay off, or they'd have the place full of feathers. Angus retired outside with an injured air.

At about ten-thirty Roy locked the door of the chalet behind him – this was becoming quite a habit now – and whistled for the dog, who was not in sight. He had to whistle again before Angus appeared, shaking soil from him in all directions.

'You filthy pup!' Roy said in disgust, and bundled him, protesting, into the pool, from which he emerged snorting vehemently and shaking himself like an energetic housewife with a dusty rug. He looked so reproachfully at his master that Roy burst out laughing.

'Sorry, old man,' said Roy, bending and patting him, 'but

you were a mess. Never mind, you'll soon dry. Come on, let's have a race.'

He set off at a fast trot up the cliff road, Angus barking excitedly, but it was Roy who tired first and he slowed down to a walk while the dog chased ahead.

The deep gold of the morning sunshine and the piercing blue of the sea dazzled the eyes. The sea, which seemed barely to have strength to turn over in tiny wavelets on the beach at the foot of the cliffs, looked more inviting than he had ever seen it. This would be a perfect day for sunbathing and swimming, alone or in company, provided it were the right company.

That set him thinking of Karen Silvers, who, he was forced to admit when he thought about it frankly, had never really been out of his thoughts since she had made him feel such a fool when he kissed her at the mine entrance. He still felt resentful when he recalled her unfeeling attitude, and yet he could not drive her out of his mind. Perhaps it was because she had rebuffed him, and no man likes being rebuffed, especially by an attractive woman. And she was attractive, there was no denying that. Attractive for him, anyway. A pity, though, she wasn't a bit more human and less scientific. Didn't she ever have fun? he wondered. For a moment he entertained a mad idea of going to the mine, yanking her out of the laboratory, where he felt certain she was slaving away, and carrying her off to the beach. That was what she needed – a bit of relaxation. He sighed and turned his eyes away from the alluring sea.

He could not see any signs of life as he approached the Cliff Top Inn. Tod was usually to be seen pottering about somewhere in the yard or the garden. He went up to the door and knocked. He waited a moment, but no one came, so he knocked again. There was still no response. He listened with his ear close to the door, but there were no sounds of movement inside. Funny, thought Roy. Perhaps Tod had gone into Torcombe.

He stepped back from the door and looked up at the bedroom windows. As he did so a head – and it looked like the head of Tod Murdock – dodged hurriedly out of sight behind the curtains of one of the windows.

'Tod,' he called. 'It's Roy.'

Nothing moved at the window. Perhaps, he thought, Tod's on his way down to let me in. But no one came. He stood for a moment or two wondering if he should knock again, more loudly this time, or try to find some way of entering the house in case Tod was not well and could not come downstairs. He hadn't been looking too good the day before. He peered up at the bedroom window again, but there was nothing to see except the motionless curtains, and he began to wonder whether or not he really had seen Tod.

'Oh well, I can call on my way back,' Roy said aloud. 'Blast,' he added, remembering that he had intended 'phoning Charlie at the garage from the 'Cliff Top'. Now he'd have to walk into Torcombe to tell him about the bike. He called Angus and set off. After he had gone about thirty yards he turned suddenly and looked back at the inn. This time there was no doubt about it. There was someone at the bedroom window and he had dodged back out of sight. It didn't look like Tod, either, though from this distance he could not be sure. He paused irresolutely, wondering whether or not to go back, but thought better of it. It was damned queer all the same.

By the time he got to Charlie's Roy was mopping his brow and even Angus was glad to sink down on a pile of sacks in a corner of the garage, his tongue lolling out. Charlie smiled as he eyed them both.

'Warm, isn't it?' he remarked. 'Why all the exercise?'

Roy liked Charlie. He had been a fisherman before the war, but had always preferred boats with engines to boats with sails, much to the contemptuous amusement of some of Torcombe's old salts. He had also suprised them when the war came by enlisting not in the Royal Navy or the Merchant Navy, as did most of the Torcombe men, but in the Tank Corps. He had won the M.M. at Sidi Rezegh and, judging by all Roy had heard about him, he'd be a useful man to have in a tight corner. When Charlie came out of the Army he had left the sea for good and started his garage business. There was nothing he loved more than tinkering with engines and there was hardly a repair job of any kind he couldn't tackle. His was the only garage in the village and he was doing well now. Charlie also knew something of Roy's war record and a firm friendship had sprung up between them.

'If you can manage to find a bottle of nice cool beer,' said Roy pleadingly, 'I'll tell you why the exercise, but you won't get another word out of me till I've had a drink.' He mopped his forehead.

Charlie disappeared into the office, returned with two bottles of beer and two glasses and poured out the drinks. Roy emptied his at one gulp. 'Thanks,' he said feelingly. 'You've saved my life.'

'Don't mention it. But why Shanks's pony on a day like this?'

'That's why I've deigned to come and see you in person. The bike's smashed up.' He saw Charlie's look of surprise and wondered whether to tell him of his suspicions, but contented himself with a straightforward description of the

Francis Durbridge

accident. If Charlie suspected anything, thought Roy, it would be his own idea, not planted in his mind by someone else.

'That's funny,' said Charlie, when he had finished. 'The tyres and brakes were all right when I had her in a couple of months ago. What the deuce have you been doing to her?'

'Nothing,' replied Roy casually. 'Things wear out, don't they?'

'Not my new brake cables,' retorted Charlie indignantly, 'at least, not with ordinary wear and tear. Anyway, why did you walk all the way in? Why didn't you 'phone me from the "Cliff Top", as you usually do? It couldn't have been because you were pining for a glimpse of my pretty face, could it?'

'No, Charlie, it wasn't, much as I cherish and admire you. I just couldn't get into the "Cliff Top". Nobody would answer the door.'

'What do you mean by "would answer"? Do you mean Tod was there, but wouldn't let you in?'

'Well, I can't swear it was Tod, but I'm sure I saw someone duck out of sight behind the bedroom window curtains. He hasn't got anyone staying with him, has he?'

'Not that I know of. Odd. It doesn't sound like Tod's way of behaving – if it was Tod. You haven't upset the old boy, have you? You know, he's a bit touchy sometimes.'

'Not that I know of,' said Roy. 'He seemed to me to be behaving a bit queer the other day, but I put it down to the fact that he was probably worrying about his missus. Heard how she is, by the way? Have she and Modwen got back yet?'

'Not yet, I think. I haven't been up this week, but Harry Broad, the postman, was in here yesterday and said he'd taken Tod a letter with a London postmark, so that was probably from them. Now you mention it, Harry also

84

thought Tod was behaving a bit queer – anyway, more so than you'd expect in the circumstances. Still, I don't suppose it's anything. This illness of his wife's probably upset him more than we thought.'

'Well, I'll call in on my way back and see whether he's about yet. When do you think you'll be able to fetch the bike in, Charlie? Tomorrow?'

'I'll do it now and give you a lift at the same time, if you like. I don't suppose anyone will tamper with the bike – it won't go, anyway – but I want to have a look at those cables and I'd also like a word with Tod. I'm a bit worried about him. He's been a good friend to me. Put up some of the money for me to start this business, you know, though I've pretty well repaid him by now.'

Charlie got out his breakdown lorry, which he had built himself from the remains of a couple of jeeps and heaven knew what other wrecks. Angus returned from a private rat-hunt at the rear of the garage and jumped up on Roy's knee.

'Tod should have opened up by now,' remarked Charlie, as they climbed the hill out of the village, 'that is, if he's really at home.'

'Or if he hasn't been taken ill,' put in Roy. 'That possibility did occur to me, and I wondered whether I ought not to try and get in and find out, but if there hadn't been anyone there it might have been rather hard to explain.'

As Charlie stopped the lorry outside the inn they saw that the door was open. They got down and went into the bar. It was empty.

'A bit early for the fishing lads yet,' remarked Charlie, looking at his watch. 'What'll you have?'

'No, this one's on me. I've had one on you already this morning.'

'All right,' said Charlie. 'I'm not going to argue about who pays for a pint, which is what I'll have if there's anyone here to serve it.'

He banged on the bar counter. 'Shop, Tod!' he called.

There was no response for a moment or two and then Tod Murdock appeared in the doorway leading from the living quarters. Roy thought he looked even more haggard and worried than he had done the day before, and he saw that Charlie, too, was looking very concernedly at his old friend.

''Morning, Tod,' said Roy. 'I've brought an old friend to see you. Or, rather, he brought me. Two pints, if you please, and whatever you'd like yourself, of course.'

''Morning, gentlemen,' said Tod. He spoke in a hoarse whisper, and Roy again noticed that, as he drew the beer, he glanced furtively towards the living-room door. 'I'll have a whisky, if I may.'

'You may,' said Roy, 'but if it's not a rude question, when did you start drinking whisky at this time of day? I thought you preferred it as a nightcap.'

'I do usually,' whispered Tod, 'but I haven't been feeling too well lately. Been worried about the wife, you know.'

'How is she, Tod?' asked Charlie. 'Any news?'

Tod again glanced towards the door before answering. 'No,' he said, 'I haven't heard anything from them. It's very worrying.'

'Well, here's hoping everything will be all right,' said Roy, raising his tankard.

'Me, too,' said Charlie, and looked significantly at Roy as Tod tossed off his drink; he had poured himself a double – neat.

'This is the second time I've called this morning,' said Roy, 'but I couldn't make anyone hear the first time, though

86

I thought I saw you at the window.' He added laughingly: I nearly decided to break in and see if there was anything wrong.'

A look of alarm came over Tod's face. 'I'm glad you didn't do that, sir,' he said. 'That might have been very awkward—' He stopped, and again Roy had the feeling that the man knew he was being watched. 'What was it you were wanting, sir?'

'Oh, I only wanted to 'phone Charlie to bring the old bike in,' said Roy casually. 'You see, after I left here yesterday morning my brakes failed going down the hill and I smashed up at the bottom of the cliff road. Damned lucky I didn't go into the sea.'

Roy had watched Tod's face closely as he told him this. The alarm was still there, but this time the look was mingled with one of curiosity.

'Nice place to tamper with a bloke's bike, this,' said Roy deliberately, 'that is if you wanted him to smash himself up. You don't have much of a chance once you've got speed up down that hill.'

There was fear in Tod Murdock's face now. 'I'm very sorry about the accident, sir, but I'm sure no one here would have tampered with your bike.'

Roy laughed. 'Well, naturally, I wasn't suspecting you, Tod. Or did you think I was?'

'Oh no, sir,' said Tod hastily.

'Well, drink up, and let's have another for the road,' said Charlie. 'All's well that ends well. I'll soon be able to tell you whether that bike was tampered with or not.'

Tod refilled their tankards and poured himself another double whisky, they noticed. Charlie put down a ten-shilling note. Tod turned away to the till, glanced quickly towards the side door, appeared to be fumbling for the money and murmured something about the till not working properly.

Then he turned to the bar again and put down the change, covering it with his hand. He lifted it significantly and they both saw the ten-shilling note and a few silver coins.

'Here, it was a ten-bob note—' began Charlie, thinking Tod had taken it for a pound. Then he stopped as he saw the look on Tod's face. It was one of such anguished pleading that, bewildered, he glanced at Roy, who nodded for him to pick up the money. Charlie did so and put it in his pocket without looking at it. Quietly they drank their beer, and after one or two casual remarks about the weather and exchanges of village gossip, they left.

'What the devil . . .' began Charlie as soon as they got outside, but Roy motioned him to get into the lorry and they moved off down the cliff road to where the cycle was still resting against the cliff wall where Roy had left it. Roy jumped out, and after turning the lorry Charlie followed him.

'Now,' he said impatiently, 'do you mind telling me what the deuce this is all about – that is, if you know.'

'All in good time, my lad,' said Roy, glancing up the road to see if there was anyone in sight. 'Now let me have a look at that ten-shilling note.'

Charlie pulled it out of his pocket and gave it to him. Roy examined it closely.

'Well, I'll be damned!' he exclaimed. 'Look at this.'

Charlie looked. Scrawled on the back of the note in indelible pencil were these words:

Wife and daughter hostages. Am being held prisoner.

'What on earth does that mean?' asked Charlie, bewildered.

'I'm not absolutely sure yet,' said Roy slowly, 'but it's all beginning to tie up.'

'It's tied up all right – in knots as far as I'm concerned,' said Charlie drily.

'On second thoughts,' said Roy, 'I think I'd better tell you all I know, though what Leyland will say about it when he hears I can imagine only too well.'

'Never mind Leyland, whoever he is. Concentrate on me at present.'

Roy told him the whole story from the beginning – his adventure in the mine, his meeting with Karen Silvers and Chief Inspector Leyland, the booby trap set for him in the chalet, the vicar's theory about the old Priory and the 'Cliff Top', the cycle crash, and now Tod Murdock's message.

It was characteristic of Charlie that his first comment should be about the cycle crash, because it involved his professional skill, of which he was inordinately proud.

'I darned well knew,' he said, after examining the cable ends, 'that there'd been some monkey business with these. They could never have worn out in that time. Well,' he added, as the significance of the rest of what Roy had told him sank in, 'this is a ruddy fine business you've got me in to. What do we do now?'

'Got yourself into,' rejoined Roy. 'I didn't ask you to take me out to the "Cliff Top", and it was your ten bob, not mine, on which Tod wrote the message.'

'What about returning it to its rightful owner, then?'

'Better let me keep it for the time being. Leyland will want to see it. But what worries me is that he won't be back until tomorrow night, and I feel we ought to do something to help old Tod as soon as possible. The question is – what?'

'Don't you think we ought to try and find out a bit more about this message – what it means exactly? Where are his wife and daughter held hostage and who by? Why is he being held prisoner – in his own pub, mind you – and again, who by? The same people who've got his missus and Modwen or someone else? You don't suppose the poor old chap's gone off his head with worry and that he's imagining all this, do you? If you took it to the police they'd probably just laugh at you. Such things don't happen in quiet English country pubs.'

'Yes, but the local police don't know what Leyland and I know,' Roy pointed out. 'All the same, I agree that we've got to find out more before we can act. We must have a talk with Tod whether he's held prisoner or not. What about you and me going back there tonight and seeing if we can't get to him without being spotted? Unless, of course, you'd rather keep out of it.'

'What the hell do you take me for?' asked Charlie indignantly. 'Of course I'm not keeping out of it now. Even if Tod wasn't one of my best friends, you couldn't keep me out of this.'

Roy laughed. 'I was just thinking,' he said, 'of what Leyland said before he left last night. He told me not to get impulsive and try to clear up the whole business by myself. Well, if we do clear it up I shan't have done it on my own, so perhaps he won't mind after all. But what he'll say when he finds there's another outsider in on the secret, I don't know. Anyway, I don't think we ought to wait until he gets back, do you?'

'I'm not waiting,' said Charlie determinedly, 'whatever you do.'

'Now don't you start going all tough on me,' Roy warned him. 'This is more my cup of tea than yours, and these are tough babies we're up against, if Leyland's right. Look, I tell you what we'll do. I'll meet you at midnight at the back of the "Cliff Top". Everything should be quiet enough by then. Do you know which room Tod sleeps in?'

'I know which room he used to sleep in,' said Charlie, 'but, of course, he may have had to change if some unexpected guests have moved in on him.'

'Well, we'll have to take a chance on picking the right one. I'll bring along my old Army revolver just in case we barge into the wrong boudoir, but I don't want any shooting party if we can avoid it. OK?'

'OK by me,' said Charlie. 'And now let's get this bike shifted.'

Roy gave him a hand in lifting it on to the lorry.

'How long do you think it will take to fix it?' he asked. 'You never know, but I may need it urgently.'

'Oh, a couple of days,' said Charlie, 'providing you don't keep me out all hours of the night.'

'Well, if everything goes according to plan, tonight's little job shouldn't take long. See you at midnight – and don't be late,' he called, as Charlie roared off up the hill.

Roy and Angus walked back to the chalet, Roy deep in thought.

CHAPTER XIII

Midnight Rendezvous

Angus again took a poor view of being left behind when Roy set out to meet Charlie and he could hear him whining piteously as he walked away from the chalet in the crêpe-soled shoes he had put on to ensure quietness and, if necessary, quickness of movement. He left the cliff road before he reached the inn and approached it from the back. As he got near, the figure of a man smoking a cigarette detached itself from the shadow of a tree, and came towards him.

'Beat you to it,' said Charlie in a low voice as they met.

'Yes, but if there's anyone watching you've probably given the game away with that cigarette,' retorted Roy. 'Put it out, for heaven's sake.'

Charlie grunted, but did so.

'Any signs of life?' asked Roy.

'No,' replied Charlie. 'There were no lights in the place when I got here ten minutes ago, and I haven't seen or heard anything.'

'Come on, then.' Roy led the way towards the garden wall, pulled himself to the top, looked around for a moment, then dropped over the other side. Charlie followed.

'Which used to be Tod's bedroom?' asked Roy.

'The one over the outhouse, but goodness knows whether he's in there now or not.'

'One of us ought to have watched the place earlier to find out,' said Roy. 'but it's too late now. We'll have to take a chance. I'll go first, shall I?'

'Better let me. I know the lay-out better than you do, and if we run into any trouble it's more important that I take care of it and that you get away.'

'It's very likely I should do that and leave you holding the baby, isn't it?' asked Roy scornfully. 'Anyway, lead on.'

Charlie led the way through the garden, Roy following closely on his heels, until he reached the wall of the outhouse. There they both paused for a moment or two and listened, but no sound came from the inn.

'Hope this roof's strong enough to bear us,' muttered Charlie as he prepared to pull himself up. 'You'd better wait here till I've got Tod to open the window and let me in – that is if he's there. If he isn't, it'll be just too bad.'

'OK,' said Roy, giving him a leg up. 'Take it easy.'

Charlie crawled gingerly on hands and knees up the sloping roof of the outhouse and rested a moment with his hands on the window-sill. Roy, stepping back a little so that he could see what was happening and also keep an eye on things generally, heard him tap gently on the window-pane. His own heart thudded a little more quickly as he waited for the response they hoped for, but none came. Charlie tapped again, this time a little louder. A moment or two later the window slid quietly up and Charlie climbed through, leant out again and said in a loud whisper, 'OK, come on up.'

Roy was soon standing in the bedroom beside Charlie and a still sleepy and somewhat puzzled Tod Murdock.

'So far, so good,' he murmured. 'Now, Tod,' he went on quickly, in a low whisper, 'what's the layout here? Is there anyone here besides yourself?'

'Two guards,' said Tod. 'One sleeps next door and the other further along the passage. They used to take it in turns to watch outside the door when they first came, but they don't now. I suppose they think I can't do anything,' he added ruefully. 'By God, I'd like to show 'em!'

'When did they first come?' asked Roy.

'About a week ago. So much has happened in the last few days,' said Tod, wearily passing his hand across his forehead, 'that I can't rightly remember, but there were three of 'em, the two who are here now and another, very commanding fellow. The other two seemed frightened to death of him.'

'But how did they get here? Where did they come from? Did they just walk in like we did this morning, or what?'

'That's the most puzzling part of the whole business. I'd locked up one night after closing-time and went into the parlour and there they were, sitting down as comfortable as you please, with Mary and Modwen looking scared as anything by the sideboard. I'll swear they hadn't come in through the public entrance, or I'd have noticed them.'

'And what happened then?' asked Charlie.

'I remember beginning to say "What the devil's the meaning of this?" when the leader pulled a gun out of his pocket and said quietly and very politely, just as if he'd been ordering a drink like, "I'm very sorry, Mr Landlord, but I'm afraid we shall have to take over your inn for a while." "Take over the inn!" I exclaimed. "Don't be a damned fool!" and made a dash for the telephone on the sideboard. I never reached it. Something hit me and I passed out. When I came round I was on the settee. The leader and one of the other men were still there, sitting watching me like cats watching a mouse, but Mary and Modwen and the other man had disappeared. "That was very foolish of you," says the man with the gun, "so we've had to take steps to see that nothing like that happens again while we're in, shall we say, occupation? Your wife and daughter are going to be our guests – and nothing will happen to them if you do as you are told. I shall leave two of my men to keep you company and see that you don't use the telephone, or try to communicate with any of your friends. They have strict orders to shoot you immediately if you make an attempt to do so. If anyone asks where your good wife and daughter are, you will tell them that Mrs Murdock is not well and has gone up to London to see a specialist, that your daughter has gone with her and that they are staying with relatives. You have relatives in London, have you not? Good. Otherwise, you go on with your daily life here as if nothing had happened. We are sorry to inconvenience you like this, but I trust it will not be for long."'

Tod paused for a moment, obviously still baffled by the monstrousness of it all.

'I remember,' he went on, 'telling him that they couldn't do things like that in England, that I'd find some way of telling people what had happened. Then he got very stern and said, "Mr Murdock, if you do, I assure you that the bodies of your wife and daughter will be delivered to this inn within one hour of your making such a move and you will join them immediately afterwards." I think he meant it, too. That's why I've had to be so careful.'

'I think he meant it, too,' said Roy solemnly,

'I asked him who he was,' resumed Tod, 'what he was doing here, where they'd taken Mary and Modwen, and lots of other questions, but he just laughed and said perhaps I'd find out one day. Then he left and the other man returned. Since then I've hardly had a second to myself. They've watched me night and day, but I managed to get that note to you without being seen, I think. Thank God I did. What's it all about, Mr Benton? Do you know?'

'I've an idea, Tod,' said Roy, who had been touched by this recital, 'but I'm not absolutely sure yet.'

'Well, do you know where Mary and Modwen are? I'm worried to death.'

'We don't yet,' put in Charlie, in a tone Roy had never heard him use before, 'but we're damned well going to find out. Of all the ruddy nerve! They don't really think they can get away with this, do they?' he asked, turning to Roy.

'I'm afraid they do,' said Roy gravely, 'and it isn't going to be easy to stop 'em now they've got Mrs Murdock and Modwen. That complicates things considerably, but we'll do our damnedest, Tod. I can't tell you all I know yet, but the authorities are aware of it and a good friend of mine from Scotland Yard is on the case. You'll have to trust us. Tod. In the meantime, you carry on as you are doing. Let me or Charlie know if anything happens here – the note in the change is as good a way as any, especially as you've got away with it once – and we'll try to get word to you about Mrs Murdock and Modwen as soon as we can. It's a good job we're both regular customers, so that we can come and go without arousing the guards' suspicions. Well, let's be off, Charlie. There's nothing more we can do here at present.'

'What about scaring the pants off those guards?' asked Charlie truculently. 'I'd like to get my hands on 'em, and I'll bet Tod would, even more so.'

'I'll say I would!' said Tod vehemently.

'No,' replied Roy firmly. 'Nothing would please me more

than to drop 'em both over the cliff, but we've got to think about those women. Do either of the guards ever leave the place, Tod, or does anyone come to see 'em?'

'One of 'em disappears occasionally,' said Tod, 'but he's always back by nightfall to relieve the other one. I've no idea where he goes or how he goes. I've never seen him outside the inn. That's the mysterious part of it.'

'It's very mysterious, I agree,' commented Roy, 'and I've a little theory about that, but I want to put it to the test first before I say anything about it. No, we'd better go while the going's good, I think. Come on, Charlie. So long, Tod, and try not to worry. We'll get some news to you as soon as we can.'

Roy turned away to the window, felt his leg bump into something, made a wild grab at it to stop it falling to the floor, and missed. It was a small bedside table, and he cursed as it hit the floor with a crash.

'Hell's bells, that's done it!' exclaimed Charlie. 'Let's get out of here, p.d.q.'

'I'll tell 'em I knocked it over as I was getting out of bed,' said Tod, 'but hurry. I think I heard the guard in the next room.'

Roy and Charlie scrambled hurriedly through the window, slid down the outhouse roof and lay still in the shadow of the wall, concealed from the view of anyone who looked out of the window. They heard noises and excited voices in broken English. Evidently the guards were questioning Tod, for the window was thrown up and someone looked out.

Raising himself cautiously, Roy saw the upper half of the figure of a man. Something gleamed in his hand. For several seconds he stared into the garden, while they both lay dead still, hardly daring to breathe, and they heard Tod's voice saying: 'I tell you no one is there. I knocked the thing

Francis Durbridge

over as I was getting out of bed to get a drink. I couldn't sleep, and no wonder.'

The man at the window grunted, but finally seemed satisfied and pulled down the window. For fully five minutes longer Roy and Charlie lay couched against the outhouse wall, in case anyone was still keeping an eye on the garden, but nothing further happened and finally they crawled away, remaining in the shadow of the inn, and then following the garden wall to the point where they had first climbed it. Again they paused for a moment and looked back at the inn, but there was no sign of movement and quietly they climbed over.

They were just beginning to move away from the wall, when a voice said quietly: 'Don't move, either of you. Put your hands up and face the wall.'

CHAPTER XIV

Coffee for Three

Roy and Charlie slowly obeyed. 'Well,' said Roy, 'no one can say we're having a dull evening.'

There was an exclamation behind them, and then a soft laugh. Roy started too when he heard the laugh.

'Well, well, if it isn't Miss Silvers,' he said, turning, and saw the scientist holding a small automatic in her hand. She was still laughing.

'And may I ask what you are doing here at this time of night? I thought you scientific girls weren't allowed out of the dormitory after Mistress Leyland had tucked you in bed. Or is this a special midnight spree? Suppose I tell him when he gets back?'

'Suppose I tell him I found you snooping away from Cliff Top Inn at one o'clock in the morning, and, moreover, doing it so carelessly that I could have shot you both easily if I'd wanted to?'

'Oh, could you,' said Charlie indignantly at this reflection on his Commando technique. 'This is all very interesting to you two, no doubt, but do you mind letting me in on it?'

'A thousand apologies, Charlie,' said Roy. 'Miss Silvers, may I present Charlie Gibson, ex-tank expert, now motor-tinkerer-in-chief of Torcombe? Charlie, this is the Miss Silvers I was telling you about this morning.'

'How do you do, miss?' said Charlie. 'You can forget the Gibson, if you don't mind. Everyone calls me Charlie.'

'How nice!' said Miss Silvers. 'And now perhaps you'd tell me just what you two have been up to. The Chief told me he'd warned you to keep out of trouble while he was away and not to try to solve the case off your own bat. Incidentally, this doesn't seem to be a very good place to be holding a conversation. Hadn't we better move?'

'Just what I was thinking,' said Roy. 'What about coming back to the chalet with me? I'll make some coffee, and I daresay I can rustle up a few sandwiches. I'm hungry.'

Miss Silvers hesitated.

'More work to do?' asked Roy. 'Oh, you needn't worry,' he went on rather bitterly. 'There's safety in numbers, I believe.'

He saw Charlie look quickly at them.

'I really ought to get back,' said Miss Silvers. 'I told Joe I wouldn't be long. He'll get worried if I'm overdue, but . . .' she hesitated.

'Oh, come on, miss,' said Charlie. 'We shall be running into trouble if we stand here talking much longer.'

He moved away towards the cliff road, and Roy and Miss Silvers followed him.

'You haven't told me what you were doing here,' she reminded them as they walked towards the chalet.

'Nor have you told us,' Roy retorted. 'It's rather a long story. Did the Chief tell you I thought there was something funny going on at the inn?'

'He did.'

'Well, it got a little funnier this morning when we dropped in on our way to collect my bike.'

Roy described the morning's happenings and told of their decision to go back that night to see old Tod and of his strange story.

'It all ties up,' commented Miss Silvers when she had heard the story, 'but I don't like the news about those two women one little bit. It makes things very awkward.'

'You're telling us,' said Roy. 'The question is what ought we to do about it?'

'I think we ought to wait till the Chief gets back. He may have some news for us.'

'Well, I don't,' said Charlie flatly. 'The sooner we start looking for 'em the sooner we'll find 'em.'

'But where are you going to start?' Miss Silvers demanded. 'We haven't a clue as to where they are.'

'I have,' said Roy. He told them of his visit to the vicar, of his stories about the old smugglers, the underground passages and the chart. 'I'd like to bet,' he added, 'that they've made the old Priory their headquarters.'

'Then why the devil don't we go and winkle 'em out?' demanded Charlie.

'But it would be suicide to go there on your own,' protested Miss Silvers. 'If the gang *are* there, the place is sure to be bristling with guards. You'd never get near the place without being spotted, or, if you did, they'd probably get you, too, and that would only make matters worse.'

'Oh,' said Roy with ill-concealed glee, 'you do care just a little about our personal safety, then?'

Miss Silvers did not reply to this, but went on: 'You know

the Chief Inspector would be furious if you did anything that might spoil his plans. Any independent action by you now might ruin the whole thing.'

'That's true enough,' admitted Roy, 'but how much longer is he going to wait?'

'Every day's delay seems dangerous to me,' said Charlie. 'I'm all for doing something now.'

'But you must trust him,' protested Miss Silvers. 'After all,' she went on, appealing to Roy, 'you know him. You've worked with him before. Has he ever let anyone down yet?'

'No, of course not,' said Roy, 'but this waiting does rather get on one's nerves.'

'I should have thought you'd have been used to it after your experiences with the underground forces,' Miss Silvers reminded him.

The discussion went on until they reached the chalet, where Angus greeted them rapturously. Roy set about making coffee and sandwiches, while Miss Silvers wandered around and Charlie sat glumly in a chair and smoked his pipe.

'Nice place you've got here,' remarked Miss Silvers, when Roy returned with a tray. 'An ideal spot to write a book, I should say.' She sat down and played with Angus's ears. 'I could do with a place like this for my own research.'

'Well,' said Charlie rudely, with his mouth full of sandwich, 'what *are* we going to do about Mrs Murdock and Modwen?'

Miss Silvers sipped her coffee appreciatively. 'I still think we should wait until the Chief returns before we decide on anything drastic. In fact, I would say that we *must* wait. After all, he's in charge of the case and acting under orders from Whitehall. We're only the amateur helps, or rather you are, and much as I sympathize with the Murdocks, we just simply can't risk anything which might mess up the whole works.'

'While I rather object to the word "amateur",' remarked Roy, 'seeing that I've done most of the investigating since I was co-opted in this case, I must say I think you're right. It isn't just a case of getting Mrs Murdock and Modwen away and clearing the guards out of the inn. There's far more at stake than even their lives. What do you say, Charlie?'

Charlie finished off his cup of coffee before replying. 'I suppose you're right,' he said reluctantly, 'but it goes very much against the grain with me to sit still and do nothing.'

'But it's only until tonight,' Miss Silvers pointed out. 'As soon as the Chief gets back he'll come on here, I expect, to find out if there've been any developments, and you can have a round-table conference and decide what's the best thing to do.'

'That's settled then,' said Roy, 'though there's no need for us to sit around and do nothing. Charlie, you're better known around these parts than I am and wouldn't attract so much attention. Suppose you go out and have a scout round in the direction of the old Priory on your motor-bike? I'll take Angus for a walk in the same direction, only approaching it from the combe here. I'll go this morning, and you this afternoon. That'll give you time to fix my bike.'

'And what about some sleep?' asked Charlie indignantly.

'Oh, a couple of hours should do for an old soldier,' replied Roy pointedly. 'Besides, I thought you were pining for action.'

'OK,' said Charlie resignedly.

'Then tonight,' went on Roy, 'we can all meet here and compare notes. How will that do? Meantime, Miss Silvers can be catching up on her research – down the mine.'

'Suits me,' said Charlie, hastily stifling a yawn. He looked at his watch. 'Ye gods, nearly two o'clock! Time I was getting off if I'm going to get any sleep, get that bike done and do some snooping round the Priory. I can't please myself when I work – like some people I know.'

They all got up. 'I'd no idea it was so late,' said Miss Silvers. 'Thanks for the coffee and sandwiches. They were most appetizing.'

'Don't mention it,' said Roy. 'What about coming to dinner sometimes? I'm rather a good cook, you know.'

'I'll consider the invitation carefully,' she said with a smile. It was the first smile Roy had seen since their embarrassing leave-taking at the mine, and his heart gave a little leap at the sight of it.

'I'll see you on your way, then,' he answered casually. 'Angus would like a walk, too, I'm sure. Wouldn't you, old boy?'

Angus was already by the door making crooning noises as he always did preparatory to going out.

'There's really no need, you know,' said Miss Silvers. 'I can take care of myself. I'm armed, don't forget.'

'I hope that isn't intended as a warning to me,' said Roy, and she laughed again.

Outside, Charlie said good night and set off up the cliff road to the village, moaning that he hadn't his bike with him now.

Karen Silvers and Roy walked slowly along the path to the old mine. A soft, cool breeze was coming in from the murmuring sea and a young moon that looked like a slice of silver melon was riding over the water, linked to the shore with a path of silver. Involuntarily, impelled by the beauty of the night, they both stopped. Neither spoke for a moment or two. Then Karen said quietly, 'It's incredible, isn't it, to think that somewhere not very far from here that awful gang are up to goodness knows what, that Mrs Murdock and Modwen are their prisoners and that the peaceful-looking Cliff Top Inn is virtually a prison for poor Tod?' She sighed. 'What a mess we make of a lovely world!'

'And what a still greater mess we may make of it!' Roy reminded her. 'In a way, it's even more incredible to think that down an old mine a lot of very intelligent people are working to perfect something that could darned near blow the whole bag of tricks to pieces – and not thinking a thing of it.'

'That's not fair!' she cried, with a note of anguish in her voice that surprised him. 'We're always thinking of it. We're all terribly concerned to see that it falls only into the right hands.'

'That's the tragedy of it. Who can ensure that it falls only into the right hands? Are there any right hands fit to have a deadly thing like this entrusted to them? I doubt it. Oh, I know that you're terribly concerned about it, but there are others not so scrupulous. Man always tends to use the weapons provided for him, no matter what the intentions, however blameless, of those who do provide them. Look at Nobel and his dynamite.'

'But this is different,' she protested. 'This thing is so deadly, so devastating, that it's very existence ought to prevent anyone ever going to war again.'

'I seem to have heard that before about other weapons, but it hasn't prevented other wars. Still, I can see I'm preaching to the converted. I'm sorry. And I'm sorry, too,' he went on rather diffidently, 'about my behaviour the other night. Believe me, I don't usually go around kissing comparatively strange, if very attractive, young women the first time I meet them. In fact, I usually fight shy of them, but there was something about last night – perhaps it was the curious circumstances in which we met, perhaps it was just something in the air, like there's something in the air tonight – which made me forget myself for a moment. I do apologize.'

There was silence for a moment or two. They were both watching the moon over the sea. Then she said quietly: 'I don't think there's any more need for you to apologize than for me. After all, I could have stopped you, but I didn't.'

'Why didn't you?'

'I don't know. Perhaps I felt something in the air, too.' She paused a moment, then laughed softly. 'I'm afraid I didn't respond very well, did I?'

Roy laughed too. 'I'm afraid you didn't,' he said. 'My masculine pride was very much offended. It was rather like kissing a . . . shall we say a scientist?'

'It was exactly that. You see, my life hitherto hasn't taken me very much into the company of men, except in laboratories, and they don't go in very much for love in the lab. It was a rather novel experience for me and I was just trying to analyse reactions, as I would in an experiment, only this time they were my own reactions, not those of a guinea pig, or a rat. That's why, if there's to be any asking for forgiveness, I'm the one who should be doing it. It was unpardonable of me, I'm afraid.'

'Oddly enough,' said Roy, 'I find it very easy to pardon you. But would it be impolite of me to ask what the reactions were?'

'I'm afraid the experiment was not conclusive. Some day, perhaps, when all this is over, I'll . . .' She did not finish the sentence.

'Why don't you chuck all this?' asked Roy suddenly. 'I'm serious. It's no job for a woman. You ought to be leading a happy, natural life.'

'I suppose by that you mean bringing up a family. Well, perhaps I will one day, but don't you see that I couldn't now? I've been given a job to do, a terribly important job, and I must finish it. You wouldn't back out of it now, and I'm in it much more deeply than you are. You could no more go back to the chalet and get quietly on with your book, knowing Mrs Murdock and Modwen were still in the hands of that gang, than you could have refused to go on a mission during the war. Could you?'

Roy did not reply for a moment or two. Then he sighed. 'No,' he said, 'I couldn't.'

'And no more can I leave my job unfinished.'

'But I wish to God it was all over,' said Roy. 'It would be such a relief to get back to sanity again. And that seems a long way off, even at this moment, in this setting, with you here – a woman instead of a scientist, for the time being, at any rate.'

They walked on in silence for a little while. Then Karen stopped and said: 'Don't come any farther now. And do please be careful. I'd hate anything to happen to anyone else.'

'What about you?' asked Roy. 'It's a pity you ever got mixed up in this. As I said before, it's no game for a woman. And that reminds me, you haven't told me yet what you were doing sneaking round the Cliff Top Inn earlier this evening.

'Oh, I just had a hunch after what the Chief told me, and, like you, I thought I'd do a little private investigating. You beat me to it, that's all.'

'Just as well, too,' commented Roy, 'or goodness knows where you'd have been by now.'

'Well, you weren't particularly brilliant yourselves,' she taunted him, 'knocking over that table and bringing the guards about your ears.'

'Better us than you, though. So remember what I told you. No more private snooping. You stay safely down your little mine. Promise?'

'I promise,' she said solemnly, 'but I'm not sure that the mine's going to be a very safe place much longer.'

'Don't worry about that. We'll take care of it. Good night. See you tomorrow, I hope.'

'Good night.' Karen held out her hand and he took it firmly between his for a second or two. Then she turned and went on towards the mine. He watched her until she was out of sight. Then he turned and walked thoughtfully back to the chalet.

CHAPTER XV

The Man in the Combe

'Confound you, Angus! Come on!'

Roy called and whistled furiously, but the dog showed no sign of having heard. Instead he went on barking.

'Down a blessed rabbit-hole pretending he's trapped a bear. I suppose,' grumbled Roy to himself. 'Ah well, I suppose I'll have to rescue him.'

He began scrambling down the steep side of the combe towards where the barks were coming from, muttering curses about the delay as he went. They had set out towards the Priory far later than he had intended because he had over-slept, and now here was Angus making a fool of himself and causing further delay. They wouldn't be back until afternoon if they didn't get a move on, and he wanted to put in some work on the book, which had been rather neglected lately,

Roy could not see the dog because of the trees and the thick undergrowth that covered both sides of the combe, at the bottom of which flowed the stream, which found its way to the sea past the door of his chalet, but the barks were sufficient guide. As he got nearer to the place they were apparently coming from, the ground levelled a little and he soon came out into a clearing fringing the stream.

Angus, he saw, was at the far side of it, barking and pushing at what looked like a bundle of clothes. Roy strode towards him and then stopped dead, a startled exclamation on his lips. The bundle of clothes, he now saw, was the body of a man, who was lying face downwards, his arms spread out and his face towards the stream.

Roy knelt down beside him. He was wearing only trousers, shirt and boots, and was apparently unconscious, if not dead. He turned him over on his back, and when he saw the man's face he turned away and wanted to be sick. It was a puffy mass of bruises, and blood was trickling from his nose and mouth. The hands, too, he saw, were mangled and bleeding, and when he opened the man's shirt to feel if his heart was still beating he saw that the chest was criss-crossed with livid weals.

The heart was still beating, but very feebly, and it was only too obvious that he was in a bad way. Roy hesitated for a moment, wondering what to do for the best. Who was he? How had he got here? Had he managed to struggle here by himself, or had he been brought here by someone and just dumped? He felt in the man's pockets to see if there was anything which would give him a clue to his identity, but they were empty.

That, however, would wait. That the man needed immediate medical attention if he was not to die was only too evident; the problem was how to give it to him. To move him might be dangerous, especially if he also had internal injuries, which Roy was not sufficiently expert to be able to detect with any certainty; on the other hand, if he were left lying here until it was possible to get a doctor to him he would probably die.

He shook the man very gently by the shoulder. If he could speak only a few words in response to his questions he might be able to indicate how badly hurt he was and where, but though the man groaned and winced away from him he did not open his eyes. That wince spoke volumes to Roy. He had seen it before – in victims of the Gestapo. These terrible injuries had not been suffered in an accident; of that he was certain.

There was only one thing to be done, he decided. That was to carry him to the chalet and then get help as quickly as possible. He stooped and very carefully lifted the man in his arms, carrying him like a baby. It needed a great effort to lift the inert body in his arms from this position, and the man groaned heavily, but Roy slowly staggered off towards the chalet, Angus, now silent, running ahead.

The going in the bottom of the combe was rough, and though he picked his way as carefully as possible, Roy often stumbled, and once he went down on one knee, but managed to save himself from falling. Several times in the mile and a half to the chalet he had to stop and rest, and once he thought his burden had died on him, but the next stumble brought a groan from him. It was a nightmare journey, but somehow he managed it though when he finally staggered across the threshold of the chalet and laid his burden down on the divan, Roy's clothes were damp with perspiration and his arms and legs felt like lead and ached intolerably.

He sat for a moment or two until he recovered his breath, and then went to look at his patient. The man was far gone, and Roy fetched the flask of brandy he kept for emergencies and managed to get some into his mouth. After a moment or two a little colour came back into the face and then the eyes opened and stared wildly about. Roy

111

had never seen such an expression of mingled horror and
fear on a man's face before – and he had seen some gruesome
sights in his time. This man must have gone through some
very terrible experience.

'That's better,' said Roy, when the man opened his eyes.
'Have a drop more?'

He put the flask to the man's lips again, and he managed
to swallow a little more. I'm probably doing the wrong thing,
thought Roy, but I've got to find out something about him. He
had formed a theory about this man, a theory he did not as yet
dare put into words; it was not a very nice one. But he could
not be sure he was right unless he knew who the man was.

'Can you speak now?' he asked him. 'Who are you? What
happened to you?'

The man made a slight gesture with his hand, but the
effort was too much for him and his arm fell limply back
on the divan again and his eyes closed. They opened again
in a second or two and his mouth began working as if he
were going to speak. He seemed to be screwing himself up
for a great effort. This time he succeeded in raising his hand
to his mouth, from which came ghastly noises.

Roy bent over him as his mouth slowly opened. Then he
turned away – and this time he *was* sick, sick as he had never
felt sick before. The man's mouth was empty, empty of tongue,
of teeth, empty of everything except gaping, bloody holes.

Roy at last stopped retching. There was no need to ask
the man's name now. He had never seen him before, but if
this was not Pat, the missing steward, then he felt he had
never been right about anything in his life. And if he had not
been tortured – abominably, excruciatingly tortured – then
he had never seen a victim of the Nazis. Pat must somehow
have fallen into their hands and they had done these things

to him to make him speak, to tell all he knew of what was happening in the old mine.

And, of course, he had not known. The terrible irony of it struck Roy like a blow. What was it Leyland had said? 'Only a few of the staff know why they are here. The guards and servants certainly don't.' Poor devil! He had suffered all this for nothing; he didn't know anything. Roy shuddered. He had remembered something else Leyland had said – that only Miss Silvers knew the whole thing from A to Z. If ever Delouris and his crowd got their hands on her— But he couldn't bear to pursue the thought.

The man on the divan was making signs to him again. His hand moved slowly as if he were writing. Roy hurriedly got him a pad and a pencil. He put the pad on his knee and the pencil between the bruised fingers and held him up. Making a great effort, the man scrawled some letters on the pad, then fell back exhausted. Roy took the pad from him and gave him some more brandy. He knew that he ought to have gone for help long ago, but if the man had anything to tell him it was imperative that he tell him now. If he waited until he had got help it might be too late, and the man might have information that, if it could not save him, would possibly save others.

The man tried again, scrawled a few more letters and collapsed. Roy looked at the pad. The letters were faint and ill-formed, but so far as he could make them out they read:

P O P.   W o m   t u

That was all. The man groaned again, and Roy bent over him. His pulse was very weak. He could not delay any longer

Francis Durbridge

in trying to get help. It was too far to Torcombe and would take too long even if he had got his bike, which he hadn't. His only hope was the mine. Surely among the scientists there was someone with some medical knowledge, though the chances were that by the time he got back even from the mine the man would be dead.

The man's eyes were closed, but he was still alive. Roy touched him gently, and he opened them.

'I'm going to try to get help,' Roy told him. 'A doctor. Do you understand? I'll be back as soon as possible.'

The man tried to shake his head, and as plainly as human eyes could speak they begged that he should not be left alone.

'You'll be all right,' Roy assured him. 'I shan't be long, and I'll leave the dog to look after you and the brandy where you can reach it.' He put it on the table within reach of the man's hand and where he could see it, and was turning to go, when he felt his own hand feebly grasped by that of the man on the divan.

Once again those piteous eyes pleaded that he should not be left alone, and Roy had not the heart to desert him. He sat down by the divan, holding the man's hand and trying to comfort him. He had relaxed a little now that he seemed sure that he was not going to be left, and his breathing seemed easier. Roy thought that he might be falling into a sleep, and for a time appeared to doze, but it was a fitful slumber, and once the man pitched convulsively and nearly rolled off the divan, groaning and moaning piteously. Roy could guess only too well the nightmare of torture through which he was once more passing. Finally the shuddering ceased, the pulse grew more and more feeble and then Roy could not feel it at all. The man was at peace now, thank God.

He got up, gently detached his hand from the other's grip,

crossed his pitifully mangled hands on his chest and covered him with a blanket. That was that, and there was nothing more to be done, except to get someone at the mine to identify him, so that his relatives, if he had any, could be notified.

He decided to go up to the mine at once. He tore the sheet on which the man had written his painful scrawl from the pad and stuffed it in his pocket. He'd try to decipher that later. Telling the protesting Angus to keep an eye on the place and not let anyone in, he locked the door of the chalet, and after a quick look round to see that no one was watching he set off for the mine, with Angus's barks echoing dismally after him.

Once or twice he turned round to see if he was being followed, but saw no one. He slowed down a little as he approached the entrance to the mine, or rather where he imagined it to be, having no desire to be jumped on and assaulted again. This time, as he got near where he had been knocked out before, the voice of a man he could not see told him to halt and put up his hands. He did so and heard someone quietly approaching him from behind. These blokes certainly keep well hidden, thought Roy. Although he had been on the look-out, he had not seen a sign or a suspicion of anyone. He turned round at the man's command and saw a guard armed with a Sten gun.

The guard grinned. 'Oh, it's you again, Major, I see. Not got your dog with you this time?'

'No,' said Roy. 'I suppose you're Joe?'

'Right first time,' said Joe. 'How did you guess? Sorry I had to knock you out before, but we've got very strict orders about strangers. I thought I recognized you this time, otherwise I might have had to do it again. I hope you weren't too badly shaken, sir, the time before?'

'I was shaken all right,' said Roy feelingly, 'but no apologies are necessary. You were only doing your duty, and after what I've seen today, I hope you'll go on doing it as efficiently as you did with me that day.'

'Anything wrong, sir?'

'I think I've found Pat, and he isn't exactly a pretty sight.'

'The missing steward?'

'Yes, poor devil.'

'You mean he isn't all right?'

'He's very far from being all right – in a worldly sense, that is – he's dead.'

'Dead, sir? How?'

'In about as filthy a way as one can put a man to death. Our friends have been trying a few of their tricks on him.'

The look that came over Joe's face was not pleasant to see. 'You don't mean they've tortured him, sir, do you?'

'That's exactly what I do mean. And now will you take me in to Miss Silvers? I'm pretty certain the man is – or was – Pat, but I've never seen him and someone who knew him had better identify him. He's at my chalet.'

'Right, sir,' said Joe. He whistled softly and another guard, Spud, whom Roy had met on his previous visit to the mine, came out from among some bushes and joined them.

'Just taking the major in,' said Joe. 'He thinks he's found Pat. Take over from me, will you, and keep your eyes skinned in case the major's been followed.'

'OK,' said Spud.

'Right. Come on, Major.' Joe led the way into the mine, the entrance to which was so skilfully concealed that Roy doubted whether he would have found it even in daytime. They went along the tunnel they had traversed before, and came to Miss Silvers' room. Joe tapped on the door and they

116

went in in response to her call. Karen was alone and very surprised to see them.

'What on earth brings you here at this time?' she asked. 'I thought the Chief said you hadn't to come here during the daytime, and in any case—'

Roy rather rudely interrupted her. 'It was important,' he said. 'I think I've found Pat.'

'Oh, good,' said Karen delightedly. 'I'm so glad. Where is he?'

'He's at the chalet,' replied Roy, 'and it's not good; it's very bad.'

'What do you mean?'

'I mean,' he said, moving towards her and taking her hand, 'that Pat is dead. That's bad enough, but it's the way he died that's the awful part of it.'

She looked stunned. 'Do you mean he's been killed in an accident?'

'No,' said Roy grimly. 'It was certainly no accident. He was murdered. And I don't mean they shot him, or anything nice and clean like that. They tortured him, presumably to make him tell what he knew of this place and what is going on here.'

'Oh no!' said Karen, covering her eyes with her hands. 'Poor, poor Pat.' She was silent for a moment, and then looked up, a ray of hope in her eyes.

'But are you sure it was Pat?' she asked. 'You never saw him. Couldn't you be mistaken? Couldn't it be someone else – not that it would be any the less horrible – but Pat . . . I can't believe it, somehow.'

'I'm afraid I'm only too right,' said Roy, 'but I think, all the same, that someone here who did know him should identify him. That's why I came at once. I thought perhaps you would come, as he was your servant. It isn't going to be pleasant, I'm afraid, but it ought to be done.'

'Of course I'll come,' she said instantly, 'and you'd better come with us, Joe, I think, just in case. Have you left a covering guard?'

'Yes, miss.'

'Very good, then. Let's go.

Joe led the way down the tunnel to the entrance, and they followed him. On the way to the chalet Roy described his morning's adventures, Angus's discovery of the body, the trip back to the chalet, his attempts to revive the man, his efforts at writing, and finally his death. He did not dwell much on the man's injuries, thinking that those would speak only too plainly for themselves, but he gave Karen a plain hint of what to expect.

'I'm not absolutely certain, of course, but if poor Pat hasn't been in the hands of that gang, I'll be very surprised. The irony of it is that they can't have got what they wanted to know, if what Leyland told me is correct – that only you know the whole secret.'

'That's true,' admitted Karen. 'He couldn't have told them anything that would be of value to them, even if he did speak, and somehow I can't believe he did, no matter how they made him suffer.'

'If he didn't' said Roy, 'then he must be one of the bravest men I've ever seen.'

He whistled for Angus as they neared the chalet, but there was no answering bark.

'I don't like this,' exclaimed Roy, and broke into a run. 'He always barks when I whistle like that,' he flung back over his shoulder to the others, who were close on his heels, Joe with his gun at the ready.

As he approached, Roy saw that the door of the chalet was slightly ajar. Joe noticed it, too, and caught him by the arm.

'Hold on a minute, Major,' he said. 'It looks as if you've had visitors. This is a job for me.'

Roy and Karen waited impatiently as he carefully approached the door. He kicked it open and, as nothing happened, went inside. He came out again in a moment.

'There's no one here,' he said.

CHAPTER XVI

Charlie gets a Shock

Charlie, like all old soldiers, was a man who liked his sleep, and he was in none too good a temper when the alarm clock woke him the morning after the visit to the Cliff Top Inn. He yawned and stretched and nearly decided to turn over and go to sleep again, but the knowledge that he had a job to do gnawed at him and forced him grumpily out of bed.

Charlie had never had much time for women – he was too interested in engines – so that although there were one or two Torcombe girls, daughters of fishermen, who would have been only too glad to come and share the little cottage in which he lived next to the garage, Charlie had so far managed to steer clear of them and remained a simple contented bachelor.

He put an old Army greatcoat, which served him as a dressing-gown, on top of his pyjamas, went downstairs, raked out the ashes of last night's fire, lit another one and put the kettle on while he went upstairs to dress. As he got into his clothes Charlie thought over the strange happenings of the night before. He decided he didn't at all like the way they were going about helping poor old Tod when he felt sure that he and Roy, with perhaps the assistance of a pal or two he, Charlie, could count on, were quite capable of taking good care of the guards at the inn.

It was a rum go and no mistake, men who were probably ex-Nazis occupying an English inn in peace-time and nobody able to do a thing about it! It went all against the grain with him. He knew he had always been inclined to be a bit impetuous, but it was what had won him his medal at Sidi Rezegh, even though the C.O. said he oughtn't to have done it. He was a bit disappointed in Roy, too. His war record didn't show that he was afraid of a bit of action. Not that he supposed that he was afraid now. Maybe it was working with that Scotland Yard chap and this Miss Silvers that had made him cautious. Red tape and all that, instead of seeing there was a job to do, and going and doing it without any fuss.

Charlie went downstairs again and made himself a mug of tea, which he took upstairs again with a jugful of hot water to shave. As he scraped his face with an old 'cut-throat' which had been his father's, Charlie wondered idly if there was anything between Roy and Miss Silvers. They hadn't always seemed on very friendly terms last night, but that wasn't always safe to go by. He'd known women whose blokes knocked 'em about and still they loved 'em! That was a queer thing, come to think of it. Some women enjoyed a beating-up; others rushed to the divorce courts screaming 'mental cruelty' if their husband's didn't look at their new hat.

Charlie had a good swill in the bowl of cold water on the dressing-table, put on an old pullover – he never wore a collar and tie if he could help it – and went downstairs and made himself some breakfast. Well, I'm mixed up in it now, he thought, though so far it hasn't busted any tank armour.

Nor did he expect that his little reconnaissance in the direction of the old Priory this afternoon would lead to much. He'd much rather have had a crack at shifting those guards out of the inn and finding Mrs Murdock and Modwen. That would be a job worth doing. And if something didn't happen soon, he would have a crack at it, even if he had to do it on his own.

He left the breakfast pots in a bowl and poured some water over them. Then he went out to the garage and started to work on Roy's bike. As he put new brake cables in, he again felt a vague resentment that anyone for a moment could have thought that *his* cables could have worn out so soon. They'd been cut all right, and he'd like to get his hands on the blighter who'd cut 'em.

He wondered as he worked what had happened to those women, where they were and what they were doing now. He experienced a sudden pang as he thought of Modwen in the hands of those swine, and felt ashamed as he realized that he wasn't as much concerned about her mother. There had been a time when he had thought of asking Modwen to marry him. He felt she liked him, and certainly it would have been OK with Tod and his missus, but then he had thought of what it would have meant to him to give up his freedom, and he had not spoken of his feelings. Indeed, he had even stopped going to the 'Cliff Top' for a time, until they began to wonder if they had offended him, but he had made that all right, and it was Tod who had helped him set up the garage business. He had paid him back now, of course, but it had been a great help then. Maybe when all this business was cleared up . . .

Charlie worked all morning on the bike, but by half past twelve he was able to straighten his back, look down on his handiwork and pronounce the machine as good as new. Then he washed his hands, put on an old jacket and went down to the 'Harbour Bar' to have a couple of pints with the boys. He passed a pleasant half hour in the back parlour and came away feeling very pleased with himself because he felt he had bested Sam Consley, the archopponent in Torcombe of engines in fishing boats, in an argument.

He walked back to the cottage, had a meal, smoked a pipe while he looked over the latest number of the *Motor Cycle*, got out his own machine, which he had tended and tuned like a mother with her child, and set out for the old Priory. He roared up the hill out of the village, passing Doc Tremlow's groaning and battered two-seater as it carried him protestingly on his way to see a patient, no doubt, and waved cheerily to the vicar, who, as usual, was working in his garden. He'd be surprised, reflected Charlie with a grin, if he knew where I was going and what for.

The motor-cycle covered the distance to the Priory in quick time. Charlie throttled her down as he approached the ruins and coasted quietly past. There was no sign of life. He braked and stopped the machine and dismounted. Then he wheeled it into some bushes on the verge of the road and sat down in a clump of bracken. He himself could not be seen, but by raising his head slightly he found he had a good view of the road in both directions and through the trees he could see a part of the ruins.

He had just lit a cigarette when he heard a distant chugging – the unmistakable sound of Doc Tremlow's car as it racketed past. Charlie stifled a temptation to stand up and call out to the doctor. Instead he stayed where he was, lying on his stomach and keeping an eye on the road with an occasional glance towards the ruins.

The cigarette finished, he ground out the butt in the peaty soil in which the bracken grew so luxuriantly, and was thinking about lighting another one, when he heard a sound which he could not at first identify. It appeared to come from the other side of the road where the ground began to descend towards the combe leading down to No Man's Cove.

Charlie lay dead still and listened. He heard a twig crack as if someone had trodden on it and then what sounded like grunts and heavy breathing. Cautiously he raised his head slightly and parted the fronds of bracken so that he could see the road. As he did so he saw two men peer over the top of the wall which bounded the opposite side of the road. They glanced in both directions and listened for a moment or two. Then, evidently satisfied that it was safe, they bent down and lifted on to the wall what looked like a bundle of clothing. As they lifted it, however, Charlie had a glimpse of something pink, and he realized that the bundle was a man whom they were carrying.

They rested their burden on top of the wall while they themselves climbed over and then they picked it up again, one taking the head and the other the feet, and started to cross the road.

Forgetting all his Army training in the excitement of the moment, Charlie stood up and cried out, 'Hey, there!' 'Want any help?' and started out on to the road towards them.

The two men stopped dead and turned sharply in his direction. Then the man in the rear dropped the legs he was holding as if they had been red hot, put his hand in his hip-pocket, whipped out something that flashed in the sun and pointed it at him.

Charlie heard no sound, but he felt a searing pain in his head and knew no more.

CHAPTER XVII

Two Casualties

'What do you mean – no one there?' exclaimed Roy, dashing past Joe into the chalet.

But Joe was right. The chalet was empty. The body of the man he had left lying on the divan had gone.

'How the devil . . .' began Roy. A whine attracted his attention to the corner of the room farthest from the door. He moved towards the sound, Joe, who had come back into the chalet with Karen, following.

The whine had come from Angus, who was struggling pathetically and ineffectually to get to his feet. Roy bent down beside him and saw that his off hind leg was curiously bent. Muttering curses under his breath, Roy patted the dog's head and gently felt the leg. It was broken, and he could see on closer examination that one of the ends of the bone was sticking out through the flesh.

'The devils!' he exclaimed to Karen, who had knelt down beside him. 'They must have been watching when I left to go to the mine, got in somehow and taken Pat away. I expect Angus tried to stop them and got a broken leg for his pains, poor old chap. I don't think there's anything else wrong with him, but this is a bit beyond me. I'll have to get him to the vet.'

'Aren't you forgetting there isn't a vet in Torcombe?' she reminded him. 'Here, let me have a look. I used to do a bit of this sort of thing when I worked on a farm in Yorkshire years ago.'

She examined the leg. 'Well, it's a clean break at least,' she pronounced, 'probably done with a stick, or the butt end of a gun. And talking of sticks, if you'll find me a couple of short ones that'll do for splints and something to bandage them with, I think I can fix it until we can get Dr Tremlow to have a look at him.'

Roy found the sticks and tore up an old shirt for a bandage.

'I'm afraid this may hurt a bit, old chap,' she said to Angus, then turned to Roy. 'Perhaps you'd better hold his head.'

Roy did so, but the dog bore the setting of the broken bone, the fixing of the splints and the bandaging without a murmur.

'Good boy,' said Karen, patting him when she had finished. 'You'll soon be all right.'

Angus wagged his tail gratefully and Roy picked him up carefully, put him on a rug by the hearth and gave him some milk with a few drops of brandy in it. The dog lapped it up eagerly.

'Well, at least I'm thankful they left me the flask,' said Roy. 'It came in useful for the dog, if nothing else.'

'Knows good stuff when he tastes it,' commented Joe approvingly. 'Seen the door, sir?'

'No,' said Roy. 'I haven't had time to see anything yet, except that Pat has gone. What about the door?'

'Come and have a look.'

Roy and Karen went over to it. The lock had been forced and the jamb splintered.

'I'll soon get someone to fix that for you, sir,' said Joe.

'Evidently they weren't standing on ceremony,' commented Roy. 'They must have wanted him badly; but why? I don't see how they could have thought he was still alive, the way I left him, even if they were in a hurry and hadn't time to investigate. And he wasn't any further use to them dead, that I can see.'

'Perhaps they had orders to bring him back dead or alive,' suggested Karen. 'Presumably he managed somehow to escape from wherever it was they were keeping him a prisoner. They wouldn't know where he had gone when they sent out the guards to recapture him. I suppose they thought it might be very awkward if a man in his physical condition were found by one of the villagers. They haven't finished the job they came here to do – at least so far as we know. They wouldn't want to risk anything interfering with that.'

'I suppose that must be the explanation,' said Roy. 'It isn't often one can say it and mean it, but thank God he was dead. At least they can't do anything more to him now, poor devil. And he may have given us more information about them than they got out of him about the mine. I'd almost forgotten it.'

He pulled out from his pocket the now rather crumpled page of the writing pad. 'What do you make of that?' he asked, handing it to Karen.

She studied it for a moment. 'It's a bit of a poser, isn't it?' she asked. 'Probably the first "P" stands for Pat – I expect he was trying to tell you who he was. Then "O. P." what could that be?'

'It must be "Old Priory", of course,' said Roy. 'Why didn't I see it before? I'll bet a thousand to one we're right, and that's where they're hiding out.'

'"W o m", even though there are spaces between the letters, is probably as much as he could write of "women",' said Karen, 'and women in this connection could only mean Mrs Murdock and Modwen. He was trying to tell you where they are.'

'And "t u" are the first two letters of "tunnel",' said Roy excitedly, 'and if the vicar's right, there're plenty of tunnels at or near the old Priory, so it looks almost certain they're imprisoned somewhere near there, if not in the ruins themselves. We'll obviously have to do some investigating there now all right. I wonder if Charlie stumbled across anything this afternoon.'

'You'll probably have to wait until tonight to know that,' said Karen. 'We all arranged to meet here, remember, when the Chief got back.'

'Yes, unless he has discovered something and comes on before then.'

She looked at her watch. 'I don't see there's anything more Joe and I can do here if we stayed, so we might as well get back to the mine. What are you going to do till tonight?'

'I think I'll take Angus into Torcombe, to see Doc Tremlow. I'm not casting any aspersions on your first aid,' he added hastily, 'but I shall be happier if he has a look at him in case there are any complications. I wouldn't like to lose that dog, you know. As a matter of fact, now that this has happened, I've a good mind to ask the doctor to look after him for me for a while. I'd be more relieved if he were safely out of the way now that the chalet has become such a popular rendezvous for visitors.'

'But you haven't got your bike,' said Karen. 'You can't carry a dog all that way.'

'Oh yes I can,' said Roy. 'I've carried him farther than that when we've been out on really long hikes together and his short legs have got tired more quickly than my long ones – even though he has four to my two. I've got a nice big shopping basket I can put him in. He'll be perfectly comfortable, won't you, old man?'

Angus wagged his tail. Karen bent and twiddled his ears. 'All right,' she said, 'if you're so bent on having exercise I won't stop you, though I should have thought you'd had enough for one day. I'll come back later with the Chief. And for goodness' sake take care of yourself. Goodbye.'

Roy watched Karen and Joe out of sight from the door of the chalet. She'd be safe enough with Joe, he thought. Then he came inside and got himself a belated lunch. He sat down for a smoke before starting out to Torcombe. He reflected that it wasn't really necessary for him to go that afternoon. Angus seemed perfectly all right and a rest would do them both good, but he did not feel like lounging around doing nothing, or even working on the book. Too much was happening for that sort of concentration, and he was afraid that a good deal more was going to happen before this business was finished.

He began to go back in his mind over what had happened from his first finding the footprints and following them to the old mine to the horrible incidents of that morning and the fate of poor Pat. He started to sketch idly on the writing pad – first No Man's Cove and the coastline, stretching on the one side to Shingleton and on the other to Torcombe. He marked the chalet, the combe and the stream, the cliff road and the Cliff Top Inn, the road inland from Torcombe which went past the old Priory, the route he had taken to the mine entrance concealed among the bushes.

Somewhere, linking the mine with the Priory and the Priory

with the 'Cliff Top', were underground passages. He traced them with dotted lines, as far as he could remember how they went from the vicar's chart. But did they exist any more, or were they merely fallen heaps of rubble now? If the Chief's theory about the reasons for the robbery from the mine was correct, one of those tunnels was being opened up by Delouris and his men right now. As for the others, who could say?

He tossed the pad on the table, stretched and got up. He got the shopping basket from the pantry and lifted Angus, rug and all, into it. 'There, my lad, how's that?' he asked, and the dog crooned at him. 'Doc Tremlow'll wonder what on earth I've brought him when he sees this lot.'

Rather to Roy's surprise, it was an uneventful walk to the village. He had come to expect something happening almost every time he went out now. There was no one about when he passed the Cliff Top Inn, and though he would have liked to make a call to see if there had been any developments there, he thought he had better not go there out of opening hours.

As he had anticipated, Dr Tremlow was a trifle nonplussed when Roy arrived with his basket and apologized for troubling him.

'No trouble at all, my boy,' said the doctor. 'My patients bring me all kinds of jobs to do for 'em. I'm vet and everything else around here.'

He took off Angus's bandage and splints and examined the leg.

'Not bad work for an amateur,' he said. 'I didn't know you went in for first aid, but I expect you had to know a bit of everything in your job, like me.'

Roy forbore to tell him who had done the first aid.

'He'll be all right in a few weeks, won't you, old chap?' said the doctor to Angus, who wagged his acknowledgments. 'Why don't you leave him here so that I can keep an eye on him? My wife would be delighted to have the little fellow.'

'Well, as a matter of fact I was going to ask you if you'd mind doing just that,' said Roy, 'but I didn't know whether it would be convenient.'

'Perfectly all right. No trouble at all. He'll probably be spoiled to death by my wife. She's a fool where dogs are concerned, especially sick ones. He probably won't want to leave here when he's better! By the way, I've been attending a friend of yours this afternoon.'

'Oh, who?'

'Charlie.'

'What!' exclaimed Roy. 'When, where, how?'

'Found him lying on the road near the old Priory when I was coming back into Torcombe from seeing a patient. Damned nearly ran over him. Got a nasty mark on his head. Said it was caused by falling off his bike, but I didn't believe him. Did you ever hear of Charlie falling off a bike? If that injury wasn't a bullet crease, I've never seen one. What are you two up to? Not been poaching, have you? Or fighting a duel?'

'Good lord, no,' said Roy, 'but how about Charlie – is he all right?'

'He'll be right as rain tomorrow. I patched him up, sent him home and told him to rest. Funny business, though. Still, I suppose it's no concern of mine, though if he's in some trouble, I wouldn't mind being in on it – that is, if it's strictly legal. I could do with a bit of excitement. A country doctor's practice gets a bit tame sometimes, you know. So if you want any help at any time, just let me know. Only don't tell the wife,' he added with a wink.

131

For a moment Roy was tempted to take the doctor into his confidence. He'd certainly be a useful sort of chap to have on one's side in a tight corner, if all he'd heard about him was correct. He'd been a naval surgeon during the war, and Roy had heard bits about some of his exploits, official and otherwise. But he decided that he had better not say anything for the time being. Leyland would probably be annoyed at his having told Charlie, without his bringing any more outsiders into it. Still, the doctor would be well worth bearing in mind if they wanted extra help some time.

'Well, if you're sure it'll be all right about Angus, I think I'll go and call on Charlie before I go back,' said Roy. 'Bye-bye,' he said, patting the dog. 'I'll come and see you soon. Thanks a lot, Doctor.'

He went straight to Charlie's cottage and found him sitting in front of the fire with a bandage round his head, smoking a pipe. Charlie started to his feet on seeing him.

'Sit down, invalid,' said Roy. 'What the dickens happened to you this afternoon?'

'How did you come to hear of it so soon?' parried Charlie.

Roy told him of the incidents of the morning, of the discovery of the man they believed to be Pat and of his disappearance.

'I'll bet that was the chap I saw,' said Charlie, slapping his thigh in exasperation. 'What a b.f. I was! I ought to be kicked. If only I hadn't stood up and attracted their attention! I could have trailed them and found out where they were taking him. Instead, I had to go and act like an idiot and let them take a pot at me.'

'Oh,' said Roy. 'So it was a bullet wound. The doc suspected as much.'

132

'Yes, I rather thought he would. He's seen too many to be deceived by my tale.'

'Aren't you forgetting I haven't heard your tale?' asked Roy. 'What the deuce did happen to you?'

'Sorry,' said Charlie. He went on to describe how he had seen the two men carrying another one crossing the road and how he had stood up and called to them and been fired on. 'I'm damned lucky to be here at all,' said Charlie, 'but I'd have had only myself to blame if the doctor had found a stiff on the road instead of merely a stunned one. That gun must have had a silencer on it because I never heard a thing. But what a chance I missed of finding out where they were really going.'

'Never mind,' said Roy, telling him about the note Pat left. 'I'm pretty sure it's the old Priory. Anyway, I'll find out tonight.'

'What do you mean, "I"?' asked Charlie indignantly. 'Aren't you forgetting I'm in on this, too? You don't think I'm going to be left at home now, do you, after what happened this afternoon? I've all the more reason now to want to get a bit of my own back.'

'The doctor told me you had to rest,' Roy reminded him. 'I think you'd better stay at home tonight.'

'Not on your life,' snorted Charlie. 'I'm all right. I've had cracks on the head before – and,' he added, with emphasis which made Roy smile, 'it's about time I started dishing a few out.'

'All right, you old fire-eater,' conceded Roy. 'Be at the chalet about ten o'clock and we'll see what the Chief says. In the meantime why don't you try and get a bit of sleep? It would do you good. You can't have any objections to that, unless you've changed a heck of a lot since I last saw you.

By the way, did you manage to fix the bike before you got yourself knocked out?'

'When I say I'll do a job, I do it,' said Charlie. 'It's in the garage and it's as good as new. Mind you take better care of it this time and watch out for nasty men who want to monkey with your brake cables. They were cut all right, you know.'

'Right,' said Roy. 'I'll be glad of the lift. I wasn't particularly looking forward to walking all the way back. See you about ten. So long.'

'So long,' grunted Charlie. 'And don't you dare start without me or you'll have more trouble on your hands.'

On his way back Roy looked in at the Cliff Top Inn. There were about a dozen customers in the smoky bar and Tod Murdock was serving them. Roy ordered a pint and Tod looked at him hopefully as he saw him.

'Nothing yet,' he said, as Tod pushed the tankard towards him. 'Any change here?'

Tod turned back to the till and got his change before answering. 'Nothing,' he muttered, 'except that there was only one guard last night and he's keeping a very close eye on me.'

Roy nodded and turned to talk to one of the fishermen. He had a quick look at the door to the living-room. It was slightly ajar and he guessed that there was someone behind it listening. He drank up, called 'Good night' to Tod and went out.

'Only one guard, eh,' he said to himself as he mounted his machine and coasted off down the cliff road. 'Very interesting. I think we shall have to do something about that.'

It was a grim-faced Chief Inspector Leyland who listened later that night to Roy's recital of the day's events. He had already heard some of them from Karen, and Roy contented himself with filling in the details and adding the story of Charlie's adventure.

As he had anticipated, Leyland was none too pleased at yet another outsider being let into the secret.

'I suppose this chap's to be trusted?' he asked dubiously.

'You can trust him as you would me,' said Roy rather indignantly. 'As for bringing in outsiders, if it isn't expedient, as you say it isn't, to bring in police or troops to round up this gang yet, it seems to me you've got to depend on outsiders to do your dirty work, and I can't help saying that so far they've done most of it.

'All right, all right,' said the Chief. 'There's no need to get annoyed. I appreciate what you've done, believe me, but I've told you that the authorities, rightly or wrongly, take the view that we can't afford to take a chance on any of this gang, especially Delouris, getting away, and that this mine and what's being done here must serve as the bait for the trap into which we hope they'll stick their noses. After all, this is what they're really after. They've got to make a move here sooner or later and we think it will start soon. Delouris, if our information is correct, hasn't returned here yet, but we think he will when they're ready to send the balloon up. That's the man we've got to wait for. The rest is only incidental.'

'Pretty grimly incidental, though,' commented Roy. 'It's a pity you didn't see what they did to Pat. I feel badly enough about him and I'd never even seen him before then. If anything should happen to any of the women . . . to Karen . . .'

He saw the Chief look up sharply and wished he had not used her Christian name. 'By the way,' he added, partly to cover up his slight confusion, 'where is she? I thought she was coming with you.'

'She wanted to,' rejoined Leyland, 'but after I'd heard what happened today I gave her strict instructions not to leave the mine again unless she is escorted by you or me, or one of the guards.'

'I'm glad to hear it,' said Roy. 'I'd hate to think of her as part of the bait of the trap, or that she'll be here when it's sprung.'

'So that's how the land lies, is it?' said Leyland softly, more to himself than to Roy.

'That's how it is so far as I'm concerned,' said Roy, 'and I hope she feels the same way about it.'

'Well, well,' said the Chief, for want of something better to say.

Any further exchange of confidences was prevented by the arrival on his motor-bike of Charlie. Roy introduced them, and was glad to note that the Chief immediately liked the look of his friend and took to him at once.

The Chief questioned him about his experience that afternoon, but Charlie could not add anything to what he had already told Roy, except an apology that he had acted so rashly, instead of trailing the men.

'Still,' he said, 'I know exactly where they crossed the road and I think we can pick up their trail from there.'

'I don't suppose you recognized either of the men?' asked Leyland.

'No, never seen either of 'em in my life before.'

'You're sure they were making for the Priory?'

'Well, I couldn't swear to it, of course, but there isn't another building within miles in that direction. I think we ought to investigate the place tonight, and I must say I'm rather looking forward to a bit of fun. If they didn't guess it before, they must be pretty sure by now that we suspect they're there, so they'll probably have a reception committee all lined up to greet us. Well, that suits me. I don't care very much for people who take pot shots at you when you offer 'em help.'

'And talking of help,' put in Roy, 'don't you think we need reinforcements? Doc Tremlow would come along with pleasure if we asked him. No,' he went on hastily, as he saw an annoyed look come over the Chief's face, 'I haven't whispered a word to him, but I think he suspected this afternoon that Charlie hadn't been scratched by an angry rabbit, and he as good as invited himself into any trouble there might be in the offing. There's probably at least a dozen, if not more, men at the Priory, and only three of us at present. Not that any of us have ever minded a few odds, but if we're hoping to get Mrs Murdock and Modwen away it won't be exactly a cake-walk. What do you feel?'

Leyland drew hard at his pipe before replying. 'I've been thinking about that a lot,' he said, 'and I'm still of the opinion that we stand a better chance of getting in there – and getting out again in one piece – if there are only a few of us instead of a small army, which they're probably expecting.'

'I agree,' said Charlie. 'This is a small patrol job, if ever I saw one. We've a much better chance of surprising 'em if there are only a few of us.'

'All right by me,' said Roy. 'I only thought I ought to mention it. Maybe we'll need the doc to patch up our wounds.'

'Cheerful blighter, ain't he, sir?' asked Charlie.

'If there was one thing more than another I learnt in the Service,' said Roy, 'it was never to take unnecessary chances. I was only thinking about the women folks. I don't want them to be let in for anything more than they've already had to bear, through our miscalculating. It wouldn't help them any if we went and got ourselves caught. Well, what's the plan of campaign? I'm ready if you are.'

'We'll make that when we see how the land lies,' the Chief decided. 'One thing I've learnt in the Service I belong to,' he added with a twinkle in his eye, 'is not to create problems before they exist. But one problem has already arisen – food. What about something to eat before we set out, Roy?'

'Right, sir,' said Roy promptly. 'Coming up in a jiffy.'

CHAPTER XVIII

The Old Priory

'This is just like old times, eh, Charlie?'

Roy, leading the way up the combe, paused for a moment to allow the others to catch up.

'It sure is,' said Charlie, as he and Leyland came up with him, 'except that it's a bit quieter. Still, we don't want any guns popping on this trip, or flares to light us up.'

They stood listening for a moment. The night was quiet, except for the usual noises of the countryside and the far-off chuffing of a train. The moon had not yet risen, and the bottom of the combe, from which they had just emerged, was as black as the inside of a bag, as Charlie put it, though if they looked up through the trees they could catch glimpses of the stars.

'Well, come on,' said the Chief. 'Surely you young chaps aren't exhausted already? I'd like to get some sleep before the night's out.'

Roy, ignoring this sally, turned and resumed the climb to the road which separated them from the Priory. They were roughly following the line they calculated Delouris' men must have taken when they were taking Pat away, and aiming to come out on the road where Charlie had surprised them.

Roy stopped again a few minutes later. 'We're nearly up to the road,' he said in a low undertone. 'Don't make any noise.'

He had gone on about a dozen yards further when he paused again and sniffed the air. 'Smell anything?' he asked the Chief.

'Yes,' said Leyland. 'Someone's having a smoke, and pretty foul stuff it is, too.'

'That means they've probably got a guard out on the road, or, more likely, under cover on their side of it. Unless, of course it's a poacher. I'll soon find out. It's just my cup of tea. I'll give you a whistle when the coast's clear.'

'All right,' whispered Leyland, 'but for heaven's sake be careful.'

'Want me to come with you?' asked Charlie. 'I used to do a bit of this sort of thing, too, you know.'

'No, thanks,' said Roy. 'You stay here with the Chief. He'll need you if anything goes wrong.'

He moved silently forward, and the others waited, tense in the darkness. The seconds after he had gone seemed minutes. At last they heard a few scuffling sounds, followed by a grunt and a strangled groan. Then silence, broken by a low whistle. Leyland and Charlie climbed cautiously up to the road and saw a dark figure on the other side.

'It's all right,' said Roy in low tones. 'I've got him here.' 'Him' was the figure of a man slumped at his feet. 'It was a guard all right. He never knew what hit him. Here, give me a hand with tying him up. We don't want him coming to and giving the alarm at an inconvenient moment.'

Charlie produced one of several lengths of rope they had

brought with them and the man was soon trussed and gagged. They rolled him out of sight under some bushes, then stood listening for a moment or two, but there were no sounds in the night and they moved cautiously forward, still in single file.

Soon the bushes and the trees began to thin out. Roy halted them. 'You can see the old Priory now,' he whispered, pointing through a gap in the trees at a black pile silhouetted against the sky.

'Ugh!' said Charlie with a shiver. 'It looks a grim old place. Any ghosts, I wonder?'

'The only ghosts you'll see tonight, my lad, if you see any at all, will be flesh-and-blood ones,' said Leyland. 'What now?'

'I think we'd better separate here,' answered Roy. 'I'll go straight ahead, and I suggest you, Chief, take the right flank and you, Charlie, the left. OK?'

'OK,' repeated the Chief. 'We'd better meet here in, say, an hour. That ought to be long enough for us to see what's what.'

They split up and moved away, each on his own course. Roy paused as he came to the last bushes before the ruins, sank to the ground and looked carefully around him. There might be another guard hereabouts, he thought, but there was no sound, or sign of movement, so he crawled silently on, then got cautiously to his feet.

He had gone only a few yards through the long rank grass when suddenly his feet shot from under him and he found himself dropping as if into the very earth. Then the exclamation of surprise he had half stifled as he lost his footing changed to a grunt which was forced out of him as his feet hit something solid and his body piled up on top of them.

The breath driven momentarily out of him by the fall, he lay still for several moments, listening, feeling certain that the noise of his fall must have warned any guard who might be near, but no sound of alarm came to him through the gaping hole several feet above his head through which he could still glimpse the stars. Roy had no idea where he might be, but he calculated that he must have fallen fifteen or twenty feet. There was a dank smell in the air about him and the stones and earth he could feel under him were damp and slimy.

Some sounds now came quietly to him, apparently on his own level, but they were too indistinct to be identified. He felt in his pocket and was relieved to find that his torch was intact. He debated for a moment whether or not to switch it on, then decided he must take a chance. He had to find out where he was, or else risk more unpleasant shocks. The sharp beam of the light showed him that he was in what appeared to be a low tunnel, the earthen floor and rough stone walls of which were covered with moss and dripping with moisture. The tunnel to the mine! Or perhaps a branch of it? He could not be sure, but there was something, evidently, in the old legends after all, and this tunnel at least hadn't been filled in, though there appeared to have been several falls from the roof.

Excited by his discovery, he moved forward, bent double to avoid hitting his head on the low roof, in the direction he calculated would take him towards the Priory. It was slow and rough going, for the floor was littered with earth and stones which had fallen from the roof and sides and he had to pause occasionally to clear a way. It was after one of these pauses that he again heard sounds, plainer this time, so he was evidently moving in their direction, or they in his.

He went cautiously on until he became pretty certain that the sounds were being made by men digging. He identified the clink of metal on stone, stertorous breathing, and finally the sound of voices.

Crawling now because he dared not use his torch, Roy moved slowly on. The sounds, which got louder as he advanced, seemed to be coming from his right, almost as if they were behind the wall of the tunnel. Roy was trying to puzzle this out when he heard sharp words of command and then the sound of marching feet, apparently coming in his direction. He huddled closely against the wall of the tunnel, hardly daring to breathe. At first the feet seemed to be making directly for him; then he realized with relief that they were passing what seemed to be only a few yards in front of him and then going away.

He tried to count how many pairs there were, but it was hopeless. Ten or a dozen men he calculated, but he could not be sure. The sounds died away and all was quiet again except for the drip, drip of moisture from the roof. Roy waited a little and then crawled on. He dared at last to switch on his torch and found that he was almost at the junction with another, and much broader and higher, tunnel, into which the passage he was in ran diagonally. That explained why the sounds he had heard of marching feet had seemed at first to come from behind the right-hand wall of his tunnel, then move towards him and finally away from him.

He risked getting to his feet before moving stealthily out into the main tunnel. The floor, roof and walls were of earth and the roof was supported by baulks of timber and props, but what interested him most was the narrow-gauge railway lines which ran down the centre of the floor. There was mining going on here all right. He paused and tried to work out his direction. If he had guessed right, the main tunnel he was in now ran roughly between the Priory and the mine. It was beginning to look as if the Chief's theory was right and that the gang was trying to get into the mine this way.

Hugging the wall and flashing his torch only at intervals, he edged his way along the tunnel to the right in the direction, he reckoned, of the mine and away from the Priory. He wanted to see how far the Germans had got with their operations. He passed tubs filled with earth and stones waiting to be moved and emptied. He wondered where on earth they could be putting all the stuff, and then reflected that there were probably plenty of places in the bowels of the ruins where it could be dumped.

Switching on his torch again, he saw that he was no more than a dozen yards from the face of the working. Picks and shovels were lying about where the diggers had dropped them. They were having to do it the hard way, instead of blasting, which would undoubtedly have attracted attention. This was where the stuff stolen from the pit had gone all right, and if he was not very far out in his estimate they hadn't much farther to dig before they were through into the mine itself. The balloon might go up quicker than they bargained for.

Roy looked at his watch. Twenty minutes had passed since he left Leyland and Charlie. He debated for a moment or two whether to go back and try to locate them to tell of his discovery, but then he remembered that he'd literally fallen into this, and without a ladder he could not think of any way he could get out of the shaft down which he had dropped. He'd got to find another way out now, so he might just as well do some more investigating in this direction. Even if he found out nothing else, he had discovered enough to have made the expedition worth while, but he wanted some news of Mrs Murdock and Modwen, too.

Keeping his torch on now that there seemed no immediate danger of detection, but shading it with his hands, he moved swiftly but silently back in the direction in which he had come. Passing the entrance to the side passage by which he had entered the main tunnel, he went on in the direction taken by the diggers, who must have just finished a shift, he decided. He had not gone more than fifty yards past the junction when, feeling his way along the left-hand wall, he encountered stone instead of earth. He examined the walls closely with his torch. They were of stone all right, great slabs of it, and the floor too. That could mean only one thing – that he was now within the boundaries of the old Priory walls, probably in what had been the cellars or the crypt.

He took out the pair of fisherman's stockings he had brought with him and drew them on over his boots so that he would make less noise. He moved forward a few yards and then stiffened as the light of his torch showed him a massive door set back in the left-hand wall. He crept up to it, paused, and listened with his ear close to the woodwork. For a moment or two he could not hear anything; then there was the sound of movement, followed by what sounded like a woman crying softly.

'Mrs Murdock and Modwen – for a pound,' muttered Roy under his breath. He listened a little longer, then decided to risk it, and tapped gently with his knuckles on the door. The sounds inside the room stopped instantly. He tapped again and spoke quietly and distinctly.

'Mrs Murdock? Modwen?'

There was a faint sound of movement. Then a woman's voice asked:

'Who is it?'

'Roy Benton. Are you all right? Can you open the door?'

What a damfool question to ask! thought Roy. As if they'd still be in there if they could!

'Oh, thank God somebody's come,' he heard the older

woman say tearfully. 'Yes, we're both here. We're all right so far, but they keep threatening us. Get us out, for God's sake!'

Roy pressed against the door, more to reassure the women that he was trying to help them rather than in the hope that it would budge. It didn't. It was very solid and immovable – for him at least. A shot of dynamite would probably be required to shift it.

'I can't now,' he said. 'I'll have to get help to break this door down, but I'll be back soon, I promise. Tod's all right. Try not to worry. I'll tell him you're unharmed.'

'Oh, don't go and leave us now,' Mrs Murdock pleaded.

'I must,' said Roy, 'but I'll be back, never fear.'

'Well, be careful,' urged Mrs Murdock, and the thought that in her plight she could still spare a thought for others touched Roy oddly. 'These men are fiends,' she added. 'They'll do anything.'

Thank heaven she doesn't know how fiendish, thought Roy. Aloud he said: 'I'll watch out. Keep your chins up. 'Bye now.'

He moved reluctantly on a few yards, then hesitated. Ought he not to abandon the investigation now that he knew the whereabouts of the two women and try to get help? But from where? Once more he reminded himself that he'd still to get himself out of this place – and to find a way – so on he went.

Another twenty yards or so farther on he saw another door on the opposite side of the tunnel. He froze against the wall and put out his torch as he heard the sound of voices and the clink of crockery and cutlery. Suddenly the door opened and Roy dropped flat on his face as a man was framed in the light that poured from the room into the tunnel. The man paused for a moment and looked along the tunnel in Roy's direction. He felt sure the man must see him, but he turned, said something in German to the others in the room

and strode off down the tunnel away from Roy, whistling
Die Lorelei. Roy found himself remembering the version of
the song he had sung at school in a translation that he had
always loved. How did it go?

> The air is cool in the gloaming
> And calmly flows the Rhine,
> The thirsty summits are drinking
> The sunset's flooding wine.

The sound of the whistling died away in the distance, and
Roy let out a slight 'Phew!' of relief, but stayed where he
was. He could not be sure that the man had gone for good,
or whether he might not be coming back. It was as well that
he did so, for in a few moments the man, still whistling,
returned and re-entered the room. Roy waited a little while
in case there were any others in the room who felt like taking
a sudden walk along the passage, but the sounds of talking
and eating were resumed. Supper break, evidently, thought
Roy, and moved cautiously past the door.

Ten yards farther on, still feeling his way along the wall
because he dared not risk switching on his torch with the
men so near, he found his hand moving away from the stone
wall into space. He stopped and, risking a quick switch on
and off of his torch, which he shielded with his jacket, he
saw that the tunnel forked, one branch going straight on;
the other to the left ended about six yards ahead in another
door. He decided to investigate the door, and moved quietly
towards it until his outstretched fingers gently touched the
woodwork.

Putting his ear close to it, Roy listened intently, but no
sound came from the other side. He quietly switched on his

torch again and saw that the door had a ring handle. Very cautiously he moved it ever so slightly. It did not make a noise. Evidently well oiled, he thought, and went on turning it, making no sound. He turned it a full half circle and then, with an unspoken 'Now for it', he pressed gently against the door with his shoulder.

Immediately he saw that there was a light on in the room and hastily but quietly pulled the door shut again, but kept the handle turned. Nothing happened. Slowly he pressed the door open again. He put his eye close to the widening crack he was making and gradually saw coming into view a table at which a man, with his head resting on his hands, was seated. There were some papers spread out between his elbows. They looked like drawings of some kind.

The man did not move. Was he asleep? Roy wondered. He continued pushing open the door, and had got it wide open enough to slip his body through it, when the man at the table raised his head and looked full at him. Then he smiled, and at that smile Roy found himself unaccountably wanting to do something he had not done since he was a small boy, when he was chased by another small boy holding a grass snake, of which he had a horror – he wanted to turn and run. The man spoke.

'Ah, Major Benton,' the man at the table said, in a voice in which there was just the slightest trace of an accent. 'Come in, please. We've been expecting you.'

CHAPTER XIX

Ordeal by Torture

Roy stood stock still for a moment. Then slowly he pushed the door farther open and stepped into the room. A cry broke from him. Seated in a chair near a glowing brazier on the side of the room opposite the table was Karen. She jumped up as she saw him and in the expression on her face were mingled shock, dismay and warning.

'Get out, quick, for heaven's sake!' she cried.

Roy turned swiftly, realizing the trap he had walked neatly into, but it was too late. Two men, who must have been hidden on either side of the door as he came in, closed in behind him and stood with their backs to it. They had revolvers in their hands.

Karen ran quickly to him. 'Oh, Roy,' she whispered – and her use of his first name gave him a thrill of pleasure even in this unpleasant situation – 'what a mess I've made of it!'

'You have indeed,' said the man at the table, in his precise voice. 'Permit me to introduce myself – Fabian Delouris. I imagine you have heard of me, Major Benton.'

149

'I've heard of you all right,' said Roy grimly, 'and what I've heard – and seen – I don't like very much. But,' he turned to Karen, 'how on earth did you get here? I thought the Chief had left you at the—' He stopped short.

'. . . at the mine?' Delouris finished the sentence for him. 'No need for security, Major. We know all about it.'

'He did,' said Karen tearfully, 'but I felt I just had to come out and see what was happening and I ran into one of the guards. He brought me here.'

'And then Major Benton walked right into our little parlour to make everything perfect and complete,' said Delouris. 'Quite a comfortable parlour, too, all things considered,' he added, looking round with evident satisfaction.

'Are you all right? Have they hurt you?' Roy asked Karen anxiously.

'Really, Major,' said Delouris deprecatingly, before she could reply. 'To suggest that we should wish to harm so charming a lady – well . . .'

'Well, what?' asked Roy bluntly. 'Or perhaps you don't know that I saw Pat after you'd finished with him.'

Delouris' face darkened. 'That was different,' he said harshly. 'He was obstinate. I have no time for such men who are so pigheadedly loyal to their country. But Miss Silvers . . .' He smiled.

'You are a woman of beauty, charm and, I hope, good sense. You are perfectly free to go when you have given us a little information. It may be necessary to keep you here a little while after you have given us that information until we have completed our plans for leaving your delightful country, but after that . . .' He shrugged.

'What information?' asked Roy, though he knew the answer to the question before he asked it.

'But about her work, of course,' replied Delouris. 'Miss Silvers is a very clever scientist and she has made some very interesting discoveries, I believe, in a field – in which I, too, have long been interested. It is only natural, surely, that, as a fellow scientist, I should wish to understand the nature of the work she has been doing. It is a very simple request, and one which, I am sure, Miss Silvers can very easily satisfy.

'You won't get any information from me,' said Karen firmly.

Delouris made a deprecatory gesture. 'And I was so hoping,' he said almost resignedly, 'that you were going to be co-operative. I do not wish to alarm so charming a person, but may I point out – though I should hardly have thought it was necessary to do so – that you are hardly in a position to defy me? Do I make myself clear?'

'Perfectly,' said Karen, 'and my answer is still that you will not get any information from me.'

Delouris sighed, as an indulgent parent might sigh at the waywardness of a child, but there was no trace of annoyance in his voice when he spoke again.

'How tiresome,' he said. 'But I will try again. No one shall say that Fabian Delouris was ever lacking in gallantry where a lady was concerned.' The smile on his face as he said this made a shiver run down Roy's back, but he did not speak. 'Miss Silvers,' went on Delouris, 'you do not look a stupid woman. Indeed, the evidence of my eyes, if not my ears, is all to the contrary, and also, in view of your reputation in the scientific world, I do not see how you can be, though, of course, it is true that some people have their blind spots. You are, I may say, very charming and attractive.'

He moved nearer to her and his eyes ran up and down the length of her body. The look in them made Roy want to hit him. Delouris went on in silky tones: 'In pleasanter

151

circumstances I should have very much enjoyed working – and playing – with you. Very much.'

He stretched out his hand slowly towards her, but his fingers had barely touched her shoulder before Roy moved. He knocked Delouris' hand down, and before the guards at the door could lift a finger he had him by the throat and was forcing him back across the table. Delouris gasped and struggled, but he could not shake off that iron grip, and he was beginning to make horrible gurgling noises before the guards, recovering from their surprise, tore Roy away, and one of them clipped him behind the ear with the butt end of his revolver. He sank to the ground.

Karen went down on her knees beside him and took his head in her lap, but he was out cold. She looked up and saw Delouris, a look of intense hatred on his dark face, which was suffused with blood, massaging his throat. He coughed once or twice and then muttered a fierce command to the guards.

They picked Roy up and, brushing Karen out of the way, threw him in a chair and securely tied him with a rope. She went over to him and with her handkerchief staunched the blood which was trickling from the cut in his head. Delouris, still shaken, moved uncertainly round to the other side of the table and sat down facing them.

'Your friend Major Benton,' he said, and his voice was still rather hoarse, but made Karen think of ice tinkling in a glass, 'is either very brave or very foolish. But perhaps he is not merely your friend? Perhaps he is already your lover?' He ignored her negative gesture. 'It does not matter, though I have no doubt he would like to be. And you, perhaps you love him a little and won't admit it.' A curious race, you English. But never mind, we shall see how much you love him. I am asking you for the last time whether you are prepared to co-operate with me and give me the information I want.'

'Don't tell him a thing.' It was Roy, who had recovered consciousness in time to hear this last remark.

'Very well,' said Delouris. 'You can't say that I did not give you every opportunity to speak freely and without pressure. Now I am compelled to try other methods.'

'If you lay a finger on Miss Silvers again,' said Roy, and his voice had an intensity which made even Delouris hesitate a moment, 'I will personally kill you, and in a very unpleasant way.'

'So,' said Delouris suavely after a pause. 'Oddly enough – and this may surprise you – I really believe that you would do what you say – or try to do it, which, of course, is a very different thing, especially in view of your – er – present circumstances. But I have not the slightest intention of hurting a hair of the charming Miss Silvers' head. That would be too crude, but . . . there are other ways. It would be interesting, for instance, to discover just how tough – I believe that is the word your American allies used, is it not? – just how tough is the famous Major Benton.'

'You wouldn't dare! You couldn't!' cried Karen.

Delouris smiled. 'May I point out,' he said very politely, 'that neither you nor Major Benton is exactly in a position to tell me what I dare not, or cannot, do.'

He snapped a command to one of the guards. The man strode across the room to Roy's chair and hesitated a moment. Delouris shook his head.

'No,' he said. 'I have thought of a better idea. We are in mediaeval surroundings, are we not? I don't suppose our good friends, the monks, who once lived in this Priory would ever have thought of it, but somehow it seems more appropriate to the setting. Also, it seems to me that it would be more likely to be effective before the senses are dulled to pain. Fritz, in that jar over there on the shelf you will observe a number of wooden spills which I keep for lighting my pipe. You will doubtless have observed that I take a spill and light it at the brazier and then apply it to my pipe. You and Ludwig will each take a few spills, light them and apply them, not to my pipe, but to Major Benton's fingernails – a very sensitive part of the anatomy, I have always understood.'

Karen stared in horror as the guards did as they had been bid, and approached Roy's chair. They each took a hand and spread out his fingers along the arm of the chair. He was powerless to prevent them.

She could stand it no more. 'No, no!' she exclaimed. 'What is it you want to know?'

'Don't say a thing!' shouted Roy. 'If you do, everything you've worked for will be ruined. You might just as well have built it for them. Keep quiet, whatever else you do. He's only bluffing.'

'I really thought you would have credited me with more intelligence than that, Major,' said Delouris. 'Do as I told you,' he added curtly to the guards.

The spills they had lit before had gone out now, but they rekindled them and this time they did not stop. Roy strained and struggled in his chair until the sweat stood out on his forehead in great beads from the effort and the pain he was enduring, but no cry escaped him. Indeed, all was quiet in the room, except for the quiet sobbing of Karen, who had covered her face with her hands.

Delouris noticed this. 'Oh, you must not turn away, my dear,' he said. 'I am doing all this for your benefit.'

He got up from the table and came round to her and forced

her hands away from her face. The guards were lighting more spills. The agony went on.

'I can't bear it, Roy,' the girl sobbed. 'Please let me tell them. Please!'

'No,' he said between clenched teeth. 'Never! Do you hear, Delouris? Never!'

Delouris motioned to the guards. They stood away from Roy's chair and Karen collapsed moaning at his feet, her arms round his legs.

'Perhaps,' said Delouris, 'my original idea was not so good. Perhaps the sight of blood might have the desired effect.'

He signed to the guard again, who picked Karen up and handed her to his companion, while he stood by Roy's chair waiting for Delouris' signal.

'See whether you prefer this sort of treatment, Miss Silvers,' said Delouris, and motioned to the guard. He hit Roy in the mouth with his right fist, then with his left. He went on hitting. Delouris went on smiling.

'When this guard is tired,' he said, 'there is another and another and another. We can keep this up for quite a long time – longer, I think, than Major Benton can – and after that there are other methods, even more painful, as your friend Pat the steward discovered. He paid with his life. You wouldn't want your gallant major to die, would you, Miss Silvers?'

She had turned away, her face hidden in her hands, moaning and sobbing at the same time, half hysterically, and saying 'No, no, no,' over and over again.

'I am sure that the guard will be only too grateful if you will tell him that he can rest, won't you, Fritz?'

Fritz, his fists smeared with blood from Roy's battered face, turned and grinned at Delouris and went on hitting.

'You know, Miss Silvers, your friend will lose some of

his good looks if you let this go on much longer. Then you might not find him so attractive. He's not very pleasant to look at now, for instance.'

She slowly took her hands from her face and looked at the mass of bruised and bloody flesh that was Roy's face. Suddenly she screamed, and even to Delouris the scream seemed to go on for a very long time. It was almost as if it also reached down into the depths of unconsciousness into which Roy was fast sinking, for he stirred, lifted his head for a moment, opened his eyes and looked at Delouris, who shivered slightly at what he saw there. Then Roy's mouth seemed to twist into a grotesque caricature of a grin and his head sank on his chest.

The guard had stopped hitting as he saw Roy apparently come to, and he was standing looking at Delouris, who did not move for a moment or two. Then he got up, went to Karen and led her to a chair. She sank into it, her eyes closed, her breath coming in great sobs. Delouris went back to the table, opened a drawer, took out a flask and poured something from it into a small glass. He forced it between the girl's lips.

After a moment she stirred and sat up. She looked wildly round the room, her eyes resting on Roy, whose head was sunk low on his chest.

'He cannot tell you to say "no" now,' said Delouris softly.

'Very well,' she managed to get out at last, and there was no tone or feeling in her voice. 'Very well, I'll tell you all you want to know.'

Delouris began to smile . . .

'Don't say another word,' put in a voice which seemed to come from the sky and was like sudden music in Karen's ears.

'Put up your hands, Delouris,' the voice went on, 'and tell your guards to do the same. And don't any of you make any other move or you're dead men.'

CHAPTER XX

This Way Out

The voice did indeed come from the sky, or, rather, from the roof. Karen, staring wildly about her, saw the faces of the Chief and Charlie framed in what appeared to be a trap-door in the roof of the cellar. The startled Delouris and his guards looked up, too, and saw a couple of revolvers pointing at them. Slowly they raised their hands above their heads.

'I'll keep a close eye on them, Charlie,' said Leyland, 'while you drop in and pay our friends a call. You're better equipped than I am for these athletic pursuits.'

Charlie grinned. 'It will be a pleasure,' he said.

Charlie lowered himself through the trap-door until he was hanging by his hands, then dropped to the floor of the cellar. He gave Karen a reassuring pat on the shoulder, roughly swept the sullen-looking guards out of the way and crossed over to Roy, who had come round and tried to smile at him through his swollen and bleeding lips.

'Only just in time – as usual.'

The words were slurred, for it must have been agony to Roy even to move his mouth. Charlie bent over him to untie the ropes with which he was bound to the chair, and as he did so Karen saw that there were tears in Charlie's eyes and the look of tenderness on his face touched her to the quick. She had not realized until this moment how fond these two men were of each other – or how much they meant to her, too.

When Roy was free he tried to get up from the chair, but fell back. Charlie, with a delighted grin on his face, helped himself to the brandy flask which Delouris had left on the table, and moistened Roy's lips with it. He even managed to swallow a little of it, though the movement made him wince.

'There,' said Charlie, and his tone made Karen think of a mother talking to her child who had fallen and hurt himself,' 'that should make you feel a bit better. You'll need to, as well. We've got to get out of here, p.d.q. Keep an eye on him, Miss Silvers, will you, while I see if these gentlemen have got any firearms on them? Somehow, I don't think they're to be trusted.'

'Lock the door first, Charlie,' advised the Chief. 'We don't want any interruptions for a moment or two.'

Charlie went over and locked the door. Then he turned his attention to Delouris and the two guards, handling them roughly as he searched them for weapons. Each had a gun, and the two guards blackjacks. Fritz said something to Charlie which Karen did not catch as he relieved him of it, and he was rewarded with a beautiful right uppercut to the jaw which sent him sprawling in a corner.

'I don't usually hit people when they've got their hands up,' said Charlie, 'but if ever a blighter asked for it you have tonight. How do you like a bit of your own medicine, eh?'

'That's enough, Charlie,' warned the Chief, though the expression on his face suggested that he would like to join in. 'We haven't time for getting our own back now. Truss 'em up and let's get out of here.'

Quickly and efficiently, Charlie roped and bound the two guards. When it came to Delouris' turn he said coolly:

'Tying us up won't avail you for very long, my friend.'

'P'raps not,' said Charlie, 'but it'll keep you out of mischief long enough for us, and we haven't finished with you yet, mark my words.'

'You are an optimist, I see,' remarked Delouris, 'but then, the English always are, surprisingly enough, though what they have to be optimistic about I never could see.'

Delouris had no chance to continue, for Charlie slipped a knotted handkerchief between his teeth and tied it as tightly as he could behind his neck.

Delouris glared at him, but the look was wasted on Charlie, who was serving the two guards in similar fashion. Then he went over to Roy, who had managed to get to his feet.

'I don't think you'd better risk trying to get out through the door,' said the Chief. 'How do you feel, Roy? Do you think you can make it through the roof if we help you?'

Roy nodded. 'OK, then,' said Charlie. 'I'll put the table under the trap-door and we'll help you on it so the Chief can give you a hand up.'

He suited the action to the words. 'You'd better go first so that Miss Silvers and I can help you.'

They each took one of his arms and helped him on to the table. Totteringly Roy stood up and held out his arms to the Chief. Charlie climbed on to the table with him, and between them they hauled and pushed him up through the trap-door.

'You next, Miss Silvers.'

Charlie gave her a hand also, and before he, too, pulled himself up out of the cellar he paused and looked at the three men.

'*Auf wiedersehen*,' he said. 'We'll be back.'

Then he, too, went out and helped the Chief to drop back the trap-door in its place, shutting the three helpless prisoners from their sight.

But they won't be helpless for long, thought Leyland, as he stood up and brushed the dirt off his hands. 'Everyone all right?' he asked. 'How about you, Roy?'

Karen answered for him. 'He's pretty well all in,' she said, 'but I think he'll be able to make it with some help.'

'Good,' said the Chief. 'We've just *got* to make it. Those boys down there will soon be loose again when the guards are changed, and they'll be after us. We've got to be well away by then.'

He looked round to get his bearings. The broken walls of the Priory were all around them.

'How on earth did you manage to find us?' Karen asked him. 'I don't know what—'

Leyland cut her short. 'No time for explanations now,' he said. 'The sooner we get to the mine the better. I think the way we came will be the quickest, don't you, Charlie? At least we know the guards in that direction are all taken care of. I think you'd better lead the way, as you know the country best, and Miss Silvers and I will give Roy a hand.'

It was not easy going, with Roy in his weakened condition, but the moon had risen now and that helped them to avoid many of the pitfalls into which otherwise they might have stumbled, though Leyland cursed the help it might give to their pursuers, if any.

They had one shock when there came a startled cry from Charlie and they hurried up to find him bending over the body of a man near the ashes of a fire.

'I thought he was a guard and socked him,' said Charlie, 'but he looks like a tramp. He's all right, but when he comes round he'll wonder what on earth hit him. He'll think the keepers round these parts are very unfriendly!'

They hurried on, pausing only when they reached the head of the combe and turning to listen for any sounds of pursuit. But nothing broke the silence of the night, except the cry of an owl and the distant murmur of the sea.

'They've probably decided they hadn't a chance of overtaking us,' said Leyland, apparently satisfied that they were not being followed. He turned as he felt a touch at his sleeve. It was Roy and he was trying to say something.

'More likely they are digging like hell,' he said falteringly through his battered mouth. 'I found tunnel and trucks. Reckon they must be very near mine. Mrs Murdock – Modwen there, too. Safe, so far.'

'They are, are they? Well, thank heavens for that. But it looks as if I've no time to lose in preparing that reception committee. Let's get on.'

It was a tired party which eventually reached the sanctuary of the mine. Karen was near exhaustion, so she guessed how Roy must be feeling. He sank gratefully on the camp bed on which – it seemed so long ago now, though it was only a few days – he had awakened when he first found himself in the mine. Karen was looking after him then and she was doing so again. Despite her own tiredness she had summoned the steward, asked him to prepare some food and herself begun bathing his bruised and battered face and bandaging his hands.

Leyland had disappeared, saying he must do some urgent telephoning, and Charlie sat in his chair and lit his pipe with the satisfaction of a man who has been parted from it for a long time and feels he has deserved the reunion.

161

'There,' said Karen, as she put away the bowl of water and the towel. 'That feel any better?'

'A lot, thanks. Light me a cigarette, will you, Charlie, there's a good chap?'

Charlie did so, but Roy found difficulty in holding it between his lips and he had to abandon it.

'Bringing me back to life seems to be getting a habit with you,' said Roy to Karen. 'I think I'll have to consider appointing you my permanent personal nurse. What about it?'

'Don't thank me,' said Karen, her eyes suspiciously moist. 'I ought to be asking your forgiveness for getting you all into so much trouble.'

'I should darn well think you should,' put in Leyland, who had re-entered the room in time to hear this last remark. 'What the devil do you mean by disobeying my orders like that? I'm not joking. You're the scientific brains of this organization, but I'm responsible for the safety of all of you, including Roy and Charlie. I gave you strict instructions to stay in the mine and you disobeyed them. I could make serious trouble for you for that. You know that, don't you?'

She nodded humbly.

'If I'd gone through what Roy's just taken on your account, I'd put you across my knee and give you a damn' good hiding,' Leyland went on angrily. 'Why did you leave the mine, anyway, if I'm not being too inquisitive?'

'Because,' said Karen rather defiantly, 'I got rather tired of seeing you take all the risks, and my staying at home playing the role of the weak, defenceless female. I'm in this as much as any of you, more in fact. I resent being told to stay at home like a good little girl because there are some gipsies in the wood.'

'Oh, you do, do you?' said Leyland, still incensed. 'Gipsies in the wood, indeed! Hasn't it dawned on you yet what sort of people we're dealing with? What do you suppose would have happened to all this if Roy and then Charlie and I hadn't happened along when we did? Charlie and I were lucky, but Roy took a beating all right. Perhaps that pleased your vanity?'

'Here, steady on, Chief,' objected Roy, who had been surprised at Leyland's severe tones. 'That wasn't her fault – my beating up, I mean. That would probably have happened any way, whether she'd been there or not. I walked straight into the parlour.'

'All right,' said Leyland. 'I'm being unfair, I know, but I can't help thinking of what *might* have happened tonight. How did you fall into it?' he asked her.

'I'm ashamed to confess I walked right into one of the guards,' she said contritely, 'though he *was* lying down. I'm afraid it wasn't very bright of me.'

'I'll say it wasn't.'

'By the way, how did you and Charlie happen to be so conveniently on the roof?' asked Roy.

'Oh, we both wandered around after we'd separated, but without finding anything,' put in Charlie, who had been rather enjoying the spectacle of the Chief letting off steam. 'Then we happened to meet. We waited a bit, thinking we might see you, but you didn't show up, and we were just going back to the rendezvous when we heard a God-awful scream which seemed to come from just under our feet. It shook me, I can tell you, We scraped around a bit, guessing there must be a cellar or something just underneath us and imagining that they were torturing Mrs Murdock and Modwen. We never imagined, it could be you, let alone Miss Silvers. I found what looked like a trap-door and together we managed to lift it.

You can imagine the shock we had when we we looked down. Fortunately, Delouris and his pals were too busy with you to notice us and that enabled us to get the drop on them.'

'And a damned good job, too,' said Roy. 'I'd have come back for help, but I didn't know the way out! I must have fallen down an old disused shaft of some kind and I couldn't possibly have climbed out that way without a ladder. So I had to go on. It was just as well I did, despite what happened. They're mining all right, Chief, and I reckon they can't be far away from us this very minute. I should say that another day or so, unless you stop 'em, will see 'em through into the mine. Can't we round 'em up now? We know Delouris is back all right. Why wait any longer?'

Before Leyland could reply, the door opened and the steward came in with a big tray piled with food and drinks.

'Ah,' said Leyland, rubbing his hands with satisfaction. 'I'm starving, and I'll bet you are, too. Let's eat. Then we can discuss what we're going to do next.'

CHAPTER XXI

Council of War

Roy found chewing too painful a process, so he had to confine himself to a bowl of soup with bread dipped in it. He enviously watched the others as they finished their meal and consoled himself by making sarcastic remarks about their alleged gluttony.

'Well,' he said finally, as they sat back with sighs of repletion, 'now that you've finished guzzling, perhaps we can get down to business, because if we don't make a move soon we shall have our friend Delouris dropping in on us – and it won't be a social call.'

'I've made all necessary arrangements for a reception worthy of him if he does,' said Leyland. 'I don't think we shall be taken by surprise. Indeed, I'm hoping there'll be one or two surprises for him – unpleasant, needless to add.'

'That's all very well,' objected Charlie, 'but don't you think he'll have figured you're preparing something like that? He's no fool who's going to walk straight into any little trap we set for him. What's wrong with our making a direct attack on the Priory? Why wait for them to come to us?'

'Just what I was going to suggest,' put in Roy. 'Delouris is back now. We know that.'

'He may have gone away again after what's happened tonight,' the Chief reminded them, tapping his pipe-bowl thoughtfully.

'I don't think so,' said Roy. 'They're too nearly ready to send up their balloon. He's sure to want to stay for that. He's the one who's got to be here if and when they come into the mine. He's the boss, and he's anxious to see for himself what's been going on here.'

'Possibly you're right about that,' replied Leyland, 'but haven't you both forgotten that he's still holding Mrs Murdock and Modwen? If we made a direct attack there, goodness knows what they might not do to them before we could round them all up. So long as they're hostages, he'll make the best possible use of them, you can gamble on that. I know we mustn't let ourselves be side-tracked into forgetting that this mine and what it contains is his Objective Number One – and ours, too – but I don't want anyone else tortured and killed like poor Pat was. And there's also Tod Murdock to think about.'

'Well, what do you think is the best thing to do?' asked Karen.

'I think that Delouris, after what's happened tonight, will be expecting an attack on the Priory and will have made all preparations that he can make to meet it. Well, I don't think we should oblige him by doing what he expects us to do, but go in by the back door – that is from the Cliff Top Inn. I don't think he'll be expecting an attack from that quarter. He no doubt thinks he's well covered by his guards.'

'We can take care of the guards easily enough,' agreed Roy, 'but I don't think we can necessarily count on getting through to the Priory from the "Cliff Top". The tunnel, if there is a tunnel, may be blocked.'

'In that case,' asked Leyland, 'how did their men get in there in the first place? Haven't you forgotten that Tod Murdock said he was certain they didn't come in the public way? And how are the guards changed? Tod says he's never seen one of them outside the buildings, but they change all right.'

'True enough,' admitted Roy, 'but we still don't know how they manage it. And they may have rigged up doors or some sort of barriers in the tunnel.

'Well, we've just got to find out,' said Leyland. 'If we can take them by surprise at the Priory, Delouris won't have time to think of doing anything unpleasant to the womenfolk. Also we shall be able to free Tod of his unwelcome guests and close up one of Delouris' bolt-holes. What do you say?'

'H'm. Sounds a bit of all right to me,' said Charlie, 'but I think we ought to do it soon.' He looked at his watch, which showed 2 a.m. 'What's wrong with now? The guards at the inn won't be expecting visitors at this hour. We should be able to dispose of them pretty quickly and get on to the Priory right away. We could be there well before dawn. Always the best time for an attack.'

'I agree,' said Roy. 'I don't think we can afford to delay for one moment, otherwise they will be through into here, and that would be extremely unpleasant for all of us.'

'No,' said Leyland firmly. 'I think we've all had enough for one night. We all need a few hours' sleep and we shall feel all the better for it. I suggest we leave here about six-thirty. That means we should be at the inn before seven. That should still leave us time to surprise them before breakfast. Even Delouris has to eat sometime. I suppose,' he added, looking at Roy – 'I suppose it wouldn't be any use my suggesting that you're in no fit shape to come on this trip, that you should leave it to us and remain here and see that Miss Silvers really stays put this time?'

'You suppose rightly,' said Roy. 'Nothing would give me greater pleasure than to keep an eye on this young woman, at the proper time, but if you think you're going to drop me quietly at this stage of the proceedings, you're crazy. Aren't you forgetting I've some unfinished business to attend to with Monsignor Delouris and at least one of his friends?' He gently caressed his jaw.

Leyland smiled. 'I rather thought you'd say that, but I insist that if there's any scrapping you keep out of it. As for you, Miss Silvers, you may be the scientific genius of this outfit, but I'm in charge of this operation and I'm ordering you not to leave this mine under any circumstances. You jeopardized the whole thing tonight by acting on your own not very bright initiative, and we can't afford to risk that happening again. There's too much at stake and we've reached the crucial point of the whole business. So what about it?'

'I promise,' said Karen humbly, looking feelingly at Roy, who grinned painfully back at her.

'That's settled, then,' said Leyland. 'Any other points? OK, then. Let's get some sleep. We're going to need it before we've finished this job – and let's hope it soon will be finished.'

'Hear, hear,' said Roy and Charlie together.

'Will you be all right on that camp bed?' Karen asked Roy, and he nodded. 'I'll ask the steward to bring in another one for you, Charlie.'

'Have him call us all about six with some coffee,' suggested Leyland. 'We shan't feel much like eating, but a hot drink would be very welcome. Good night, everybody,' He went out to his own room.

The steward brought in another bed and some blankets, which Charlie busied himself putting into shape.

'Sure you'll be all right?' Karen asked Roy. 'I wish I were coming with you, but . . .' Her voice trailed away. Then she added: 'But you will be careful, won't you? It will be awful waiting here, wondering what on earth is happening.'

'We shall be all right,' he reassured her. 'Don't you worry. I shan't so long as I know you're safe and sound. That's the important thing to me.'

He looked around the room. 'Just think,' he said: 'when we get back here, in a few hours, it will be all over.'

'Hey, break it up, you two,' said Charlie, who had climbed into bed. 'I want some sleep even if you don't.'

'Sorry, Charlie,' said Roy. He turned to Karen. 'Good night, my dear. Your worries will soon be over, I hope. Then maybe you'll relax.' He took her hand and kissed it. Karen bent low over him and he felt her lips brush his hair.

'Good night, my sweet,' she said, and was gone.

Roy lay awake for what seemed a long time.

CHAPTER XXII

The Bolt-Hole

'However do you manage to look like that at this unearthly hour?'

Roy and the others were sipping steaming cups of coffee when Karen came in, looking fresh and lovelier than ever, he thought.

'Ah, that would be telling you the secret of my schoolgirl complexion,' she smiled. 'One of the advantages of being a chemist. Did you all sleep well?'

Leyland growled. Charlie grunted and Roy tenderly massaged his bruised jaw, now projecting in several different colours.

'We've all got that six-o'clock-in-the-morning feeling,' he said, 'and if you don't know, someone ought to tell you that it isn't the time of day when a man feels his best, especially after less than four hours' sleep.'

'Never mind, you'll all be able to sleep for hours tonight, and after that maybe I'll take up on that invitation to have a before-breakfast swim.'

'That's a promise,' said Roy, 'but the way I feel at the moment I shall need a week's sleep before I'm fit to go bathing.'

170

Leyland shot him a sharp glance. 'Sure you'll be all right?' he asked. 'It's not too late to change your mind if you'd rather not go.'

'Change my mind nothing,' retorted Roy. 'Do you suppose I could rest here wondering whether or not you were making a mess of things?'

Leyland grinned and put down his cap. 'Right,' he said. 'Then we'd better get started.'

Karen accompanied them to the mine entrance, where the Chief gave Joe, the guard, strict instructions to see that Miss Silvers did not leave on any account. 'And keep your eyes skinned,' he warned. 'You may have visitors before the day's out, though I hope not. If you do – well, you know how to accommodate them. All my orders been carried out?'

'Yes, sir,' grinned Joe. 'We'll make 'em welcome.'

'But not too welcome,' growled the Chief. 'Let's go.'

The early morning mists had not cleared away when they emerged from the mine and they shivered a little as the cold air struck them.

'Brrr!' said Charlie, turning up his jacket collar. 'Still, it will be useful cover in case there's anyone stirring; not that that's likely.'

They did not, in fact, see anyone as they covered the distance to the inn at a smart pace. As they neared it, Charlie went ahead to reconnoitre. He returned and reported that there was not a soul about.'

'Good,' said Roy. 'I suggest, Chief, that you take the front entrance and Charlie and I the back, as we did before, and try and attract Tod's attention, so that he can let us in. Then we'll let you in. What do you say?'

'Sounds all right to me,' said Leyland. 'Mind, no shooting unless it's absolutely necessary to prevent the guards getting away, though at all costs neither of them must get back to the Priory to warn Delouris and the others.'

They separated and Roy and Charlie cautiously approached the back-garden wall. They climbed over it, after a preliminary look round, then darted rapidly across the garden and gained the cover of the outhouse. They halted there for a moment, then Roy gave Charlie a leg up and the latter crawled gingerly up the sloping roof and tapped at the window.

Tod must have been up and about, for Roy saw the window open almost immediately. Charlie climbed in and Roy quickly followed, shutting the window after him.

'I'd just finished dressing and was going downstairs when I heard the tapping,' said Tod. 'What's happening? And what on earth have you been doing to your face and hands?' he asked Roy.

The latter quickly told him. 'What about the guards?' he asked.

'There's only one,' Tod replied, 'and has been for several nights. He's usually up and about before this, but I haven't heard him this morning. Maybe he's got a hangover. He made me give him a bottle of whisky last night, so he's probably sleeping it off.'

'Taking an awful chance with you, isn't he?' said Charlie. 'How does he know you wouldn't clear out and tip off the police?'

'Probably thinks I'm too scared after all the threats they've made to me.'

'Well, let's see what sort of a state he's in now,' said Roy.

They went outside on to the landing and stole on tiptoe to the door of the guard's bedroom. They did not need to listen at the key-hole. They could hear snores from where they stood.

'He's well on,' whispered Charlie.

'We'll let him enjoy his beauty sleep a bit longer,' said Roy, 'Tod, will you slip downstairs and let in Chief Inspector Leyland? He went round to cover the front entrance in case this bird made a break for it. I think we could handle him all right,' he added to Charlie as Tod went downstairs, 'but I suppose we'd better wait for the Chief.'

They did not have to wait long. When Leyland came upstairs a few moments later, followed by Tod, Roy explained the position to him. Leyland listened carefully and came to a rapid decision.

'Right, then, let's go in and wake him,' he said. 'You, Roy, and Tod cover the doorway in case he makes a bolt for it and you, Charlie, when we get inside the room, had better move over to the window before I wake him in case he has any ideas about getting out that way.' They all nodded and moved towards the door.

Leyland quietly opened it and walked in, Charlie following, and striding swiftly to the window. Roy, standing just inside the room, with Tod behind him, could see that the guard, a burly figure under the blankets, lay with his face buried in the pillow in a bed which was placed with its head to the wall on their left. The room smelt strongly of whisky and stale tobacco fumes, and there was an empty bottle lying on the floor. The guard was snoring heavily.

The Chief took a gun out of his pocket, bent over the bed and shook the guard by the shoulder. The man stirred in his sleep and shrugged the hand away from him, as a sleepy child will sometimes do. Leyland looked up at Roy and grinned. This time he was not so gentle. The guard groaned, turned over, opened his eyes and saw Leyland bending over him. Realizing that something was amiss, he sat up with a

173

muttered exclamation, stared wildly round the room for a moment and then, surprisingly swiftly for one so recently awakened from a heavy sleep, moved.

The suddenness of it and the direction in which the man moved so surprised Leyland and Charlie that neither tried for a moment to stop him. Instead of going for the door or the window, as they had expected he might, the guard dived straight out of bed across the room towards the fireplace, grabbed the mantelpiece and, to their amazement, pulled the whole structure back from the wall.

It was Roy who acted first. In a flying tackle that would have done credit to an England full back, he flung himself past Leyland and grabbed with his right hand at the guard's ankle just as he was disappearing into the opening. He felt a searing pain shoot from his burned fingers up his arm, but he clung desperately.

Leyland had moved too, now, if not so quickly, and as the guard turned round, kicking violently to free himself from Roy's grip, the Chief stepped across and with the butt end of his gun clipped the guard firmly behind the ear. He gave one gasp and fell backwards into the bedroom.

Leyland leaned over him. He was out all right. Then he turned his attention to the breathless Roy, who had had all the wind knocked out of him by his dive and the guard's struggles to free himself. He helped him to his feet. Roy wrung his burning hand.

'I thought I told you to keep out of it if there was any scrapping,' Leyland growled. 'Still, p'raps it's as well . . . He might easily have got clean away and I wouldn't even have got a shot at him. Sit down on the bed while we see to him. Got any rope, Tod?'

Tod was staring open-mouthed at the fireplace. 'So that's

how they got in and out!' he exclaimed. 'Well, I'm jiggered! I've kept this inn for twenty years and never knew that before. No wonder he insisted on having this bedroom.'

'Well, now that you know,' said Leyland, laughing at the expression on his face, 'what about fetching that rope – unless, of course, you'd like our friend here to get away?'

'Sorry, sir,' said Tod. 'I'll be right back.' He hurried out of the room.

'Give me a hand with him, Charlie,' said Leyland, and they slung him on to the bed.

Tod returned in a moment or two with a coil of rope. 'It's the missus's clothes-line,' he said, 'but I don't think she'd mind it being used to tie up one of these blighters. Are they all right, sir – the missus and Modwen, I mean?'

'They were the last time I spoke to them last night,' said Roy reassuringly, 'and I hope you'll be seeing them today.'

'Thank God for that,' said Tod fervently.

Leyland and Charlie had tied up the guard thoroughly and fastened him to the bed, where he showed no sign of returning consciousness.

'There,' said the Chief, tying the last knot. 'That ought to take care of him until we can make other arrangements. Now let's have a look at this fireplace.'

Tod held the mantelpiece back while the Chief Inspector investigated the opening with his torch. Its light showed them a flight of stone steps leading downwards.

'We'll see where they go to in a moment,' said Leyland, switching off the torch, 'though I've not the least doubt that this is the entrance to the tunnel which leads to the Priory, and that this is the way the guards came and went. First, though, we'd better see how this thing works.'

Charlie had been feeling all over the front of the fireplace.

175

'I rather fancy this knob does the trick,' he said. 'It moves, anyway.'

Leyland turned it backwards and forwards. 'I think you're right,' he commented. 'Let's try it.'

They pushed the mantelpiece back into position and it clicked home.

'We shall look well now if it doesn't,' said Roy, 'but we'll get through if we have to tear the damned thing down.'

Charlie turned the knob to the right and the fireplace swung slowly open again.

'There's another knob on the inside,' said Leyland, 'so that it can be opened by anyone coming up the steps. Very neat.'

He looked at his watch. 'Quarter to eight,' he remarked. 'Quarter of an hour to spare before the others get here. We might as well see how the land lies.'

Switching on his torch, he led the way down the steps, followed by Charlie and Roy, Tod remaining to keep an eye on the guard. The steps were well worn and slippery with damp. Roy counted twelve of them, then there was a turn and he counted ten more. At the foot of this last flight they found themselves in a flagged passage which sloped downwards for a little way before it levelled itself out and appeared to go straight on. There were one or two fallen stones about, but an investigation with the torch showed that the roof seemed fairly safe.

Leyland stopped. 'I don't think we need go any further now,' he said. 'It seems pretty plain sailing from here on.'

'Let's hope you're right,' remarked Roy. 'But I have an uneasy feeling that we may run into trouble.'

'Feeling all right?' asked Leyland, as they retraced their steps to the bedroom.

'Yes,' said Roy, 'but I think I'll ask Tod if he's any whisky left. A shot would do me good, I think. That dive shook me rather.'

'I don't wonder after what you went through only a few hours ago,' said Charlie.

The guard had slowly recovered consciousness, and glared furiously at them as they came through the opening into the bedroom. They grinned at him and went downstairs into the bar parlour, where they found Tod pouring out four cups of steaming coffee.

'Thanks, Tod, you've saved my life,' said Roy. 'Any chance of a drop of something in it?'

Tod grinned and unearthed a bottle of rum. 'I've been keeping this out of sight of them blighters,' he said. He poured a stiff shot into each cup. 'Just the thing for a job of this kind.'

They all drank gratefully. 'Seems a long time since I ate,' remarked Roy.

'And it may be a long time before you eat again,' rejoined Leyland, 'so make the most of this. How long, by the way, do you reckon it will take us to get through the tunnel to the Priory?'

'Difficult to say,' said Roy, sipping his coffee. 'I saw only some very old plans, remember. The distance as the crow flies is about a mile and a half, I should say, but we shall be going as the mole burrows, so to speak, and it will naturally depend on the state of the tunnel.'

'Still, they're hardly likely to have made the tunnel wind about,' said Charlie. 'And it can't be in such bad shape as all that, or they wouldn't have been able to use it.'

'True,' said Roy. 'I should say that, all being well, we ought to get there in three quarters of an hour, or thereabouts.'

'Then we should arrive just before nine,' Leyland estimated.

177

'I don't know what your friends' habits are, but I should say it's rather an inconvenient time of the day for callers, especially if your attention is concentrated on a job you want to get finished in a hurry, so there's a good prospect, it seems to me, of giving them an unpleasant surprise.'

'If they haven't finished it already,' said Roy gloomily. 'I'm sure they couldn't have had more than a few more yards to dig.

'Well, even if they have finished the job,' said Leyland, 'I told you there was a reception committee waiting for them, so I'm not worried on that score.'

'Let's hope you're right,' said Roy.

There was a rap on the inn door.

'That will be the reinforcements,' said Leyland, going to open it. Outside, Roy saw, there were about a dozen men, some in uniform, some in plain clothes. Among them was Sergeant Trelawney, who grinned at Roy and Charlie. The man in charge of them introduced himself.

'Inspector Dearson reporting, sir,' he said. 'My men are all here.'

'Good,' said the Chief, 'bring them in.'

'In here, sir?' Dearson was surprised. 'I thought we should be going across country.'

'Well, we shan't. We're going to do a little underground exploring.'

'Right, sir.' Dearson was the imperturbable police officer again. He marshalled his men into the bar parlour and the Chief introduced him to Roy and Charlie.

'Well, men,' said the Chief Inspector to the gathering at large. 'The position is this. We've found the entrance to an underground tunnel which we're almost certain will lead us to the old Priory and the men we want. You know all about them

178

now, and I'm sorry I couldn't let you into the secret before, but very important issues were at stake and I wasn't free to do so. They had a guard here, but we've taken care of him, so it's fair to assume, I think, that they won't be expecting us from this direction – which is the reason we chose this way instead of making a frontal attack on the Priory. That should give us the element of surprise. Nevertheless, I want you all to understand that this may be a tough assignment. These men are desperate and we shall probably have to use force, even guns, if necessary, though I don't want any shooting unless it can't be avoided. I'd much prefer to round up the whole lot alive, especially their leader. In fact, he *must* be taken alive. Still, it's as well to be prepared. You're all armed, I take it?'

'Yes, sir,' Dearson answered for his men.

'Good,' said Leyland. 'Then I think that's all, unless anyone has any questions.'

Nobody had. 'Oh, there's one thing more. I want two men to remain here with Mr Murdock just to cover this bolt-hole in case there's an attempt to break away through here. Will you see to that, Dearson?'

'Very good, sir.'

'Can't I come with you, sir?' asked Tod anxiously.

'Sorry, Tod. I know how worried you are about your wife and daughter, but I think it will be best if you stay here. I'll get word to you about them as soon as I possibly can. Better still, I'll get *them* to you. Ready, Dearson? Charlie and I will lead the way, with Mr Benton behind us, and you and your men can follow in two's if the tunnel is wide enough; if not, in single file. All clear?'

'Yes, sir,' said Dearson, who had detailed two men to stay behind.

'Right, then. Let's go.'

179

CHAPTER XXIII

Through the Tunnel

Considering that they had to go in pairs and sometimes, when there were obstructions, in single file, they made good progress through the tunnel. Roy kept a close eye on his watch, so that he could estimate when they should be nearing the Priory, and after they had been walking about half an hour he called a halt.

'I think the rest had better wait here,' he told Leyland, 'while we go on ahead and reconnoitre. We can't be very far from the Priory now and they probably have a guard at their end of the tunnel. If so, we shall have to dispose of him without giving the alarm, and that's a job for one or two men at the most, not a whole army. I suggest you arrange with Dearson to flash your torch three times as a signal for them to come on when we want them to.'

Leyland gave Dearson his orders, and he and Charlie and Roy went cautiously on ahead. Once or twice they halted and listened intently for a few seconds, but they did not hear any sounds coming from the direction of the Priory. There was only the everlasting drip, drip of moisture from the roof.

'I don't like it,' said Roy. 'I don't like it at all. If they're still digging we ought to be able to hear something of it by now. Sound carries a long way in these tunnels. But I can't hear a thing, can you?'

The other two had to confess that they couldn't. 'Anyhow,' said the Chief, 'there's no point in our hanging about here. If they have got through into the mine, the sooner we get there, too, the better. Let's push on.'

They did not dare use the torch now and consequently their progress was much slower. After what seemed to Roy an age, his left hand, with which he had been feeling his way along the wall of the tunnel, suddenly found itself in space when he stretched it out. He stopped the others.

'The tunnel's changed,' he whispered. 'We must be very near, if we're not already in the Priory.'

They all listened for a few seconds, but heard nothing. 'I'm going to risk switching on the torch,' said Roy. 'We've got to see where we are.'

The torch clicked on for a moment, then off, and in the brief flash of light they saw that they were in what appeared to be a cellar, empty so far as they could see, and that the tunnel appeared to continue on the far side of it. They gropingly crossed to the opening and Roy risked flashing his torch down it, but it penetrated the darkness only a little way and did not reveal anything.

'What now?' asked Charlie.

'Well, we might as well get the others as far as this, anyway,' said Leyland. 'Will you go back and signal them on?'

Charlie did so, while Leyland and Roy waited and discussed the next move in low tones. Soon they were all together again at the entrance to the next stage of the tunnel.

Leyland told them all the position, and decided that he,

Roy and Charlie would go on ahead again and that the others had better wait in the cellar.

Roy could see that Dearson didn't like this, but he obeyed his orders like the good police officer he was and they went on into the far tunnel.

'We must be under the Priory now,' said Roy in a low tone. They had gone only a few yards when the tunnel opened out again. They stopped and listened, but still no sounds came to them. Roy flashed on the torch and this time he kept it on. They were now in a wider tunnel and there were flags underneath their feet instead of earth. The walls and roof, too, were of stone. A few yards farther on there was a branch tunnel to the right which ended in a door.

'Now I know where we are,' whispered Roy. 'That's the door of the room where they held us prisoners. The other tunnel leads straight on past the door through which I spoke to the women and then on towards the mine.'

'Well, let's see if Delouris is still at home to us,' Leyland whispered back.

'Somehow,' said Roy, under his breath, 'I don't think we're going to find him in.'

The three of them moved silently to the door and listened. There was no sound from the other side of the thick oak. Gently Roy tried the door, as he had done when he had walked into the trap Delouris had set for him. The door opened – on to blackness. He switched on his torch. The room was empty, except for the table and chairs he had seen on his previous visit. There were no files, no papers – and no Delouris.

'I knew it,' said Roy disgustedly. 'He's cleared out. We're too late.'

*   *   *

Joe stood up among the bushes outside the entrance to the mine, stretched and yawned. Gosh, he thought, I'm sleepy. I'll be damned glad when Spud gets here to relieve me. He looked at his watch. Only five more minutes to go and then – beautiful shut-eye.

He yawned again. In fact, when he came to think of it, he'd done a hell of a lot of yawning since he'd taken on this job. It was a bind. Not like the old Commando days. There were plenty of dull patches then, but when they did get some action – oh, boy! Besides, even when they weren't on a raid there was always something to do, training, or drinking in the 'local', or the Naafi.

But this job . . . the only bit of excitement he'd had had been when he caught the major bending. Joe nearly laughed out loud. That had been funny, except for the dog-bite. Good job he hadn't hurt it when he kicked it off after it had bitten him. Some of these officer types were a darned sight more particular about their pets than they were about themselves. Still, the major was OK Some officers he'd met would have played merry hell about that crack on the head he'd given him; a real sockeroo, too, even though it was in the line of duty. But he'd taken it like a gent. Realized he was only doing his job and all that. Must have been a good guy to have been with during the war, if all he'd heard about him was true. But then, he wasn't a regular. Always the worst, they were, for discipline and what not. The major had been in Civvy Street before. He could understand how a bloke felt now and again.

Joe yawned again and looked about him. Going to be a nice day again, he thought. Wouldn't be a bad place for a holiday, this, if he could only get down to the 'Cliff Top' once in a while and have a skinful. That'd been Pat's idea, though, and look what happened to him! Joe shivered. He hadn't seen Pat like the major had, but he'd seen a few of Jerry's leavings during the war and he could imagine what he'd look like. Never could fight fair and shake hands afterwards if they were licked, like anybody else. Had to go torturing and killing people. Joe sighed at the villainies of the world.

The sun was getting warmer now. He wouldn't have minded a bit of a swim before getting into kip, but he supposed he'd better not. The old man had warned him to keep his eyes skinned today, special. All the same, a lounge on the sands would suit him down to the ground. He'd have to bring the old woman here sometime when it was all over, if only to prove to her it wasn't the haunt of vice she thought it was. He chuckled. Anybody'd think, to hear her talk when he went home, that he was out with the village girls every night. Suspicious old bird, she was. Haunt of vice, indeed. Why, the only bit of skirt he'd set eyes on for months had been Miss Silvers. Nice bit of goods she looked, too, but a bit cold like, Joe fancied. Might be the major's type, though. He wouldn't be surprised if there wasn't something cooking between those two.

He looked at his watch again. Any time, he thought. He heard a slight sound in the bushes behind him. That'd be Spud now, he shouldn't wonder, and half turned to meet his colleague. Then out of a clear sky a black cloud seemed to burst in front of his eyes and he pitched on to his face and lay still.

Leyland tried to conceal his disappointment. 'Well, he isn't here,' he said, as he gazed into the empty cellar, 'but we don't know that he isn't still somewhere in the mine. He may be paying a visit to Mrs Murdock and Modwen. Let's call the others up and get on as quickly as we can.'

Charlie went back and signalled the others again.

'If they're still here,' said Roy, before the rest of the party joined them, 'you'd think we'd have come across some sign of them. I can't believe they wouldn't have had a guard posted if they were still in the mine. Delouris isn't such a fool as all that.'

Leyland silently agreed with them, but said nothing. He prayed silently that the reception committee he'd arranged had done its stuff, if, indeed, Delouris and his men had broken into the mine.

'We'd better all keep together now,' said Leyland to Dearson, as the latter came up with his men. 'The birds seem to have flown from here, but they should have been taken care of in our little nest.' He tried to make his words sound as cheerful as possible, but Dearson didn't like the way he said 'should have been'.

The column moved on, trying each door as they came to it. All were unlocked and all the cellars on to which they opened were empty. They were hurrying on now, past the entrance to the branch passage from which Roy had entered the main tunnel, towards the digging face. Trucks and picks and other mining equipment littered the floor of the tunnel, but there was no sign of the workers.

Roy halted them all as they neared the spot where he had heard the men digging, and he, Leyland and Charlie went on ahead again. This time the tunnel did not end in an earth wall. It went on through newly excavated earth and stones. Leyland signalled the others to follow and they went forward again in a body, but more slowly now until the signs of excavation ceased and they saw clearly where

185

the gang had broken through into the mine. The contrast between the newly dug soil and the old blackened walls of the mine was only too evident to all of them.

This time it was Leyland who halted them, catching Roy and Charlie by the arm.

'I don't like the look of this at all,' he said quietly, peering anxiously down the tunnel. 'If anything had gone according to plan, there ought to have been one of my men hereabouts to meet us. What the devil's happened, I wonder?'

'How should I know?' retorted Roy testily. He had been seized with dreadful new fears for Karen's safety, but he would not have given expression to them for the world.

'The sooner we find out the better,' said Charlie. 'Let's get on.'

They came slowly out into a wider chamber, off which led doors and other passages, all deserted. They halted uncertainly and the leaders conferred while the others gathered uneasily round them as if proximity gave them a feeling of safety.

'I think we'd better split up,' decided Leyland, 'and investigate in pairs, leaving one or two men here.'

'I hardly think that will be necessary,' said a voice that three of them at least instantly recognized.

CHAPTER XXIV

Trapped Again

The voice came from behind them, and it had in it a ring of triumph which made Roy feel more depressed than he had felt at any time since this curious adventure had begun.

They all swung round, Leyland with his gun already in his hand, but the voice spoke again, more sharply this time, and the Chief did not raise the weapon.

'And don't anyone move,' it said, 'unless you want to die quite suddenly. Drop your guns, all of you. You are all covered.'

Dearson glanced inquiringly at his Chief, who hesitated a moment and then set the example by dropping his gun to the ground.

'That is much better, gentlemen,' said Delouris, who was standing at the entrance to the tunnel from which they had just emerged. 'Now we can talk – or rather I can – without any feeling of nervous tension, which I find is always associated with the possibility of having to shoot someone. Don't you agree with me, Major Benton?'

Roy did not reply, but glanced all round him, questing

187

for a way of escape. He could see none. At each of the doors and passages abutting on to the chamber in which they were, there now stood a guard heavily armed.

Delouris rapped out a command and one of the guards left his post and moved among the police, picking up the weapons they had dropped. When he had finished, but not before, Delouris strolled forward until he was within a few feet of them. There was a mocking smile on his face, and Roy, for one, had great difficulty in restraining himself from trying to knock it off. But he knew it would be of no use now; perhaps his time would come later.

'Good morning, gentlemen,' said Delouris, still in that mocking tone. 'So we meet again, though the circumstances are a little different from what you imagined they would be. I trust you are feeling better, Major, and that your face and fingers are not paining you too much?'

He moved forward until he was only a foot or so from Charlie. 'And you, sir? Are you feeling quite so – how do you say it? – cocky – as you were last night?' His eyes blazed suddenly. 'You swine!' he said, and his right hand shot out and struck Charlie in the face. 'It is a long time since anyone laid hands on me as you did last night. You will be sorry for it before I have finished with you.'

Charlie's face had flushed an angry red as the man struck him, but he had himself well under control. Now he grinned. Delouris turned away and spoke to Leyland. His voice had renewed its old mockingly triumphant tone.

'And how is the genius of Scotland Yard this morning? Forgive my little display of temper a moment ago. I do not usually pay so much attention to subordinates; I leave *them* to *my* subordinates. But you, my dear Chief Inspector, are an enemy worthy of steel. Or are you? I'm a little disappointed in you, Chief Inspector. Your plans, I am afraid, have gone sorely astray, have they not? Instead of your reception committee – I believe you called it – we are the reception committee and you are the received – and deceived. Really, my dear Chief Inspector, I expected better of you than this. Surely you did not think that I should fall into your trap so easily, that I should allow myself to be thwarted at the last moment?'

His voice grew harsh. 'No,' he said. 'I have waited too long for this moment and no one is going to stop me now. No, my dear Chief Inspector, no one is going to stop me now. All your colleagues are safely under lock and key and very soon you will join them until we have finished our work here and are safely away. After that – well, I have made suitable arrangement for disposing of you – except for Miss Silvers, who will be coming with us.'

'What the hell do you mean?' growled Roy.

'Ah,' said Delouris, smiling. 'I see the gallant major is still most concerned about the lady. I am very sorry to disappoint you. It appears, Chief Inspector, that you have been too clever for me in one respect. I expected to find some plans here, the complete plans of the atomic rocket, but either they have been very skilfully hidden, or else they do not exist. I am inclined to favour the latter theory; it is what I should have been inclined to do myself. Moreover, I am satisfied, after questioning one or two members of the scientific staff here, that only Miss Silvers knows the whole secret of this new device. Consequently I am forced to ask her to accompany us.'

'Accompany you where?' asked Leyland.

'To a certain island off the South American coast, where I have established my headquarters,' said Delouris blandly.

'You see, gentlemen, I have arranged for a submarine to pick us up in No Man's Cove at midnight. I can tell you this now since there is no possibility of your being able to prevent it. Between now and that hour my men will be dismantling the rocket apparatus and moving it down to the beach so that it can be put on board as soon as the submarine reports its arrival. Incidentally, it's a U-boat.'

Delouris was obviously pleased by the surprised and mortified looks on the faces of those around him – of all, in fact, except Chief Inspector Leyland. 'You did not think there were any U-boats not accounted for, gentlemen?' he went on. 'You are still, I see, underestimating me as you have always done, and as you will doubtless go on doing until you find you have done it once too often. Well, I took very good care, before the end came in Germany, to contact some influential naval friends over there, who saw to it that several of them, including long-range types fitted with the latest Schnorkel device, did not fall into their enemies' hands. It will be one of those which will be taking us to where we can complete our work. And when it is completed . . .' There was an almost fanatical smile on Delouris' features.

Roy glanced at Leyland as Delouris continued to enjoy his triumph, but he could read nothing from his expression. He dropped his eyes and stared at the ground. Was this the end, he wondered, or had the Chief still got something up his sleeve? He suddenly felt very tired. To go through all that had happened in the last few days – or was it weeks? – for this. And only this morning he had told Karen not to worry, that it would soon be all over and they would be able to relax. Well, it looked as if it would soon be all over, but there would be no relaxing. He thought of Mrs Murdock and Modwen – what had happened to them? he wondered – and of poor old Tod waiting anxiously at the inn for news of his loved ones, which couldn't come to him now. He looked up again as he heard Leyland's voice.

'And what, may I ask,' he said, 'are the "suitable arrangements" you have made for disposing of us?'

'You may ask,' replied Delouris, 'and I will tell you. I am nothing if not informative this morning, am I not? Obviously, it would be most inconvenient to have you leaving here immediately after we had embarked in the U-boat and giving the alarm to your Admiralty, so that I am afraid it will be necessary to . . . er . . . detain you for a considerable period, if not indefinitely.'

'Indefinitely?' asked Leyland. 'What do you mean by that?'

'I see some shocked, not to say frightened, faces among you,' went on Delouris. 'I mean indefinitely. It is regrettable, I agree, especially for Major Benton, who will be losing so much else besides, but I assure you it will be absolutely necessary. Before we finally leave, charges of dynamite will be exploded at the entrances to this mine, thus effectively sealing them and preventing your exit. They will be substantial charges, to prevent any possibility of loop-holes, and, though I am well aware of the skill of the British miner, it is, of course, possible that before a way could be cleared into the mine it would take too long to benefit you gentlemen in any way.'

'But that would be mass murder!' The outburst came from Dearson.

'I see your colleague is not so familiar with our methods as you are, my dear Chief Inspector,' commented Delouris. 'No doubt you, with your greater experience, will be able to convince him that I mean what I say. I have been a dealer in mass murder and the means to it for more years than I care

191

to remember. What I am proposing to do is very insignificant and even humane compared with the sufferings that will be caused by the atomic rocket you have been working on. But I have talked enough and we are wasting time. Gentlemen, be good enough to follow the guards. I warn you that if anyone makes a move to attack them, or to escape, he will be shot down like a dog. Move on, please.'

'Just a minute,' said Roy. 'There's one question I should like to ask you before we go to wherever it is you want us to go. I'd like to know what has happened to Miss Silvers.'

'My dear Major,' said Delouris, smiling. 'I assure you that the lady is in very good hands. At this moment she is with my chief of staff explaining, I hope, the correct way to dismantle the rocket. I am sure that this time she will see that there is no point in withholding information. Does that satisfy you, Major?'

'Yes, for the time being,' replied Roy. His voice became grimmer. 'There's just one thing I'd like to remind you of.'

'And what is that, my dear Major?'

'Just this. I told you when you were having your fun and games with me last night that if you laid a finger on Miss Silvers again I would personally kill you, and that I should do it in a very unpleasant way. Just remember that, will you?'

Delouris gave a laugh, but it was not a very convincing one. 'My dear fellow,' he protested, 'you misjudge me. Besides, don't you think you are now in even less of a position to utter threats than you were last night?'

'Perhaps,' said Roy quietly, 'but I'll do it all the same – if I have to follow you all round the world, assuming that you get away from here, that is.'

192

'That's enough,' said Delouris sharply. 'Move on, please.'

Dejectedly they filed after the guards further into the mine. Dearson manoeuvred himself near to Leyland.

'Surely, sir,' he whispered, 'we aren't going to let them get away with this without a fight? There's enough of us to give them a good run for their money, even if one or two of us got hurt in the process.'

Leyland laid a restraining hand on his sleeve. 'Not now,' he warned. 'They've got us where they want us at the moment. There may be a better chance if we wait—' He broke off suddenly, as one of Dearson's men made a dash for the guard immediately in front of him. 'My God – the fool! Stop him, Dearson!'

But it was too late. A shot rang out, reverberating deafeningly in the confined space of the mine, and the man fell forward on his face. Dearson got to him first and bent over him. He turned the body over, but there was nothing to be done. The bullet had gone into his back and come out through his heart. Roy thought he would never forget the expression on Dearson's face as he looked up. It was a terrifying blend of anguish for the loss of one of his men and hatred for those responsible.

Delouris' voice cut sharply into the shocked silence which had followed the incident.

'I would suggest,' he said, 'that no one else should attempt such a stupid move. Perhaps that will convince the rest of you that we mean what we say, or do we have to kill more of you? I always knew the English were stupid, but I did not know how stupid until now. Pick him up if you wish to and get on.'

The funeral procession – for so it seemed now to Roy, as

193

two of Dearson's men picked up their colleague and carried him with them – moved on until the guards halted at one of the doors.

'The big laboratory,' Leyland said to Roy. 'There's no way out of there, damn it.'

They filed in past the guards to join the other occupants of the mine – among them, he noted with relief, Mrs Murdock and Modwen – and the door closed after them and was locked. He felt sorry for Leyland as the members of the staff of the mine and his police colleagues of the 'reception committee' crowded round him, asking for explanations of what had happened.

He went across the room with Charlie to the two women, who were almost in tears. They had hoped and hoped, after speaking to Roy the previous night, that he would come back and rescue them, but nobody came except the German guards to move them into the mine. Would they be able to get out? How was Tod? Was he all right? They pestered him with questions until he felt he could have broken away and run, but Charlie took on the burden of answering them and trying to calm them.

Thankfully Roy turned to the others in time to hear Leyland asking a big, burly inspector, whose name, he gathered, was Holmes, how the deuce the gang had managed to surprise them.

'Well, sir,' said Holmes, looking very self-conscious, 'we followed your instructions and posted our men in the gallery where we estimated they would ultimately break through. We could hear them all right and we were on tenterhooks waiting for 'em, but they never came.'

'What do you mean, "they never came"?' demanded Leyland impatiently. 'They're damned well here, aren't they?'

'Yes, sir, of course, sir,' stammered the embarrassed inspector. 'What I meant to say was that they didn't come that way – at least not till later. They came in through the front door, so to speak, and took us by surprise.'

'Do you mean to tell me they entered the mine by the main gallery from the seaward side?' the Chief Inspector demanded incredulously. 'But what about my guards, Joe and Spud? Didn't they give the alarm?'

'We didn't have a chance, Chief,' said Joe, rather shame-facedly. His head was bandaged, as was that of Spud.

'Oh, and why not?' demanded the Chief grimly.

'Well, I was just standing there keeping a look-out, an' expecting Spud to relieve me any minute, and thinking I ought to bring my old woman—'

'Never mind about your old woman,' said the Chief Inspector curtly. 'No wonder you were surprised if that is how you were day-dreaming.'

'I wasn't, sir, honest,' said Joe. 'We couldn't even whisper a warning, let alone shout or draw a gun. They never made a sound, and we was both knocked out and didn't know a thing about it till it happened.'

'That's right, sir,' put in Spud. 'I didn't think the man had been born who could have nipped up on me like that.'

'Nice work,' commented Roy drily. 'I never thought they'd do that – and in broad daylight, too. He was right, Chief, when he said we were always underestimating them.'

'Well, I haven't underestimated them,' said Leyland, rather tartly. He turned again to Holmes. 'What happened then?'

'They got the drop on us from behind, of course, our attention all being concentrated on the mine and not expecting anything from the other direction. While we were all lined up against a wall, thinking we were going to be shot, one of them tapped a message to his pals on the other side of the wall and they came crashing through and joined forces. Meanwhile they'd rounded up all the staff of the mine and put us all in here – all except Miss Silvers, that is – and here we've been ever since, hoping you'd come along and rescue us. But what happened to you, sir?' he asked, rather diffidently. He obviously did not relish taking all the blame.

'Never mind what happened to us,' said Leyland shortly. 'We're all here, aren't we? Isn't that enough?'

'Yes, sir.' Holmes subsided in a slightly disappointed tone.

'Well, thank goodness no one else has been killed or tortured except poor Thomas there,' said Leyland, glancing towards the screen in the corner behind which the body of the dead police officer, covered with an overcoat, had been placed.

He turned to the two women. 'I'm very sorry things have turned out like this,' he said, 'when you must have hoped that you would soon be rescued and able to go back home, but at least you're among friends and safe, for the time being, at any rate, and you have the consolation of knowing that Tod's all right. I'm glad now I insisted on his staying at the inn.'

'Well,' said Roy, 'the question seems once again to be "What now?" I must say, Chief, you don't seem unduly worried.'

'I'm worried all right,' he replied quietly, 'but there's no point in letting it get me down, or in showing it before the others. We've got to keep up our morale.' He glanced at his watch. 'Ten o'clock. That means they have about fourteen hours in which to dismantle everything connected with the rocket and get it down to the beach. It should be ample with the manpower they've got and Karen's technical assistance. She must be in a state, poor girl, being forced to help them. At least, I presume Delouris will have told her what's happened to us and to you, but I hope he's spared her the final gory details of the fate he has in store for us.'

'Knowing him, I think he'll have told her all right,' said Roy glumly. 'I wish to God I could get to her somehow.'

'I don't think there's much hope of that,' remarked Charlie.

'Well, as you said, "What now?",' repeated Leyland. He glanced down the long chamber. 'There's no point in our attempting to do any tunnelling from here – it won't get us anywhere except into the bowels of Cornwall. That means we've got to concentrate on the door. The best time will be when the guards bring us some food. I presume that even Delouris won't let us starve. He ought not to with all the stuff we have in this place, unless he wants it for his pals in the U-boat. They'll probably be glad of some fresh rations if they've come all the way from South America, under water most of the time, probably. I suppose they *have* left guards on the door?' He went to it and tried the knob.

'Vat you vant?' asked a gruff voice from the other side.

'I thought so,' said Leyland. 'What about some food?' he demanded in a louder voice, 'or are we going to be starved to death?'

They heard the guard grunt and then speak to someone else in German.

'Two of 'em, anyway,' commented Roy. 'What's your plan?'

'It depends what happens,' replied Leyland, 'and whether they both come in with the food. If they do we've got 'em, but I'm afraid they won't. You, Charlie, and Dearson, had better get each side of the door flat against the walls. I'll give the word if I think there's a reasonable chance of a break.'

'I'd give anything to get some word to Karen,' said Roy as they waited for the guards to return. 'We just can't let them yank her off to South America without making some effort to stop them. I'll never forgive myself if I don't.'

'I know how you must feel,' said Leyland. 'For that matter, I feel even more badly about it than you do, though in a different way, of course, since I'm officially responsible for the security of this mine and everyone and everything in it; but it's no good trying anything rash which may only make things worse.' He broke off as there was a sound outside the door. 'Quick,' he said to Dearson and Charlie. 'Here they come.'

The two men flattened themselves against the wall, one on each side of the door as it opened. A guard came in carrying a tray on which were plates of sandwiches and a steaming jug. Leyland groaned inwardly as he saw another guard outside the door with a Sten gun levelled and pointing into the room ready for the slightest move on the part of the occupants.

'No good,' he whispered to the others, and moved into the centre of the room as the guard went out and the door was closed and locked behind him. 'It would have been suicidal to have tried anything then. He could have mowed down half a dozen of us as soon as we made a move.'

They had not really wanted the food, and now that they had got it they made a poor show at eating, until Leyland advised them all to have something. 'We don't know when, if at all, we shall get any more,' he said, 'though we'd better save some of the sandwiches. Will you take charge of them, Holmes?'

The burly inspector nodded and wrapped up a bundle of sandwiches in a piece of paper. Disappointedly, Roy drank some coffee and began to munch a sandwich. Suddenly he choked and spluttered.

'What the devil . . .!' he exclaimed as soon as he got back his breath. 'What on earth are they feeding us in these things?'

He put his finger and thumb inside his mouth and pulled out a part-chewed and food-smeared piece of paper. With a gesture of distaste and a muttered 'Excuse me' he flung it from him on to the floor.

'Just a minute,' said Leyland, bending down and retrieving it. 'I thought I saw some writing on it.' He wiped the paper on his handkerchief and carefully opened it out. The others gathered round him.

'I was right,' he said finally. 'It's some sort of a message – from Miss Silvers I think. If only you'd noticed it before you started chewing,' he said to Roy. 'I expect you've swallowed the missing bits now. Still, we may be able to get the drift of it. They must have given her the job of preparing the food, and she risked slipping this into one of the sandwiches, hoping it would be noticed.'

Gingerly he spread out what remained of the note on the table. They were eventually able to decipher:

Do   or y   hi f.   ill b   w up   hol   hing r the
han   et th m ge   way w t t. ive y lov o   y.
ell   im I   sor y it ad t en   ik   his. By   ren.

They stared at it for a moment. Then a groan came from Roy. 'Oh, my God!' he said. 'No, no, she mustn't do it!'

'So you've made it out?' Leyland queried softly. Roy did not answer. The Chief looked up from the note and at the anxiously inquiring faces of the others, who were not able to see for themselves what it said. 'I think you all ought to know what is in this note,' he said quietly. 'It's from a very brave woman.' He read it out:

'Don't worry, Chief. Will blow up whole thing rather than let them get away with it. Give my love to Roy. Tell him I'm sorry it had to end like this. Bye, Karen.'

Nobody said anything. Roy sat down in a chair, his head between his hands. All he could think of at this moment, the most poignant and hopeless in their short but exciting acquaintance, was that they loved each other – and there was nothing they could do about it. But not Karen, he reflected. She was going to do a lot – she was going to destroy the work of years rather than let it fall into other hands. And in doing so she would destroy herself, perhaps all of them. Not that it mattered about them. They were doomed, anyway, if Delouris carried out his threat, as he undoubtedly would if he could, but there was no need for her to die. What did the damned rocket matter, anyway? It had always stood between them, and now it was going to be the end of her. He began to curse quietly under his breath, to utter words that he had never thought to hear from his own lips.

'Stop that,' said Leyland, putting a firm hand on his shoulder. 'That won't help her or us.'

'No, but can you think of anything that will?' Roy demanded passionately. 'You got us into this. Well, get us out, damn you.'

'Go easy, old chap,' said Charlie. 'This isn't the Chief's fault, or anyone else's. I know how you feel after all you've been through, but that sort of thing won't do any good.'

'I'm sorry, Chief,' Roy said contritely. 'You know I didn't mean it.'

'I know,' said Leyland. 'Forget it.'

'If only we could get a message to her telling her not to

do it!' said Roy desperately. 'What does it matter? Her life's more important than any rocket.'

'That doesn't sound like you,' Leyland chided him gently. 'You know that it matters a great deal, and especially to her. She cares a great deal more about humanity than she does about herself. You ought to know that.'

'I do know it,' said Roy, 'but at the moment I can think of only one member of the human race, and that at the time when she needs me most I can't lift a finger to help her.'

'Don't be so pessimistic,' said Leyland. 'We're not finished yet.'

Roy looked at him hopefully, but Leyland only smiled encouragingly and turned away.

CHAPTER XXV

No Exit?

The time dragged by. To Roy it seemed as if it had never passed so slowly. His mind went back over other tough spots he had been in, but though his wartime experiences had included, amid lots of excitement, a fair amount of tedious waiting it had never seemed to pass so drearily and slowly as the time in the laboratory. But then, he reflected, the circumstances had never been quite the same as these. There was always hope then, no matter how long a parachute drop or a message from the Resistance movement was delayed, whereas now there seemed none at all. The explosions he had heard in those days had been of his own making and he had exulted in them, knowing they would hinder the Germans and, possibly, result in the deaths of some of them. The explosion his nerves were on edge for now would be made by the woman he loved and it would almost certainly mean her death, and, possibly, their own deaths as well. He found the situation well-nigh unbearable.

The other prisoners lounged about in chairs, or on the floor, with their backs propped against the walls, or against cubicles in which experiments had been conducted. They talked and smoked, and two of the scientists were even playing chess with a pocket set. Roy envied them their apparent detachment. From time to time Leyland moved among them, talking to them, joking, trying to keep up their spirits, but it seemed a hopeless business to Roy. He had never felt like this in the war years. An atmosphere of frustration pervaded the room.

Occasionally they heard sounds from outside, of shouted commands, of heavy objects being moved, and once what sounded like a scream. It made them all jump and Roy started up, every nerve and muscle tensed.

'Did you hear that?' he demanded of Leyland. 'If that was Karen, if those devils . . .' He did not finish the sentence; he could not put into words what his mind visualized.

'We can't be sure it was a scream,' Leyland tried to reassure him. 'It might have been almost anything.'

'But it *might* have been, you can't deny that,' said Roy, distraught with apprehension. 'Supposing she's tried to do what she said she'd do and failed. Supposing . . .' But he could not go on.

'Stop it, Roy, for heaven's sake,' pleaded Charlie, 'or you'll have us all going nuts.'

Roy subsided again, but though he kept quiet he could not calm his fears. The guards came again about six o'clock with more food and drink, but once again the one with the gun stood outside the door covering them. Leyland tried to get some information as to what was happening, or had happened, out of the guard who brought the tray in, but the man merely grunted and went out again. Once again, on the Chief's orders, Inspector Holmes saved some of the sandwiches. The others welcomed the interlude and ate eagerly, but Roy had nothing except a drink of coffee. This time everyone was asked to make sure that there were no messages concealed in the food, but a careful search failed to reveal anything.

That was the final blow to Roy. He realized that, quite unreasonably, he had been banking on some further message from Karen. He hadn't stopped to think about it – he had just hoped – and now that hope was dead. Did it mean that she, too, was dead? There had not been any explosion to suggest that she had made her attempt to destroy the rocket, but perhaps she had tried and failed and the gang had killed her. He tried to put the thought from him, but it persisted.

This time the guards did not come and remove the tray and for a long time after the prisoners had finished eating there was silence both inside and outside the laboratory. Once someone tried to strike up a song, but nobody took it up and the tune perished miserably. Roy fell into a fitful doze and no one disturbed him. He woke up with a start to hear Leyland saying, 'Nearly eleven o'clock,' and realized that he had been asleep on and off for some hours.

'Has anything happened?' he asked Charlie anxiously.

'Not a thing,' said Charlie.

'They must have pretty well finished the dismantling by now,' said the Chief. 'What next? I wonder. Making sure we don't get away, I suppose.'

There was the sound of marching feet in the passage outside, and the door was suddenly flung open and Delouris came in.

'Couldn't resist a last triumphant crow, I suppose,' muttered Leyland to Roy, who got wearily to his feet.

Delouris was smiling confidently and was evidently very

pleased with himself. 'Well, gentlemen,' he said. 'We shall shortly leave your highly unpleasant country. Everything is ready down on the beach. We await only the U-boat to take us away, and' – he glanced at his watch – 'that should be here very soon. Nothing remains, I think, but to ensure that you gentlemen do not attempt to spoil my plans at the last moment. You see, *I* do not make the mistake of underestimating my enemies, as you do. I know that the English are never more dangerous, or more likely to do some mad thing – mad, that is, except to themselves and to those who do not know you as well as I do – as when the position appears most hopeless. So I take all precautions. In a few moments you will hear a series of explosions. They will be caused by my men sealing all the exits to this mine – except, of course, the one by which we shall leave. That will come afterwards. I am sorry that it has to end this way—'

'Sorry be damned, you blasted hypocrite!' burst out Roy. 'Get it over with and spare us the regrets. I assure you I shouldn't have any if I could get my hands on you.'

Delouris sighed. 'I suppose I should make special allowances for you, Major Benton, under the circumstances. It must be very distressing to you to lose so clever and charming a companion as Miss Silvers.'

'What do you mean by "lose"?' asked Roy. 'Must I remind you of what I said—'

'There is no need for excitement,' cut in Delouris. 'Miss Silvers, like you, is imbued with patriotic motives. A little while ago, under the pretence of helping us to dismantle a particularly important piece of mechanism, she attempted to destroy it. Happily for us – and for you – she did not succeed, but unfortunately I was compelled to place her under some restraint.'

'Then it *was* she we heard screaming?' demanded Roy.

'It was,' said Delouris. 'Very distressing, was it not? However, she is safely tied up now and I am hoping that the sea voyage will improve her temper and make her a little more reasonably disposed towards us. It often has that effect, I am told. If not, then I fear she will have to be persuaded when we get to our destination. Still, that is my problem. Why should I worry you with it? You have enough of your own.'

'I don't know where it is you're going,' said Roy very quietly and intently, 'but if it's the South Pole, the North Pole or the equator, I'll follow you when I get out of here and—'

The other's lips curled contemptuously. 'Don't be a fool, my dear Major. Really, I gave you credit for more intelligence. If you ever get out of here it will be when you are carried out—'

He broke off as a dull, rumbling sound came to their ears. The earth under their feet trembled and the lights flickered.

'That,' said Delouris, 'should be sufficient to show you how futile your threats are. That was the tunnel from the inn to the Priory being sealed. You thought I should overlook that one, didn't you, my dear Chief Inspector?' he added malevolently. 'Not that it would have made any difference, because we shall seal up the link we so arduously made as well. You'll no doubt hear it in a few moments. But I must be going. Good night, gentlemen.'

As Delouris turned smartly on his heel Roy moved towards him, but a guard stuck his gun roughly into Roy's chest and pushed him back. Delouris went out without a backward glance and the guards followed him. The door banged to and the key turned in the lock. The sound of their footsteps died away down the passage and all was quiet in the mine for a few moments until another explosion, this time much nearer, shook the room. The lights went out for a moment, but came on again.

'Two,' counted Charlie. 'Only one more now and we've had it.'

Suddenly one of the prisoners flung himself, screaming, against the door, battering it with his fists. It took three of them to pull him away and calm him down, and they had just quieted him when there came the third explosion from the seaward exit.

'Well, that's that,' said Leyland. 'They've sealed all the ways into and out of this place now. There's one consolation,' he added, glancing up at the lights: 'we can still see.'

'Well, let's at least make sure,' said Roy. 'You can't always be certain with explosives, even if you're an expert. You plan 'em, but they don't always work out that way. It might still be possible to wriggle our way out somewhere and make an attempt to stop them before the U-boat arrives. Anyway, it's better than sticking in here dying like rats in a trap.'

'We've got to get out of this trap first,' Dearson reminded him.

'Damn it, we haven't been able to try until now,' retorted Roy. 'We ought to have been looking around for tools instead of mooning about feeling sorry for ourselves, like I was. Well, let's do it now.'

Leyland smiled at Charlie as they noticed the change in Roy now that there was a chance of action, and the effect his words had had on the other prisoners.

'This door looks pretty stout,' said Dearson. He butted it heavily with his shoulder, but it did not give, Charlie added his weight to Dearson's. The door shook a little, but remained stolidly closed.

'Don't you keep any tools in this lab?' asked Roy impatiently. 'Everyone have a scout round, please.'

It was Charlie who found a small but stout metal lever in a corner under a bench.

'It must have been left here when we undid that last lot of packing cases,' said one of the scientists.

'Just the thing,' said Roy, thinking it was probably the unloading of those very cases, and the footprints of the men who did it, which had led him into all this.

'Here, let me do it,' said Dearson, relieving him of the jemmy. 'I used to be rather good at this sort of thing before I joined the force.'

He laughed. It was the first sound of real laughter they had heard since they entered the mine and it cheered everyone up. Dearson got to work on the door, heaving and straining. There was a sound of wood splintering, then a crack. Dearson stepped back and wiped his forehead.

'A couple of good heaves should do the trick now,' he said. 'Come on, Holmes and you, Trelawney. You're about the heaviest members of the party. See if you can shift it.'

The two burly officers charged the door together. It cracked and gave a little at the first attempt. At the second it gave way and Holmes and Trelawney went with it and fell on their faces outside. They got up coughing. The air in the passage was full of dust which had not yet settled after the explosions, and even though the lights were still on visibility was none too good.

Leyland, Roy and Dearson joined them out in the passage. 'Good work,' said the Chief, 'though I don't know whether it will get us anywhere. Anyway, we can explore a bit. I think I, for one, had better go, as I know the mine better than anyone else. Roy, you've seen a bit of it, so you'd better come, too. I suppose we haven't got a mining expert with us, by any chance, have we?'

'By Jove, yes,' exclaimed Dearson. 'Tregarrion,' he called to a short, thick-set little man with huge shoulders. 'Didn't you used to be a miner before you joined the police.'

'Yes, sir,' said Tregarrion. 'As a matter of fact, I once worked in here years ago.'

'Then you're just the man we want,' said Leyland. 'Why didn't you speak up before?'

'Well, sir, there was you, sir, a Chief Inspector, Inspector Dearson, Inspector Holmes, Sergeant Trelawney and you, Major, an' I hardly felt it was proper for me to say anything.'

Leyland laughed. 'Well, you can say something when we inspect these exits, or what's left of 'em. We'd better try the beach end first as that's the nearest to our friends. Come on.'

'Good luck,' said Dearson. 'Hope to God you find something.'

'We shall need it,' Charlie grinned back at him.

They set off along the passage towards the sea. The air was thick with dust and at Tregarrion's suggestion they tied their handkerchiefs over their mouths. They must have looked a queer crew, thought Roy, as he looked at the others. They passed through the great chamber where Karen had shown him the rocket being assembled. It was empty and bare now save for a few odds and ends of useless equipment.

'Made a clean sweep, haven't they?' mumbled Leyland through his handkerchief.'

'Thorough as usual,' replied Roy. 'Let's hope they haven't been so thorough at the entrance.'

But they had. A solid avalanche of rock faced them, and search as they would they could not find the slightest opening.

'No hope there, sir,' said Tregarrion. 'It would take days to shift that lot without dynamite.'

'And they'll have taken that with them if they didn't use it all,' said Charlie savagely.

They returned dejectedly to the laboratory and broke the news to their fellow prisoners.

'There's still the Priory entrance,' said Roy.

'That wouldn't be much use even if we could get through,' said Charlie. 'Don't forget they've sealed up the way to the inn.'

'Yes, but not the shaft I fell down,' said Roy. 'We could still get out up that if there's a way through, or we could make one. Let's have a look, anyway.'

So the party set out again, coughing and choking in the dust. Finally they came to the chamber where Delouris and his men had so unpleasantly surprised them that morning and a little farther on they began to stumble over rubble and rocks which had been brought down by the explosion. Soon they were brought to a halt.

They stood in a little bunch, as though huddled together for protection, while Tregarrion went over with a torch every inch of the fall that barred their way. At last he turned away and shook his head. 'Worse than the other one, if anything,' he said morosely.

'Surprising how big a disappointment it still is even when you weren't really banking on anything,' said Leyland. 'At least, I wasn't.'

'Well, I must admit I was,' said Roy.

'Me too,' said Charlie.

'Never give up, do you?' remarked Leyland with a smile.

'No point in it,' said Charlie philosophically. 'If we'd given up hoping in the desert where should we be now?'

'Well, not in this confounded mine, anyway,' said Roy savagely.

Slowly they retraced their steps to the laboratory. They had no need to say anything. There was silence except for the sobbing of Mrs Murdock, whom Modwen was trying to console. Leyland moved over to them and gradually she quieted.

'And what does the desert rat recommend us to do now?' Roy asked Charlie. 'Penny for 'em.'

'I've been trying to remember something,' said Charlie. 'Years ago, when we were kids, the village lads used to play a lot in No Man's Cove. We had grand times there, with an old boat, playing pirates and—'

'Ye gods!' exclaimed Roy disgustedly. 'Playing pirates!'

Charlie smiled goodtemperedly. 'I know,' he said, 'it doesn't sound much to the point, but there was a cave in the cliff side.'

'Yes, I know it,' said Roy. 'I've wandered into it once or twice, though not very far, but what's that got to do with us now?'

'That's what I was trying to recollect,' said Charlie patiently.

Dearson was looking interested. 'Go on,' he said, 'I remember that cave, too.'

'I thought you would. Did you ever get right inside it?'

'I did once, I believe,' said Dearson, rather doubtfully, 'but if I remember rightly it was a bit too creepy for me and I came out quicker than I went in.'

'Yes, it was rather weird,' agreed Charlie, 'but I was always a curious kid, and one day I went in with a torch and a rope, determined to explore every bit of it. Well, I did. There were one or two smaller caves branching off it and at the far end of one of them, there was a hole in the rocks just big enough for me to squeeze through. I found myself in another cave which led into a kind of passage. I never found out

211

where it led to, but I've always had an idea that somehow it was connected with this mine.'

'My hat!' said Roy excitedly. 'Do you mean there may be yet another way out of this place?'

'Easy, easy,' said Charlie. 'I don't know. I said I never explored far enough to find out. It's only a theory, and besides, even if I'm right, and they did connect, don't forget it's years ago and the formation of the caves and the passages may have changed a good deal.'

'Never mind that,' said Roy, 'it's worth investigating. Here, Chief,' he called to Leyland, who was still talking to Mrs Murdock, but came across to them, 'Charlie thinks he knows of another way in and out of this place.'

'He does, does he,' exclaimed Leyland. 'Well, why the devil didn't he mention it before?'

'It's only just come back to me,' complained Charlie apologetically. 'It was years ago, you know.'

'Well, where is it? What about showing us?'

Charlie explained his difficulty. 'If I had a map of this area I might be able to get some idea of where the passage might connect with the mine.'

'There ought to be one,' said the Chief. 'Have you a map handy?' he asked one of the scientists.

'I believe there's one about somewhere,' the man replied. 'I think I saw it in one of the drawers.'

He began to look for it and eventually located it. They spread it out on a table.'

'Here's the cave in No Man's Cove,' said Charlie, indicating it with his finger. 'The sea goes into it at right angles to any passage which might have led from here to the caves, but the cave where I found the hole was on the left of the main cave as you went in, so that the direction is roughly right. The nearest mine passage marked on the map isn't too far away – somewhere about here where this branch passage is shown.'

'I don't see how that can be it,' said Leyland. 'That's a dead end. All these passages and galleries were investigated before the Government took over this place and our experts reported that there was only one way into and out of the mine and that was from the seaward side, which we've always used.'

'Oh,' said Charlie. 'Then I'm afraid my theory couldn't have been right.'

There was silence for a moment. The sense of disappointment at the apparent dashing of this last hope could almost be felt.

It was Tregarrion who broke it. 'You may be right, sir,' he said to the Chief Inspector, 'but I seem to remember hearing stories when I worked here of a passage linking the mine with the seashore. They even said that once in the old days the sea broke in and flooded the mine. Of course, it may have been only a story—'

'Are you absolutely sure, Chief, that that's a dead end?' asked Roy impatiently. 'Couldn't the experts possibly have made a mistake? Experts do sometimes, you know.'

'It's possible, of course,' admitted the Chief, 'but not very likely.'

'Well, then, even if there's only the slightest possible chance, I vote we investigate. Damn it, we've got nothing to lose and everything to gain.'

'I'm game to try anything,' said Leyland. 'I'll take you to the dead end and you can see for yourselves, but I shouldn't bank on anything if I were you.'

'We won't,' said Roy. 'But let's get moving. It's nearly midnight.'

Leyland led the way, followed by Charlie, Roy, Tregarrion and Dearson, who said he wasn't going to be left out of it this time. The dust from the explosions had settled now and they made more rapid progress. Leyland led them through the same galleries they had traversed when they had made their fruitless investigation of the seaward exit, but this time, before they reached the avalanche which had barred their progress on the first occasion, he turned off down a side passage to the left.

It was obvious from its condition that it had not been used like the others. They had to stoop several times to avoid bumping their heads on the low roof and there were piles of stones over which they stumbled. The passage was bending to the right now, almost in a semi-circle it seemed to Roy, and it gradually grew narrower until they could advance only in single file and they had to bend more and more frequently to avoid the low roof.

At last Leyland halted. 'This is as far as we can go,' he said.

As far as the available space, which was not much, permitted it, they crowded forward to see the nature of the obstruction of earth and rock on which Leyland let his torch play. It looked as substantial a barrier as the others.

Dearson sighed. 'Sunk again,' he said despondently. 'There's no way out through there.'

'I wonder,' said Roy. 'Tregarrion, you have a look.'

The ex-miner made a close examination. 'I'm not sure,' he said finally, 'but I don't think this galley has been deliberately stopped up. I think this is a natural fall, in which case it might not be so thick as it seems.'

'Natural fall or not, it looks pretty grim to me,' said Leyland.

Roy had been doing a bit of probing, too. 'Can you feel anything, you chaps?' he asked.

'I feel a bit chilly, if that's what you mean,' replied Leyland, 'but who wouldn't in this place?'

'That's exactly what I mean,' said Roy. 'Can't you feel a draught?'

Tregarrion was running his hand up and down the face of the fall. 'I believe you're right, sir. It seems to be strongest here. There's nothing to see, but you can feel it all right.'

'Then it can't be so solid as all that,' said Dearson more hopefully, 'or the air couldn't get through. If only we had some tools, a pick or two and a shovel, we might be able to get somewhere.'

'Well, there were plenty about,' said Leyland, 'but if Delouris had any sense and he really possessed the thoroughness he is so fond of boasting about he'd have seen that they were removed.'

'We could have a good scout round, anyway,' volunteered Charlie. 'Maybe we'll find something we can make an impression with. You come with me, Tregarrion. You're the mining expert.'

They went back along the passage, leaving Leyland, Roy and Dearson still probing the face of the fall. Back in the laboratory, Charlie and Tregarrion organized the rest of the prisoners into search parties and instructed them to bring back anything they could find which could be used as a digging tool.

Glad of something to do, the prisoners went to work with a will and ten minutes' search produced a pick-axe and a long-handled shovel, the end of which had been seen sticking out from under the debris caused by the explosion which sealed them off from the Priory.

215

Triumphantly, Charlie and Tregarrion returned to the gallery.

'Good,' said Leyland. 'Now let's get organized. I don't think more than two men can work at the face at the same time, do you, Tregarrion? I think you'd better be one and Charlie and Dearson and the others can take it in turns to relieve you. The rest of us can help to shift the stuff you get out. I think you, Tregarrion, ought to be in charge here. I don't know much about mining, but I believe moving these old falls is a tricky business. It may bring a lot of other stuff down and we don't want anyone buried.'

'As if we weren't now,' said Roy drily.

'I'm leaving it to you, then, Tregarrion. If you say it's not safe, then stop it,' ordered Leyland.

'Right, sir,' said the policeman. 'We shall probably need some timber to shore up the roof, so perhaps the others could hunt round for anything suitable.'

Leyland gave the necessary orders.

'All clear, sir?' asked Tregarrion. 'Stand back, then. Here goes.' He swung his pick.

Tregarrion, Charlie and Dearson, taking it in turns, worked with the will that is always born of the desire to achieve something in as short a time as possible, but it was hard and tricky going. Once Tregarrion shouted a warning only just in time as more rock came slithering down from the roof and he and Charlie had to jump clear. There was a delay until Tregarrion had put in some props and announced that he thought it was safe to continue.

By the time Charlie had taken his second breather they had made a distinct impression on the face, and the draught coming through was noticeably stronger now than when they had first detected it. 'I think I can almost smell the sea in it,' said Charlie, mopping his brow, off which the sweat was pouring.

'I'm not bothered about smelling it,' retorted Roy, with a laugh. 'I'm only interested in seeing whether there's a U-boat on it. I wish to goodness I could be more use. Blast these hands!' He looked ruefully at his still bandaged fingers.

'Save 'em for when you catch up with Delouris,' suggested Charlie. 'Well, back to work. OK,' he said, taking over from Tregarrion.

'How much longer, do you think?' Leyland asked the latter.

'Hard to say. The draught's getting stronger every time, but unfortunately we're shifting rock and earth, not wind.'

But after another ten minutes' hard slogging they had their reward. Charlie carefully prised out a huge piece of rock and gasped as a blast of cold air hit him in the face. He put his hand into the hole left by the rock – and touched nothing.

'We're through – we're through!' he shouted exultantly.

'Let me have a look, sir,' said Tregarrion. Carefully he examined the gap, flashing his torch into it. 'Yes,' he pronounced at last. 'It looks like a cave at the other side, but we've got to be careful. I don't like the look of this roof. He carefully widened the gap a little and then jammed some timber in it to support the roof. Now I think it's safe, sir.'

He crawled through the gap and one by one the others carefully followed him. Leyland shone the torch around them. They were in a cave, not a passage any more.

'This looks like it,' said Charlie excitedly. 'Yes, I'm sure it is. It's a long time since I was here, but I remember it as if it were only yesterday. You can hear the sea – listen!'

They stood, a silent little group for a moment, listening

intently. The soft murmur of a quietly breaking sea not far away filled the cave. It was a moment Roy never forgot.

'Let's get on,' he said impatiently at last.

'Just a minute,' said Leyland. 'Someone ought to go back and tell the others and help them through. The sooner we get them out of the mine the better. Will you see to it, Dearson?'

The inspector looked disappointed. He was as keen to go on as anyone, but he nodded and went back.

'Come on,' said Roy. 'I want to see if that U-boat is still there.'

They hurried forward, Charlie this time leading the way. 'Thank heaven the tide's out,' he said, 'otherwise we'd be swimming by now.'

They took a right-angle turn into another and bigger cave. 'This is the big one into which the sea comes right up,' he said. 'Look, you can see the sky and the stars.'

'Thank God,' said Leyland. There was inexpressible relief in his voice.

Roy glanced at his watch in the light of the torch. 'Hurry,' he said. 'It's after midnight. That U-boat will be gone soon.'

'And how do you propose to stop it if it hasn't?' asked Leyland.

Before Roy had time to reply a beam of light flashed across the mouth of the cave and there came from ahead of them the sharp crack of an explosion.

'What the—' Roy stopped dead and turned to Leyland. There was just enough light coming from the seaward end of the cave for him to see his face. There was a curious smile on it. 'What the hell's that?'

'I think,' said Leyland quietly, 'that that will be the Royal Navy.'

CHAPTER XXVI

Curtain for Delouris

'The Navy!' exclaimed Roy. 'What makes you think so?'

'Merely that I asked them to be here,' replied Leyland mildly. 'It seems they've arrived just in time.'

'Did you hear?' Roy asked Charlie. 'He says he asked the Navy to be here. He did say it, didn't he?'

'That's what I thought he said.'

'Well, of all the . . .' Roy stuttered incoherently for a moment, though the others caught a few swear words here and there. 'Why the hell,' he asked when he became intelligible again, 'didn't you tell us, instead of letting us go on thinking we were done for?'

'For two reasons,' said Leyland. 'I didn't say anything about it before we started out from the inn because (*a*) I was hoping they wouldn't be needed and (*b*) because I couldn't be sure they'd get here at the right time. I guessed Delouris and his gang would be planning a getaway by sea, probably by U-boat – oh yes, we knew they'd got a few away – but I couldn't be sure exactly when it would be. In my original plan the Navy were to be here just in case, but I was anticipating that we should round up the Delouris crowd and that the naval boys wouldn't be needed. After they'd rounded *us* up and it looked as if we were going to finish our careers in the mine, there didn't seem much point in telling you. To be trapped without hope of escape, even though the Navy were on our doorstep, so to speak, would have been too ironical to bear, I felt.'

'Well,' said Roy after all this, 'I still think you might have taken us into your confidence, even if you didn't tell the others. Did Karen know?'

'No one knew except myself and the Admiralty and Scotland Yard, of course.'

'OK We'll forgive you this time, but . . . let's get on and see what's happening.'

The mouth of the cave was still lit by the beam of light, evidently from a searchlight, but there had not been any more firing. As they came to the cave entrance, into which the sea was gently breaking, they saw a strange sight. The mouth of No Man's Cove was almost blocked by the sleek, dark shape of a destroyer, whose searchlight lit up the conning tower and superstructure of a large U-boat surfaced between the destroyer and the shore. There were men on the deck of the U-boat and they were hoisting a white flag.

As they stood there fascinatedly watching they heard a strong English voice coming through the loud-hailer from the destroyer. 'Ahoy, there,' it said. 'No one is to leave the U-boat. If anyone attempts to do so we shall fire again. We are sending a boarding party.'

'The first shot must have been a warning,' said Roy. 'I wonder if Karen and the gang are on board her yet?'

'They must be,' said Leyland. 'The naval force was instructed to wait until they saw a boat putting off from the shore with a small party in it before taking action.'

'Hey, look,' said Charlie. 'Do you see what I see?'

He pointed to a number of figures on the landward side of the U-boat's deck. 'It looks to me as if they're lowering a boat. Yes, they are, and someone's getting into it. There's a woman – it must be Miss Silvers! I'll bet they're trying to make a break for it back to land!'

'Well, why the devil don't they do something about it?' said Roy, glancing towards the destroyer.

'Because they can't see what's happening,' put in Leyland. 'The conning tower's acting as a screen.'

'Flash your torch,' said Roy. 'They may see it.'

Leyland did so repeatedly, but no one aboard the destroyer appeared to notice it.

'Hell's bells,' exclaimed Roy, 'don't tell me that Delouris is going to get away after all, and with Karen, too.'

Dearson and the others had joined them now and they all crowded into the mouth of the cave, watching the drama in the Cove in astonishment. The boat was pushing away from the U-boat's side now and beginning to move towards the shore, but they guessed it would still not be visible on the destroyer, from which a launch had now put off.

'They'll never make it in time,' groaned Roy. 'Can't we do something to stop 'em? If only we could get to the beach first and cut them off!'

'How?' asked Leyland. 'You can't go back through the mine, because there's no other way out except the one we've just come, and we can't swim there. We're helpless. We'll just have to leave it to the Navy. They'll round them up.'

'But it may be too late then,' said Roy. 'I'm thinking of Karen. God knows what Delouris might not do to her to save his own skin.'

'Just a minute,' said Charlie. 'Dearson, didn't there used

to be a way up the cliff here by the cave? I remember once when I'd been playing in here and came out to find myself cut off by the tide. I was terrified and cried my head off for a time. Then I calmed down. I looked around a bit and found a way up the cliff. I had to swim for it, and my mother played old Harry with me, but I made it.'

'I believe you're right,' said Dearson. 'I know I used to do a bit of cliff-climbing here, too, in those days.'

'Let's have a look, then,' said Charlie. 'It'll mean getting our feet wet, but what does that matter if we can cut Delouris off? Coming, Roy?'

'You bet I am,' said Roy. 'What about you, Chief?'

'Climbing cliffs at night isn't quite my line of country,' said Leyland, 'but take Tregarrion with you if he wants to go. Four of you won't be any too many to stop that little party. They'll be desperate, you know.'

'Don't worry,' Roy assured him. 'Delouris will be well and truly taken care of this time. Coming, Tregarrion?'

'Yes, *sir*,' said Tregarrion.

The four of them, Charlie leading, waded out into the sea, hugging the cliff on the shoreward side of the cave. The water had reached their waists before Charlie, helped by the light from the torches of the party watching anxiously from the cave, began to try to climb the cliff. Once he slipped back and fell into the water with a huge splash, but he soon found foot- and hand-holds and slowly he began to climb, the others following.

Leyland sighed as he saw them out of sight. He would have liked so much to have been in at the finish – if it was the finish. He prayed silently that this time it would be. He felt very, very tired.

It was tricky going for the four climbers. Several times they had to stop and wait while Charlie searched for hand-holds, but he always found them. The moonlight helped them to some extent, but it was also deceptive, and slips and hearts-in-mouths were frequent experiences for all four. Once, while he was waiting for Charlie to find a new hold, Roy risked a glance over his shoulder at the Cove. The boat, presumably containing Delouris and some of his men – how many they did not know – and Karen, was almost at the shore now and it looked as if – yes, it was – the launch was after them. But it looked as if they would too be late to stop them landing. They probably daren't fire for fear of hitting Karen.

'Get a move on there,' said Dearson, who was immediately below him, with Tregarrion bringing up the rear.

Roy looked up and saw Charlie way ahead. He toiled after him. The cliff was beginning to slope more now and the going was easier. Soon they were at the top. They paused a moment for breath and looked down into the Cove. The boat had been beached and they saw figures disappearing into the trees lining the sides of the combe beyond Roy's chalet.

'Looks as if they might be making for the old Priory again,' said Roy, 'though what they can hope to do there, I don't know. We've got to cut them off before they do, or we'll have a deuce of a job winkling them out of there again. The naval boys'll never catch them. They don't know the ground, so it's up to us. Come on, we'll have to run for it.'

The four of them set off at their top pace towards the beach. It was downhill and easy going, apart from the rabbit-holes and gorse bushes. Roy, who was in the lead, veered off at a slight diagonal away from the cliff edge, making for the road. When, panting, they reached it, he halted them.

'I think we'd better keep straight on up the road and hope to cut them off before they cross it,' he said, breathing hard.

My guess is that if they're making for the Priory they'll keep to the cover of the combe as long as possible. That means they won't be able to travel as fast as we can and we should have a good chance of intercepting them on the road, probably about the spot where you, Charlie, saw them take Pat across. What do you think?'

'Seems the best plan to me,' said Charlie. 'If we miss them there we'll have to follow on to the Priory. If they once get there we'll need the Navy all right. Personally, I'd rather clean this up without their help. What do you say, Dearson?'

'I agree,' said Dearson. 'I've a score or two to settle with them myself. I haven't forgotten poor old Thomas.'

'Right, then,' said Roy briskly. 'Off we go again.'

They raced on down the road.

As she was hurried along by the guards, who held her tightly by the arms, Karen was silently praying: 'Oh, God, don't let them get away, don't let them get away. Please, please stop them.' Her arms were aching intolerably as she was jerked along and her feet stumbled over stones and roots.

This forced journey through the combe seemed to her the final fantastic episode in a nightmare that had begun for her that morning when, instead of Roy, the Chief and Charlie and the others returning in triumph from their attack on the Priory, she and the other occupants of the mine had been surprised by Delouris' men and she had been forced to help in dismantling the apparatus on which she had worked so wholeheartedly for so long; had learnt that she was to be taken away with it and that her friends and colleagues were to be left to die in the mine.

That had been the last straw. She did not mind so much for herself, much as she loathed the idea of the gang getting away with the rocket that had meant so much to her and to the future of humanity, but to be taken away, knowing that the others, especially Roy, were to be buried alive, was too much. It had been out of her desperation at the receipt of this news, as much as her determination that Delouris and his men should not get away with the fruits of her labours and the secret which might preserve or destroy civilization, that she had made her attempt to wreck one of the most delicate and vital parts of the apparatus.

And she had failed miserably. When they had caught her she had gone a little out of her mind for a moment or two, screaming and fighting hysterically until she was overpowered, forced into a chair and tied there. And Delouris had come gloating and deprecating, oh, so politely, what he called her tantrums, and saying how surprised he was to find that one so scientifically minded could so let her emotions get the better of her. She could have killed him then.

She had had plenty of time for reflection as she had sat there in the chair watching Delouris' men removing the apparatus out of the mine, and most of her reflections were bitter. She thought about a great many things – her home, school, the university, the war, the satisfaction she had always felt in her work because she believed that she was really doing something to help humanity, not destroy it.

She had thought about Roy Benton, about the strange way he had come into her life, in which, hitherto, men had been merely people with whom she had to work because there weren't enough women scientists. She had thought a lot about Roy these last few days. Was it only a few days since he was brought unconscious into the mine and she had bathed and bandaged his head? She felt as if she had known him a long time.

For the first time in her life she had been forced to think about a man as a man, not as someone with whom she worked as a colleague, and it had been extremely disturbing, especially when he kissed her, to note her reactions, as she automatically did. But who on earth could she have thought she was to treat him as she had done? It was in the Priory when she saw – nay, almost felt – him being tortured for her sake that she first knew that this man was to her what no other man had ever been, or ever would be. And when, a few hours ago, she had thought she would never see him again, she had known for the first time in her life the real meaning of despair.

Finally she had been taken down to the Cove and put aboard the U-boat. Then had come the shot, the sudden panic it had caused to Delouris and his men and the commander and crew of the U-boat. The hope she thought had died in her she found was alive after all, but once more she had been hurried into the boat with Delouris and three of his picked men. And the look on Delouris' face as he stepped in after her she would never forget. Nor his words. 'If I am ever caught,' he said, 'it will only be because I am dead. And you will be dead, too, my dear.'

Once in the boat she had glanced back over her shoulder and seen the destroyer and she had cried softly to herself, unashamed of her tears before these men, although under normal circumstances she would have died rather than let them see her give way. They had hurried her up the beach past the chalet – how she wished Roy could have been there then! – and into the trees. She was so tired now that she had almost ceased to care what became of her, and it was a moment or two before she realized that they had stopped. They were still in the combe and Delouris was muttering excitedly to one of his men, who went on ahead but came back in a few moments. More cautiously now, they moved on, and she felt hardness and the roughness of a road under her aching feet. They entered the trees on the far side. Then she heard a fearful yell and fainted.

The four 'harriers', as Charlie, between gasps, referred to them, had been running as quietly as they could on the grass verge, but as they approached the spot where they were expecting the other party to cross, Roy halted them for a moment or two. They stood and listened. A dog was barking somewhere in the distance, and when it finally stopped they heard, a little way to their left, the snap of a twig, followed by a muttered exclamation.

'That's them for a quid,' breathed Charlie. 'We've done it. Let's tackle 'em here as they come out of the trees.'

'No,' said Roy quietly. 'The other side of the road will be better. They won't be able to see us and they'll think they're safely across, so we ought to be able to give them all the bigger surprise. We don't know how many of 'em there are, so we may need that surprise more than you think.'

They moved swiftly and silently across the road and melted into the trees.

'You haven't forgotten that they're armed and we're not, have you?' asked Dearson. 'Miss Silvers complicates matters if there's going to be any shooting.'

'We've got to see to it that they don't get a chance to use their guns,' said Roy. 'This has got to be a—' He broke off. 'They're crossing, boys,' he whispered as he heard a sound on the road. 'This is it.'

They split up silently and waited, every nerve and muscle tensed, peering between the branches.

'One, two, three, four – and Karen,' counted Roy under his breath. 'A man apiece and Delouris is mine, don't forget. Good luck, chaps.'

As the party crossed the road and came, all unsuspecting, into the shadow of the trees, Roy let out a blood-curdling yell. One moment there had been a quiet ribbon of road in the moonlight, with trees throwing long shadows across it; the next there was a whirling pandemonium of sound and struggling.

Afterwards, none of them was clearly able to remember exactly what happened in those few hectic minutes. Roy recalled seeing Karen slump to the ground as her captors released her and thinking Thank God, she's out of it, then leaping like a maniac at Delouris, getting him round the throat and bearing him to the ground. He did not feel the pain in his burned fingers any more. Then something – it felt hard enough to be a boot or a stone – hit him on the back of the head and he blacked out for a moment. When he opened his eyes he saw a figure trying to crawl away into the bushes and he plunged wildly after it.

Charlie remembered a tangle of plunging bodies and then he was hitting out right and left and feeling the satisfaction the fighting man always has when his blows connect. Dearson sprang at a guard, who turned and put his knee into his stomach. He fell backward and lay heaving for a few seconds, all the wind knocked out of him, then pulled the man's legs from under him, banged his head against a tree and went on banging it.

Tregarrion rushed at his man with lowered head and butted him in the stomach. The man grunted and fell across him, and the Cornishman promptly threw him clean over his broad shoulders. His head hit the ground and he lay still. Then he turned to help Charlie.

It lasted roughly ten minutes, and at the end of that time two Germans lay unconscious and the other two were sitting with their backs against a tree while Tregarrion relieved them of their guns. Not one of them had had time to draw a weapon, so complete had been the surprise. Roy was on his knees beside Karen, trying to bring her round; Dearson was being sick behind a bush and Charlie was tenderly feeling an eye out of which he was having increasing difficulty in seeing.

'Well,' he said, looking slowly around as well as he could out of the good eye, 'that was quite a party. I don't remember anything in the desert that was quite as good while it lasted. How is she, Roy?'

'All right, I think. She's only fainted.'

'And no wonder, after that awful war-whoop of yours. It frightened the life out of me. Where the devil did you pick that up?'

'Oh,' said Roy, 'from a pal of mine with whom I trained. He used to live with a Red Indian tribe. That's better,' he went on, as Karen stirred. 'How do you feel now?'

She tried to sit up, but fell back again into Roy's arms and began to cry.

'Here, here,' said Roy. 'That won't do. It's all over, darling. Our friend Delouris won't ever bother you again.'

'I can't believe it,' said Karen through her tears, clinging tightly to him. 'Oh, hold me,' she whispered. 'Hold me and don't ever let go again. That's the only way I shall ever feel safe.'

Roy held her. It was very pleasant to do so. Soon she was calmer.

'You don't know what it's been like since you left me this morning,' said Karen – 'or rather yesterday morning, I suppose

229

it was. It was all like some horrible nightmare. I didn't care what happened to me if I couldn't see you again.'

'Well, none of us have exactly enjoyed ourselves during the last twenty-four hours, though the last ten minutes helped to make up for it,' said Roy, kissing her hair. He helped her to her feet. 'But the nightmare's over at last and you can go on seeing me for the rest of your life if you want to.'

'That will be lovely,' she said.

'Ahem,' said Charlie. 'I don't want to be a spoil-sport, but I think I ought to warn you that someone's coming.'

'Very tactful of you, I'm sure. It'll be the naval party, I expect.'

It was. Roy hailed them as they hesitated for a moment at the other side of the road, and they came across.

'Thanks a lot for your help,' he told the officer in charge, who looked no more than a boy, 'but I don't think you'll have any more trouble with our friends. They're all here.'

The officer looked around him, first at the uniforms, then at Roy, Charlie and the others.

'Well,' he said, 'someone seems to have been having quite a party. Sorry we missed it. Any casualties?'

'Not unless you count a prize black eye and a sore stomach,' said Charlie, pointing to his closing eye and Dearson, who was still groaning a little, but had emerged from the bushes.

'Good. Well, I suppose you'd like us to take these bodies off your hands. You seem to have other more pressing business at the moment. I'm very glad to see the lady is safe,'

'I'm quite all right now, Lieutenant,' said Karen, with a smile.

The lieutenant gave a curt order and his men dragged the others to their feet. Delouris was still dazed from his beating-up, but he managed a smile, though it was rather twisted, as he saw Roy and Karen standing together.

'Ah,' he said, 'so the lovers are re-united after all. I compliment you, Major. I don't think *you* ever underestimated me, but I am beginning to wonder if I did not underestimate you. All the same, I should be very interested to know how you got out of the mine.'

'I don't take any credit for it,' said Roy. 'It was because Charlie, here, used to like playing pirates when he was a little boy.'

Delouris looked puzzled, as well he might. 'I am afraid I do not understand,' he said.

'It doesn't matter. It wasn't due to any loophole you left, if that's what's worrying you.'

Delouris managed another smile. 'I ought to have realized,' he said, 'that you would never give in, even if Scotland Yard seemed disposed to do so. I am disappointed in the Chief Inspector.'

'You needn't be,' said Dearson. 'It was he who arranged for the Navy to turn up at the right moment.'

Delouris' face expressed his mortification. 'So? I would not have thought that the Chief Inspector would have so accurately forecast my plans. But' – he shrugged – 'next time it will be different.'

'Do you think there'll be a next time, then?' asked Karen.

'But of course, my dear Miss Silvers. You do not really suppose, do you, that you have finished with me?'

'I think I've given you enough rope,' decided the young lieutenant. 'Now come on.'

Delouris clicked his heels and bowed towards them. '*Auf wiedersehen*,' he said.

'I trust not,' said Roy pointedly. 'Goodbye.'

Delouris turned and walked away with his companions. 'And that's that,' said Charlie. 'Or is it?'

It was a happy party which gathered at the chalet a little later. Roy, Karen, Charlie, Dearson and Tregarrion followed the naval party back down the combe to the beach, where they saw the prisoners embarked just as Leyland and the others from the mine were being landed.

'Well,' the Chief greeted them, 'thank God you're all safe, especially you, my dear.' He warmly embraced Karen. 'I gather from the naval boys that you had quite a rough-house. I hope you gave them a few for me.'

'We did,' said Roy. 'I think I'll have to have my hands bandaged again. Well, what do you say to something to eat and drink? I'm famished. I think this calls for a celebration, don't you?'

'And how,' said Charlie.

'Come on, then.' He led the way up to the chalet. 'There ought to be a bottle or two tucked away somewhere. I was keeping it for when I heard that my book had been accepted. Did I say book? That must have been years ago.'

It was a bit crowded in the little chalet and the drinks didn't quite go all round, but the womenfolk made some tea and there was much laughter and chaffing, except for a moment or two when Leyland toasted absent friends, and they all thought for a moment of poor tortured Pat and Thomas, the police officer, who had lost his life in a brave attempt to turn the tables in the mine.

It was just after this that Roy noticed Karen had disappeared. He went outside and found her on the verandah looking out to sea. The stern of the destroyer was just moving out of sight behind the cliff.

He came up quietly behind her and put his arm round her. She started as he touched her and he apologized.

'It's all right,' she said, 'I must still be a bit jumpy.'

'We'll soon put that right.'

When he had put it right, she spoke again. 'I've been thinking about what Delouris said. Do you think he's right?'

'What, about seeing him again? For goodness' sake stop thinking of him.'

'I can't – yet,' said Karen, 'and I don't think we ought to if he's right in saying that there'll always be someone who'll want to dominate the world. That's why I worked so hard on my rocket because I felt so convinced that it would help to keep the peace. It didn't bring us any, did it?' She sighed. 'Now, I suppose, the Chief will want us to carry on from where Delouris interrupted us.'

'But not,' said Roy, quietly but firmly, 'until you've taken time off for a honeymoon with me here.'

Neither spoke again for what seemed a very long time.

Light-Fingers

Paul Temple, popular novelist and famous private detective, placed a red carnation in the buttonhole of his dinner jacket, flicked a fleck of dust from his trousers, and carefully adjusted his evening-dress bow. It was New Year's Eve and both the novelist and Mrs Temple – known affectionately as Steve – had been invited to a dinner party.

The party was to be held at Nicholas Hall, a delightful old manor house on the Hog's Back just outside Guildford. The Hall belonged to a friend of Paul Temple's called Sir Stephen Peters. Every year Sir Stephen gave a New Year's Eve party and both Paul and Steve were invited.

It was just after six o'clock when Steve climbed into the driving-seat of her husband's new sports car and turned the bonnet of the car southwards.

'Now drive carefully, Steve,' warned Temple. 'Remember the roads are very treacherous at this time of the year.'

Steve smiled, for in spite of the fact that she was a careful driver, they never started out on a journey without Temple administering a friendly warning. As the car glided away from the kerb and made for the open country, Steve glanced down at the illuminated clock on the dashboard.

'How long should it take us to reach Guildford, Paul?'

There was a twinkle in Temple's eye as he said: 'We may never reach there if you don't keep your eyes on the road!'

'If there are any more complaints about my driving, Mr Temple, I shall insist that you get out and walk!'

Temple glanced across at his wife and chuckled softly to himself. It was a funny thing about Steve, he reflected, although she was a very keen driver she never seemed to be completely relaxed. Even now she sat clutching the wheel with both hands, an expression of grim determination on her features.

When the car came to a standstill at the last set of traffic lights, just before they reached the open country, Steve did manage to relax slightly and remove her hands from the steering-wheel.

The lights changed from amber to green and the car moved forward.

Temple glanced into the driving-mirror and suddenly sat bolt upright.

'By Timothy,' he said, 'this fellow behind us seems to be in a hurry!'

Steve turned her head and noticed a black saloon car bearing down on them.

'You'll have to pull into the side, Steve!' exclaimed Temple. 'Or he'll force you into the hedge!'

As Temple spoke the overtaking car lurched forward and Steve instinctively reached for the handbrake. There was a scraping of metal and a sudden bump as the back mudguard of the saloon caught the wing of Temple's car. Steve skilfully manoeuvred the car into the side and as it came to a stand-still switched on the headlights. In the distance they could see the saloon roaring its way down the country road. In a little while it was completely out of sight.

Steve sat for a moment trying to regain her breath; she was obviously a little frightened.

Temple said, very quietly: 'That was excellent driving, my dear. If you'd lost your head we should have been involved in a very nasty accident.'

'Did you notice the driver of the car?'

Temple shook his head. 'He was heavily muffled and he wore his hat right down over his eyes. I doubt very much whether I should recognise him again.' He got out of the car and surveyed the damage. The wing was scratched and there was a dent near the offside lamp.

'You've had a nasty shock, Steve. You'd better let me drive for the rest of the journey.' As he climbed into the driving-seat Temple heard the sudden whir of a motor-horn and the sound of an approaching car. Steve was already staring out of the window unable to suppress her excitement.

'Here's a police car, Paul!' she shouted. 'I believe they're chasing the man who bumped into us.'

The police car came to a sudden halt and Temple recognised his old friend Chief-Inspector Brooks.

Temple lowered the window.

'What's happened, Inspector?'

The inspector was a thickset man with a jovial face and a weather-beaten countenance. He looked more like a farmer than a police inspector and because of this his enemies frequently underrated him. Brooks was in fact a shrewd north-countryman with an intimate knowledge of the London underworld.

'There's been a robbery at Malfrey's the jewellers in New Bond Street. "Light-Fingers" Layman made a smash-and-grab. He got away with a diamond necklace worth £30,000.'

Temple said: 'A black saloon crashed into us. It was driven by a man in a dark overcoat and a muffler over his face – was that the notorious Layman?'

The inspector nodded. 'Yes, that was "Light-Fingers" all right. Which way did he go, Temple?'

'He went straight down the road ahead,' volunteered Steve. 'The number of the car was UMX 829.'

'We know the number of the car, Mrs Temple,' said Brooks, 'but if he makes a get-away, ten to one he'll abandon the car or change the number plates.' As the inspector spoke the police car shot forward and before Temple had even time to wave goodbye it was nearly out of sight.

'Have you heard of "Light-Fingers" Layman?' asked Steve.

Temple changed gear and the sports car once again moved forward into the centre of the road.

'I first heard of him two or three years ago when he broke into the North Midfield Bank at Exeter. "Light-Fingers" is what they call a lone operator – he works entirely on his own.'

'Would you recognise him if you saw him?'

'I very much doubt it,' said Temple. 'I've only seen photographs of him. If I remember rightly he has rather a nasty scar across the back of his left hand.'

The car gathered speed and Paul Temple found himself thinking of 'Light-Fingers' Layman; although he had never actually encountered 'Light-Fingers', the novelist knew only too well, from the confidential reports he had seen on the Exeter Case at Scotland Yard, that he was a most dangerous criminal.

After they had been driving for about a quarter of an hour

Steve suddenly drew Temple's attention to the police car. It was about a hundred yards ahead of them, parked by the side of the road under a huge tree.

Temple took his foot off the accelerator.

'What's happened, Inspector?' he called.

There was a look of both annoyance and bitter disappointment on the inspector's face. He nodded towards the uniformed sergeant who was busy working the radio transmitter. 'We've got a cordon round the entire district but it looks as if "Light-Fingers" has given us the slip, Temple.'

'We'll keep our eyes open, Inspector. If we see anything suspicious I'll 'phone Sergeant O'Hara at Guildford.'

Ten minutes later Temple *did* see something suspicious and he was so surprised that he took his eyes off the road and grabbed Steve by the arm.

'Look where you're going, Paul!' ejaculated Steve.

Temple applied the brakes and the car came to a standstill.

He switched on the headlights.

'Do you see what I see, Steve?'

Steve turned her head and then suddenly she realised what her husband was staring at. In a little clearing, about ten or twenty yards down from the main road, stood the black saloon car. It had obviously been forced off the road, or deliberately driven off, for the front wheels rested in a narrow ditch and the radiator was embedded in the bank.

While they were watching the car a man came running up the bank and on to the road. He was a nervous, shrivelled-up little man with a clean-shaven face and long dark hair. He carried his overcoat over his left arm. The man hesitated for a moment, shielding his eyes from the glare of the headlights.

Paul Temple took careful stock of the stranger before

dimming the lights. The man certainly didn't look like the notorious 'Light-Fingers' although there was a nasty cut across the lower part of his face which added a sinister touch to his appearance. The stranger hurried across to Temple and introduced himself. He explained that his name was Professor Thompson and that he was on his way to Guildford.

'I was driving along in my car when suddenly this car,' he pointed to the black saloon, 'overtook me and crashed into the ditch. I hurried down the bank to see if I could be of any assistance but to my astonishment . . .'

'The driver of the other vehicle knocked you out and stole your car,' said Temple.

The little man nodded; he looked both surprised and relieved. 'But that's exactly what happened!' he stammered. 'How on earth did you know?'

Temple told the professor about the robbery and about 'Light-Fingers' Layman, adding: 'You'd better let us drive you into Guildford, Professor.'

The professor was highly delighted at the suggestion and lost no time climbing into Temple's car.

'I should be extremely grateful if you would drive me into Guildford,' he said. 'I have a most important appointment at eight o'clock.' The little man seemed far more concerned about keeping his appointment than about the arrest of 'Light-Fingers' and the recovery of the stolen car.

'What sort of a car were you driving?' asked Temple.

'It's a brand new Austin – this year's model. It's dark maroon and the registration number is EKL 974.'

'Well, that shouldn't be difficult to find,' said Temple. 'I'll contact the police as soon as we come to the next 'phone box.'

'Oh, dear!' said the professor. 'This is most disturbing. I do hope I shan't be late for my appointment!'

Paul Temple smiled, moved the gear into position and released the clutch. 'Your appointment must be a very important one, Professor?'

The professor nodded. 'I'm an antique dealer and a collector of rare coins,' he explained. 'Earlier this evening a lady telephoned me from Guildford with the exciting news that she had discovered a Queen Elizabeth Bank of England note and that she was prepared to consider a reasonable offer for it.'

'Is the note valuable?' asked Steve.

'Valuable?' The professor was obviously thunderstruck by such a question. 'It's unique!' he exclaimed. 'All my life I've been on the lookout for such a treasure.

Temple said: 'I suppose you're anxious to contact the lady before any of the other collectors get to hear of the discovery.'

The professor looked very worried. 'That's exactly what I'm afraid of!' he said. 'I simply must get to Guildford before any of the Bond Street collectors.'

'Well, we'll do the best we can, Professor,' said Temple, 'but I'm afraid you'll have to wait while I telephone the police.'

The nearest telephone was at the crossroads a mile or so down the road. Temple stopped the car and, after pocketing the ignition key, crossed the grass plot to the telephone box.

'I want to speak to Sergeant O'Hara,' said Temple, when the telephone operator put him through to police headquarters.

Sergeant O'Hara was delighted to hear from Paul Temple for he had known Temple in the old days when the novelist had investigated the 'Front Page Men' affair.

'Compliments of the season!' bellowed the little Irishman, 'but what in the wide world brings you down to this part o' the country now?'

Temple spoke very quietly, and as he spoke he stared out of the telephone box at the professor and Steve who were engaged in an animated conversation.

Temple said: 'Listen, Sergeant! Steve and I are on our way to Nicholas Hall and we want you to send a police car out to meet us. We should reach the outskirts of Guildford in about a quarter of an hour.'

Although O'Hara was bewildered he sensed the tone of urgency in Temple's voice.

'Is anything the matter?' he said quietly.

Paul Temple said: 'Yes, I've got the man you're looking for – I picked him up five minutes ago.'

The sergeant gasped. He knew that Temple must be referring to 'Light-Fingers' Layman. 'By the Lord Harry!' he stammered, unable to believe his own ears. 'Not "Light-Fingers" Layman?'

'"Light-Fingers" Layman,' said Paul Temple quietly.

And ten minutes later, thanks to the astuteness of Paul Temple, the notorious 'Light-Fingers' was arrested.

*

But how did Paul Temple know that the professor was an impostor and that he was in fact none other than 'Light-Fingers' Layman? There are three important clues in this story – did you find them?

Turn to page 257 to find out.

A Present from Paul Temple

One morning, two or three weeks before Christmas, the telephone rang in Paul Temple's flat and Mrs Temple – known affectionately as Steve – lifted the receiver.

'Is that you, Steve?' asked a man's voice.

For a moment Steve was puzzled, then suddenly she recognised the voice. The speaker was Dr Raymond, the Headmaster of St Conrads.

St Conrads was a famous public school at Downbeach in Sussex and Dr Charles Raymond, author of several well-known text-books on Forensic Medicine, was a very old friend of Temple's.

After a word or two with Steve, Dr Raymond said, 'I'd like to speak to that famous husband of yours, Mrs Temple!'

'I'm sorry but Paul's in the bathroom,' said Steve. 'Can I deliver a message?'

Dr Raymond hesitated. 'I'd like to see Temple,' he said quietly. 'I've a very serious problem on my hands, Steve, and I need help.' There was no mistaking the note of urgency in his voice.

Francis Durbridge

'I'll have a word with Paul the moment he comes out of the bathroom,' said Steve. 'He'll ring you back, Charles.'

Ten minutes later the famous private detective emerged from the bathroom and put a call through to St Conrads. An hour later Paul and Steve were on their way to Downbeach.

Dr Raymond was a squat little man with a high forehead and a long thin nose. He wore horn-rimmed glasses and when he smiled – which was frequently – his pale-blue eyes twinkled with good humour.

The moment Temple and Steve arrived at St Conrads he took them upstairs to his study. The study was on the fourth floor and on a clear day it was possible to see almost as far as Beachy Head.

'Now what seems to be the trouble, Charles?' asked Temple.

The doctor took an old briar pipe from his pocket and crossed over to the tobacco jar on the mantelpiece.

'I'm terribly worried, Temple,' he said thoughtfully, leaning against the mantelpiece and slowly stuffing tobacco into the bowl of his pipe. 'One of my pupils – a boy called Brian Walters – has mysteriously disappeared. Early yesterday morning Mrs Bridie, the Matron, reported that Brian had made a rope out of his bedclothes and lowered himself out of the dormitory window.'

Temple smiled. 'Well, it's not the first time I've been asked to investigate the disappearance of a schoolboy!' He was thinking of the Curzon case.

Dr Raymond said: 'I had to send for you, Temple, otherwise it meant reporting the matter to the police. I only want to do that as a last resort.'

'What kind of a boy is Brian Walters?' asked Temple. The headmaster smiled thoughtfully.

244

'I wouldn't exactly describe him as a typical boy,' he replied. 'He hates games, and spends most of his time on the cliffs chasing after butterflies. He has quite a collection. As he is not very strong I don't compel him to play games; I think his hobby probably does him more good.'

'He sounds pretty athletic to me – clambering out of windows in the small hours,' grinned Temple.

'He may have been after some special moth. He's rather an eccentric little boy. His father is a professor at Cambridge and his mother does a lot of lecturing, so Brian has been left to his own devices quite a bit.'

'Hasn't he any friend in the school?' asked Steve, anticipating her husband's question by a fraction of a second.

Dr Raymond took his pipe from his mouth and tapped it on the palm of his hand.

'Yes, strangely enough, he's on quite friendly terms with a boy named Dickson, who is the reprobate of his form. I've caught Walters helping him with his prep several times, and they work together in the lab and sit next to each other as often as they get the chance.'

Temple exchanged a glance with Steve and said:

'I think we might have a chat with Master Dickson.'

'Of course,' nodded Dr Raymond. 'I'll have him sent up immediately.' He picked up the telephone on his desk and gave the necessary instructions.

'You don't think the boy has run away because he's tired of school?' suggested Steve.

Dr Raymond shook his head.

'Walters has been very happy with us. Besides, it's only a week to the end of term. Why should he run home now?'

At that moment there came a nervous knock at the study door, and in response to the headmaster's 'Come in,' the door opened slowly and the figure of a boy of about eleven edged itself somewhat cautiously into the room. He was rather an untidy little boy with his hair over his left eye, and a tie that was moving in the direction of his right ear.

'Ah, there you are, Dickson,' said the headmaster. 'We want to have a word with you. Shut the door.'

'Please, sir,' burst forth Dickson. 'It was an accident! There happened to be a little pool of sulphuric acid on my bench, and Mr Tolworth was just leanin' on the desk, and his hand happened to . . .'

'That will do, Dickson,' interposed Dr Raymond in a severe tone, though Steve noted a twinkle in his eyes. 'We want to talk to you about Walters. This is Mr Temple . . .'

'Not *Paul* Temple?' exclaimed Dickson, his eyes widening in surprise.

'*Mr* Paul Temple,' corrected his headmaster.

'Come and sit down, Dickson,' invited Temple. 'I want to have a little talk to you about your friend Walters.'

'But I don't know anything else, Mr Temple,' protested the boy. 'I've done an hour's detention for letting him down the rope out of the dorm window . . .'

Steve could not suppress a smile at the little boy's indignation.

'Did Walters tell you where he was going?' asked Temple.

'He said he thought he could get a super moth,' replied Dickson.

'Did he say where?'

'In a little wood on the top of the cliffs by Sidley Cove.'

'Does Walters often make these night expeditions?'

'Oh no, sir. This was something special. He's a bit cracked you know when it comes to butterflies and moths,' added Dickson confidentially.

'I quite understand,' said Temple seriously. 'Now Dickson, I want you to think carefully, and see if you can recall anything in the least unusual about Walters during the past few days.'

Dickson stroked the back of his head with a grubby hand, frowning thoughtfully. Then his eyes lit up.

'He had a super new watch given him last Saturday,' he informed them. 'One of the latest Swiss wrist-watches. It looked like real gold, but of course it couldn't have been.'

'Who gave it to him?' asked Steve.

'Some artist who's always painting on the cliffs. I think he said his name was Crowther. He's painted old Walters with his butterfly net and all that, and he gave him the watch for sitting still so that he could paint him.'

All the time he was talking, Temple had been sizing up young Dickson very shrewdly, and presently he turned to Dr Raymond.

'I should be very grateful, Doctor, if you could let me have this boy as an assistant for a day or so,' he said. 'I have an idea he may be a considerable help.'

The headmaster gravely inclined his head in assent.

Dickson was unable to believe his ears.

'You mean I can cut school – and prep for a whole day?' he enquired in incredulous tones. 'Oh super! Thank you, sir,' he added,' turning to Temple.

The first thing that Paul Temple asked the boy to do was to take them to the cliffs where Dickson assured them that the artist, Crowther, was to be found.

'I always thought artists were long-haired chaps with beards and all that,' Dickson confided to Temple and Steve, as he led the way along the narrow lane which wound down to the top of the cliffs. 'This fellow isn't a bit like that.'

Master Dickson's meaning was obvious presently when they saw the artist perched on a piece of rock near the top of the cliffs. He wore an old mackintosh, a pair of shabby flannels and an ancient felt hat pulled over his eyes. He was making a rough sketch of the scene below.

When Temple told him that young Walters was missing, he seemed quite concerned. 'What *can* have happened to the little fellow?' he said.

'We thought you might have seen something of him, as he said he was coming in this direction,' replied Temple.

Crowther shook his head.

'I haven't seen him for some days,' he replied. 'Not since I finished his picture – I suppose you heard about that. He had rather an unusual face, something like Orpen's "Bubbles", and he agreed to let me paint him with his butterfly net and cyanide jar.'

'And you gave him a present?' put in Steve.

'Oh, it was only a cheap wristwatch,' said the artist, nonchalantly adding one or two strokes to his picture. 'The boy seemed to like it . . .'

'It was a smasher!' interposed young Dickson, and his elders exchanged a smile. Temple was unable to gain any further information from Crowther, so presently they left him and strolled farther along the cliffs.

'I must say I don't trust that gentleman,' said Temple to Steve, when they were out of earshot of the artist.

'You don't think he's a spy do you, Mr Temple?' piped the small voice of Dickson.

'Not the sort of spy you are thinking of, Dickson,' replied Temple. 'But I certainly think he does something else besides sketch the scenery.'

'You mean he's watching for something?' queried Steve.

'That's about it.'

Temple climbed on to a little mound to see if he could get a peep at the artist while he was unobserved. The man seemed to be busy with his drawing again, and after watching him for some minutes Temple was about to rejoin Steve and Dickson when a glint of light from out at sea caught his eye. It was followed almost immediately by another. Temple gave a low whistle.

'Someone out at sea is signalling,' he told them.

'You mean with a mirror?' asked Steve.

'That's right, and they're using the Morse Code,' announced Master Dickson, who had clambered up beside Temple.

'Do you know the Morse Code, Dickson?' asked Temple.

'You bet! I've just passed my Scout test,' Dickson informed him.

Temple whipped an envelope and pencil from his pocket.

'Is it slow enough for you to read?' he asked.

'Rather,' said Dickson, and began to decipher a series of letters, which Temple jotted down. When the message finally ceased, Dickson said disappointedly:

'It didn't make sense, sir!'

'I know,' said Temple. 'It's in some sort of code. Don't worry, Dickson, we'll fathom it sooner or later.'

'D'you think they were signalling to Crowther?' asked Steve.

'It's possible,' nodded her husband. 'Anyhow, let's get back to the school, and I'll have a shot at deciphering this code.'

They walked briskly back to St Conrads, and just as they came in sight of the familiar red brick building Dickson said:

'I say, Mr Temple, would you mind if I went off and did a bit of exploring on my own? After all, the Head gave me a day off, and I thought I might look round one or two of the places where Walters and I used to snoop about.'

'Good idea, Dickson!' nodded Temple. 'But I want you to promise me that you'll be extra careful, and if you should see any suspicious characters come back here at once.'

'Oh, yes, Mr Temple, I'll cut back like a shot,' agreed Dickson.

After the boy had departed Temple went into the headmaster's study and settled down with a pile of foolscap paper. He had always prided himself on his skill at deciphering secret codes; this particular one, however, proved considerably more complicated than he had expected, and at one time he was inclined to conclude that young Dickson had misread the signal.

In the end, he took a final scrap of paper and wrote out what seemed to be almost the complete message. It read:

WILL LAND AT LOW TIDE TONIGHT
FALCON'S CAVE HAVE CAR READY

Feeling very satisfied with himself, Temple immediately telephoned the local police station and arranged with the inspector in charge to bring a small posse of men over to the school that night at ten-thirty. He had checked that low tide would be just before eleven.

Just before tea-time, Dickson came rushing in, his eyes alight with excitement. In his hand he clutched a grubby scrap of paper.

'Walters and I have a special hiding-place in a hollow tree halfway down the cliff,' he explained. 'We keep all our things there – Walters has his butterfly stuff and I have my catapult and my birds' eggs. I went down this afternoon to see if everything was all right, and found this bit of paper.'

He handed it to Temple, who unfolded it and read in schoolboyish scrawl: 'Something queer in Falcon's Cave.'

'You see, sir,' said Dickson excitedly. 'He'd seen something in the cave, and he had gone down to investigate.'

'You know this cave?' asked Temple.

'Yes, Mr Temple. You can only get into it at low tide and even then it's a bit tricky.'

'I see,' nodded Temple, 'and showed him the deciphered message. When Dickson heard that there was to be a police raid on Falcon's Cave that evening, he was very excited.

'Can I come too, sir? I can show you the way down the cliff, and—'

'I'm afraid this isn't a job for little boys,' said Temple.

'He could stay, with me in the car,' said Steve. 'I'll keep an eye on him.'

Late that night Paul Temple, Steve and young Dickson climbed into the detective's car. They followed closely behind a police car, which carried three hefty constables, a sergeant and Inspector Eastman.

They arrived at the top of the cliffs, from where the path led down to Falcon's Cave, with about half an hour to spare, and they parked the cars about a hundred yards away in the midst of some undergrowth. When the cars were safely parked the inspector gave his instructions.

The two men were to keep well under cover until the incoming boat had landed; after that they were to close in and enter the cave.

Temple gave Steve a small torch.

'You and Dickson keep a sharp lookout, and give us a signal if anything goes wrong. But remember only to flash the torch in an emergency, because it may be seen from the sea.'

The men went off down the narrow path that led to the cave, while Steve and Dickson settled themselves in a tiny clearing surrounded by blackberry bushes. Steve spread an old mackintosh she had brought with her on the grass, and then turned to speak to Dickson. It was quite dark and she could see nothing. The boy had disappeared!

'Dickson! Where are you?' she called softly, but there was no reply.

Steve stood quite still and listened intently, but could hear nothing but the distant roar of the waves. Then came the sound of a car engine purring softly. It grew louder until the car seemed to be only a few feet from her in the stillness of the night. Actually, it was thirty to forty yards away.

Steve hoped that Dickson was keeping well hidden!

The car doors opened and closed softly, and then there was silence once more.

There was still no sign of Dickson, however, and Steve was just wondering whether to give the alarm signal when she felt a tug at her sleeve.

'It's all right, Mrs Temple,' said Dickson, looming out of the dark. 'I saw the smugglers get out of that car – and what d'you think? One of 'em is that artist, Crowther!'

'You shouldn't have gone without telling me, Dickson,' Steve reproved him. 'I thought something terrible might have happened to you.'

'Not me!' declared Master Dickson boastfully. 'Why I could go right up to anybody in the dark like . . .' he stopped speaking.

'What is it?' asked Steve

'Listen!' said Dickson quietly. 'There's the motor-boat.'

The boy was right.

They could hear the throb of the engine. After a little while it stopped and for ten minutes or more Steve and the boy sat straining their ears.

The roar of the sea on the rocks made it difficult to distinguish any sounds of human activity.

'I don't think I'd like to be a detective after all – too much waiting about,' Dickson was just deciding, when they heard Temple's agitated voice.

'Steve! Are you there?'

'I'm here, Paul. What's the matter?'

'Back to the car as quickly as you can. You too, Dickson!'

'Have they got away?' asked Dickson.

'Yes, they've made another tunnel out of the cave – we didn't know about that until young Walters told us about it. We found Walters all right – wrapped up in a blanket and fast asleep. He seems none the worse for his experience.'

They hurried towards Temple's car, moving rather too quickly for Dickson's short legs.

'How much start did they get, sir?' he panted.

'Two or three minutes, but they were carrying quite a lot of stuff which they landed from the boat.'

'They've got a car here, just along the cliff,' Steve told him, and just as she spoke, the engine roared into life, and the car in question moved off.

'Hurry! We've got to get after them!' snapped Temple. They were still over a hundred yards from their own car, and when they came up to it, the policemen were already waiting for them.

'They've got away in a car – along the lower road,' Temple told them. 'No time to lose!' He switched on the lights of his car.

'I don't think you need be in such a hurry,' piped the voice of young Dickson.

'Eh? What's that?' asked Temple, swinging round as he was about to help Steve into the car.

'They won't get very far,' Dickson informed him, proudly displaying an enormous Scout knife and opening what appeared to be a large, pointed blade.

'Both their back tyres are punctured,' he announced simply. 'This is the first time I've had a chance to use this thing – I think it's really meant for taking stones out of horses' hoofs!'

The police car overtook the smugglers less than a quarter of a mile down the road. They capitulated without any struggle, and in the back of the car the police found a small crate containing over 9,000 watches.

Temple drove two very excited boys back to St Conrads. Walters was explaining at some length to his friend how he had been on the track of a super moth when he saw a boat land near Falcon's Cave, had gone to investigate, and had been captured by the smugglers.

'They were jolly decent, really;' he told them, his mouth full of milk chocolate, which Steve had found in her handbag. 'I got plenty to eat; it was a bit like a picnic. Of course, it began to get rather boring after a while.'

'Better than school, anyhow,' decided Dickson emphatically.

'They let me roam around the tunnels – they have no end of stuff stowed away down there, Mr Temple,' continued Walters.

'So I gather,' said Temple grimly. 'I expect the police will look into that. And you are very lucky, young fellow, that things are no worse. I hope you aren't going to make a habit of climbing out of the dormitory window in the small hours.'

Walters looked worried.

'You'll catch it when the Head sees you,' said his companion, with a hoarse chuckle. 'I've had an hour's detention just for holding the rope while you climbed down!'

Paul Temple smiled.

'As we've managed to break up a gang of smugglers who have been troubling the police for some time,' he said, 'I'll have a talk to Dr Raymond and see if I can't persuade him to let you down lightly.'

Long after the boys had gone to bed, Temple and Steve sat in front of the fire in the Head's study, discussing the events of the day with Doctor Raymond.

'What made you suspect that Walters' disappearance had anything to do with smuggling?' asked Raymond.

Temple lit a cigarette and exhaled a stream of smoke.

'I suppose it was young Dickson telling me about the artist giving the boy a wrist-watch. I had to find out just how genuine the artist was, and I soon came to the conclusion that he had only been painting young Walters' portrait to keep that youngster from snooping around the cliffs at certain times when he might have discovered something.'

'How did you discover that Crowther was not genuine?'

'He gave himself away by mentioning Orpen's picture, "Bubbles". Any genuine artist would know that famous picture was the work of Millais. After, that, it was just a case of one thing leading to another.'

'Anyhow, Dickson has enjoyed it all enormously,' smiled Steve, who had taken a fancy to the mischievous youngster.

'I doubt if it will have any salutary effect in his position in form,' sniffed the Head. 'He's been bottom these past two terms.'

'My guess is that he gets an interesting view of the quadrangle from that position,' hazarded Temple with a smile.

Dr Raymond's expression became thoughtful.

'Now you come to mention it, Temple,' he said, 'I believe that is the case.'

A week later, Dickson received a small registered parcel, which he opened just before morning prayers in the midst of a noisy group of curious juniors.

'Must be something special,' said his friend Walters, as several layers of packing were torn away to reveal a neat little case.

'It's a gold wrist-watch!' cried, one of the juniors.

'Wizard! Look – there's some writing on the back.'

They crowded round and slowly read the inscription:

'To Jeremy Dickson, my partner in the Downbeach case. From Paul Temple.'

Light-Fingers

Later that night, or rather in the early hours of the New Year, Paul Temple told Steve and his old friend Sir Stephen Peters why he had suspected the bogus 'professor'.

'As soon as I saw him carrying his overcoat over his left arm I was suspicious,' said Temple. 'It was a very cold night and yet obviously he was determined not to wear his coat. I realised however that the overcoat must be serving a particular purpose – it was in fact *concealing the scar on the back of his left hand.*'

'That was Clue No. 1,' said Steve, 'but what was the second clue, Paul?'

'The second clue,' explained Temple, 'was when the "professor" said that his car had been stolen. He described the car as a brand new model, registration number EKL 974. I knew that he was lying immediately he told me the registration number. *A new car would never be registered as EKL – these letters belong to the 1938 or '39 period.*'

'And the third clue?' asked Sir Stephen.

'The third clue was the most important of them all,'

Francis Durbridge

said Temple. 'It was when the "professor" pretended to be a collector of rare coins. He said that he was going to Guildford in order to buy a very valuable Queen Elizabeth Bank of England note.'

'Well?' said Steve, obviously puzzled.

Paul Temple smiled. *'There's no such thing as a Queen Elizabeth Bank of England note,'* he said quietly. *'Such notes did not exist in the time of Queen Elizabeth. The first Bank of England note was issued in 1694.'*

BY THE SAME AUTHOR

Design for Murder

The Assistant Commissioner of Scotland Yard visits a retired detective with the news that an old adversary has struck again, strangling an innocent girl. Wyatt is reluctant to return to police work, but then another body is found – this time at his own home, with a chilling message: 'With the compliments of Mr Rossiter'.

In *Design for Murder*, Francis Durbridge adapted his longest Paul Temple serial, *Paul Temple and the Gregory Affair*, into a full-length novel. All the obligatory elements from the thrilling radio episodes were present, but in a new twist, he renamed the principal characters: Paul and Steve Temple became Lionel and Sally Wyatt, and 'Mr Rossiter' replaced the villainous Gregory. Reprinted for the first time in 66 years, fans of Francis Durbridge and of Paul Temple can finally relive this ingenious adventure.

Includes the exclusive 1946 *Radio Times* short story 'Paul Temple's White Christmas'.

Another Woman's Shoes

It was an open-and-shut case: Lucy Staines was murdered by her hot-headed fiancé Harold Weldon. But something about it is troubling ex-Fleet Street crime reporter Mike Baxter – why was one of Lucy's shoes missing from the crime scene? When an identical murder occurs while Weldon is safely behind bars, the whole case is re-opened – and everything revolves around another woman's shoes . . .

Another Woman's Shoes is Francis Durbridge's rewrite of his radio serial *Paul Temple and the Gilbert Case*, in which Mike and Linda Baxter take the places of Paul and Steve Temple in pursuing the killer. This new edition is introduced by bibliographer Melvyn Barnes and includes the short story 'Paul Temple and the Nightingale'.

Dead to the World

Photographer and amateur detective Philip Holt is asked to investigate the unexplained murder of an American student at an English university. With a postcard signed 'Christopher' and the boy's father's missing signet ring as his only leads, Holt's investigation soon snowballs into forgery, blackmail, smuggling . . . and more murder.

Dead to the World is Francis Durbridge's novelisation of his radio serial *Paul Temple and the Jonathan Mystery*, rewriting the Paul and Steve Temple characters as Philip Holt and his secretary Ruth Sanders. This new edition is introduced by bibliographer Melvyn Barnes and includes the Paul Temple Christmas story 'The Ventriloquist's Doll'.

BY THE SAME AUTHOR

Beware of Johnny Washington

When a gang of desperate criminals begins leaving calling cards inscribed 'With the Compliments of Johnny Washington', the real Johnny Washington is encouraged by an attractive newspaper columnist to throw in his lot with the police. Johnny, an American 'gentleman of leisure' who has settled at a quiet country house in Kent to enjoy the fishing, soon finds himself involved with the mysterious Horatio Quince, a retired schoolmaster who is on the trail of the gang's unscrupulous leader, the elusive 'Grey Moose'.

Best known for creating *Paul Temple* for BBC radio in 1938, Francis Durbridge's prolific output of plays, radio, television, films and books made him a household name for more than 50 years. A new radio character, *Johnny Washington Esquire*, hit the airwaves in 1949, leading to the publication of this one-off novel in 1951.

This classic edition is introduced by writer and bibliographer Melvyn Barnes, who reveals how Beware Johnny Washington was actually a reworking of Durbridge's own *Send for Paul Temple*. The book includes the short story 'A Present for Paul'.